MW00583380

A GIRL NAMED CARMEN WINSTEAD

A Girl Named Carmen Winstead

Trace Murillo

Black Water Press
An imprint of Black Water Press, LLC
71 Belgium Circle, Pensacola, Florida 32526

A Girl Named Carmen Winstead

Printed in the United States of America
First Edition, 2021

Library of Congress Cataloging-in-Publication Data
Names: Murillo, Trace, 1968- author
Title: A Girl Named Carmen Winstead/Trace Murillo
Description: Black Water Press Trade Paperback Edition.|Flor-
ida:Black Water Books, 2021
Identifiers: LCCN 2021907446|ISBN 978-1-7370683-0-3
Subject: BISAC: FICTION/Horror.|FICTION/Thriller
Record available at lccn.loc.gov/2021907446
Literary: Suspenseful Horror

Publication History
Black Water Press Edition: Epub/Print edition June 2021
Cover design by Keith Draws
Editor: Brian Paone
876543

God my maker, the devil my friend which side
will I choose in the end?

-unknown

FOREWORD

Since the release of The Patient in Room 432, I have been fast to work. I am a huge fan of horror and urban legends. I have to say, so many more legends are out there far beyond Bloody Mary or The Hook Man. Some legends will make your skin crawl, some will have you questioning your own sanity and even have you sleeping with your lights on for a very long time. Just the mere possibility that we ask if any of these legends are based on fact or fiction holds a lot of strength to their story. So, are they true narratives or just folklore? I really do not know the answer to that, but isn't this what makes the urban legends so exciting?

In January of 2019, I decided I wanted to bring some of these stories to the forefront of horror fiction and create a collection of urban legends for you to enjoy. I wanted to give them a new life, a new voice while staying close to their original storyline. A Girl Named Carmen Winstead is the first book in the collection, and The Wendigo, Hannah Crannah, and The Black-Eyed Children will follow later this year.

While writing A Girl Named Carmen Winstead, I did struggle whether to bring such a horrific topic to life. Although Carmen Winstead deserved her story to be told—and I did want it to be a part of the collection—I struggled with the fact it does detail a very real issue that many young adults struggle through daily, and that is bullying. I have written about the hopeful origins of this topic several times and its somewhat disheartening aftermath. I grappled with it at length and decided the subject deserves attention. So, I'll ignore the immemorial and be brief about the latter and assume most of you readers know this is a written form of fiction and concentrate on the history instead, so let's get down to the heart of the matter—bullying. This is a horrific crime against humanity. And although the first school anti-bullying law has been in effect since 1999, the last state to adopt it was not until 2015; this should be a reminder to us all that we still have a lot of work to do when it comes to this horrific crime.

No one deserves to be brutalized because they are different or if they are characterized as not offering some so-called normalcy to our society that thinks everyone must act the same, walk the same, believe in the same things, or be some Barbie cutout of what society thinks you should look like—whatever that means. Being different is what makes us special, isn't it?

With that said, as Carmen Winstead became more real for me—I mean, I cried with her and then cheered her on—it was imperative that I did not characterize her as a monster. I do not think anyone would agree that she was; she was a victim that, in the end, bullied her bullies. I hope everyone who reads her story will agree she was a young, lonely girl who needed a friend. She was a pleasing person who, in the end, fell to her demise because she did not stand up or did not scream from the rooftops, "Enough is enough!"

So, if you or someone you know is experiencing bullying or you are a bully and need help, please contact a parent, school counselor, or call the bullying hotline at 1-800-273-TALK, and you can connect with a crisis counselor who can help you strategize ways to get through the day. Scream from your rooftop and let people know this type of behavior is not okay.

To Jordan
For standing up to your demons and taking
them by the horns.
You inspire me.

PART I

Wednesday, Oct. 19, 2008

12:15 P.M.

armen Pigstead stinks like shit!

The words were right in front of her, engraved on the back of the chair. Someone—probably a teacher, since there was no way in hell any of the wretched kids at Somerdale High School would have—but someone had tried covering it up with black magic marker, but it was still there, regardless.

While Mr. Carlton stood in front of the class, pining over the analogies buried in Edgar Alan Poe's "The Raven," Carmen traced the words with her finger. The girl who sat in front of her, Mary Newton, had long black hair that Carmen accidentally touched every now and then as she traced the words.

Mr. Carlton was scanning the English class, which, Carmen knew, meant he was about to call on someone. He was telling them about how Poe was more famous in death than he ever was in life.

Carmen sunk lower and lower in her chair, hiding behind Mary. She was subtle about it. Though this was only her seventh day in Somerdale, she'd spent years perfecting the art of not being seen. Sometimes it even worked on teachers.

When Mr. Carlton called on an unsuspecting student on the other side of the room, Carmen relaxed. The last thing she wanted was a replay of her first day, when Mr. Carlton had requested she stand in front of the class to introduce herself—Carmen Winstead—and where she was from—Bristol, New Hampshire. She'd done it as quickly as she could, like pulling off a Band-Aid, but so meekly and quietly that several kids snickered. Pure torture. She would have much rather stood naked in front of everyone and just let them all have a look. Let them stare, they always did, stare and laugh and somehow that seemed less vulnerable than admitting she was new to school, new to town, and standing in the spotlight for all to see.

Almost immediately, the whispers had started. On the way to her assigned desk, she'd heard them.

"What the hell is she wearing?"

"Does she even comb her hair?"

"She looks like a farmgirl or something."

"Moo. Oink."

"What is it? Hermaphrodite, maybe?"

"Carmen Winstead, my ass. More like Carmen Pigstead."

The nickname had started that very first day, not that she minded much. She'd grown hardened to the whispers, the face-to-face insults. It was really the only thing she could do.

Even now, thinking of those comments, Carmen pulled at her stringy, oily hair—letting it hang down, so it framed around her face, blocking off the students around her. She was a slim girl, the sort of scrawny that looked like she had missed several meals somewhere along the way, thin but in a sick way—not the supermodel way teenage boys drooled over. Her skin was pallid and ghostlike in the unusual lightness of the room, she had a nose and forehead far too big for her face, and a set of thin lips that were perpetually dry and chapped, no matter what kind of lip balm she bought at the local drugstore to remedy the situation. It never worked.

She thought of those first-day comments as she traced the crude epitaph with her fingers. She happened to look to the right to see a boy staring at her through the thin curtain of her hair.

He sneered and made a motion like he was milking a cow.

A girl sitting behind him snickered.

Carmen pulled more hair in front of her face, effectively blocking him out. Maybe she *did* mind it, as much as she told herself she was immune. Sometimes she wished she could fight back. Sometimes she imagined tearing them limb by limb, not that she would ever hurt a fly, much less her classmates. But while their taunts hurt her feelings, while she wished people were nicer to her and that she had friends, because that's all she wanted, she'd come to accept it. Nobody likes her. And no one wanted to be her friend.

She yawned, and suddenly, her eyes felt heavy. Carmen had never been so exhausted in her life—too exhausted to even care about the jokes about her or the insults about her clothes. Her chest filled with air. Since moving here, she had not been sleeping. Something had been keeping her up at night, scratching at the bedroom walls.

Deep in thought, Carmen didn't realize when the echoes began. The catcalls first came from Tess Todd.

"Close your mouth, bitch! You're collecting flies." Startling from her daydream. Carmen slow and muddled, realized her mouth was agape and quickly clamped it shut as everyone else laughed.

Mr. Carlton turned around and glared to calm them down, but the comment had already struck the walls and bounced back and rebounded again. Mary Newton gasped a retching sound and started to laugh. "She stinks and she's sitting there drooling like she's stupid or something."

"I said enough!" Mr. Carlton yelled.

The room fell completely silent.

Carmen lowered her head and did her best to ignore them, like she always did, like she had to. What else could she do? She had no other choice.

12:22 P.M.

Joe Winstead was forty-five but looked much older. Before Carmen's mother, Nancy, had left them, she'd always claimed it was because he worked too hard. Carmen assumed this was true, because her father often came home late, and even when he was on time, he wolfed down dinner and disappeared into his office to do more work. It had gotten worse when her mom was gone. But he always made time for Carmen—checking in to see how her life was going, how she was handling being mom-less (his word, not hers). And though she knew he loved her; she also knew his first love was work. When they moved to Somerdale for his new job, Carmen had hoped this would change. And, so far, just one week after moving in, it seemed like it might.

She wanted desperately to hang onto that, since it was just about the only thing she had. The kids at school were awful, and the new house was, in Carmen's unbiased opinion, a fucking joke. But she couldn't tell her dad that, because she knew he was already feeling guilty about the move and, though he would not say it, for not being able to save his marriage, his family, as if her mom was completely blameless. She'd walked out not just on Joe, but on *both* of them and that was something else for Carmen to rationalize as nothing but a rejection. Being unwanted was familiar territory for her, something she was used to even from her mother.

When they had moved from New Hampshire to Virginia, they'd settled into a farmhouse that sat on the very edge of the rural town of Somerdale. It was in what most locals called Farmville. It was just across the tracks that went through the center of town, about a half mile from the high school. And while the land itself looked malnourished and like something from a gloomy Arthur Conan Doyle novel, the house was homey and warm.

Her father called their living situation quaint and charming. She called it monastic and miserable. She often muttered that it was amazing they got any sort of electricity out here at all. Her father, joker that he was, told her they even had a Wi-Fi signal and could one day use the internet to learn how to churn butter and make their own soap. "Live like the Amish," he would say. Carmen would just roll her eyes, but internally, she would smile at him every time. She always knew he meant well and tried his best to make things normal for her, so sometimes it opened a beam inside she couldn't understand. Maybe it was just her dad being cheery or maybe it was that he stuck around and suffered right alongside her; she wasn't sure. But what she did know is how unwelcoming she thought the house was when they first moved in.

The house's interior was somewhat cozy. There was a large living room, complete with a fireplace, and a rustic kitchen, right down to the farmhouse sink. Carmen did take pride in washing dishes in that sink, because her stupid mother had always griped about wanting a sink like that. Carmen had remarked on this, but her father had only made an *mm-hmm* in response. It was his canned response for anything that had to do with the woman he had been married to for nineteen years.

But of all the places in the new house, the one she hated the most was her bedroom. It was a decent size, but it was drafty and smelled like hay and dust. She and Joe had scrubbed and cleaned it endlessly upon moving in, but the smell never left. Joe swore that once they got fully settled, he'd have someone re-insulate that side of the house. He figured it would take care of the draft and maybe even the smell.

But the smell was nothing compared to the whistling at night. She knew it was nothing more than the wind, but in her mind, it was still freaky as hell. Her father had even explained the wind came barreling across the huge open field behind the house and hit the corner right where her room was. The whistling was the wind hissing through her partially cracked window frame— something else her father swore he would have fixed when they were finally settled. But knowing what it was at two o'clock in the morning while she stared into the darkness didn't make it any less horrifying.

That was why Carmen had slept on the couch in the living room five of the seven nights they'd lived in Somerdale. *Slept* was a bit of an overstatement though. What she did most was toss and turn and listen. On one of those nights, she could've sworn she'd heard something stalking back and forth on the porch. At first, Carmen had entertained the idea that it was her mother—that she had found out where they'd moved to and wanted to beg her father to take her back. But before her heart would allow her to hold on to such a thing, it was dashed by reality.

It was a scratching, grating sort of movement. And underneath it laid the sound of a thick, raspy breath. She wasn't sure, but, as she lay on the couch, staring at the black square of the empty fireplace in front of her, she thought whatever was making the noise had come to the front door and stopped.

It was waiting, thinking, considering.

And it didn't seem all that human.

Carmen lay awake, expecting the door handle to turn, until the first scant traces of sunlight shone through the living room window.

But it hadn't. When her father entered the living room an hour later, she almost told him about it. In the end, she decided not to. She didn't see the point in embarrassing herself. She knew he would just roll his eyes, sigh, and before walking away, he would ask her how old she was. So, she brushed it off. Besides, it was probably a bear or some other woodland creature that lived in those miserable Virginian woods. Sure, the idea of a bear stalking around there wasn't especially cheerful either, but it was far better than the other dark possibilities her mind had conjured.

That had been last Friday. When she left the house for school, she'd opened the front door, half-expecting some sludge monster from the woods to be there, waiting. She was old enough to know monsters weren't real, but if they *were* real, the world they lived in did not have rules that would cause monsters to lurk back into the shadows just because the sun was out. And a locked front door certainly would not have stopped them either. But of course, there had been no monster, nor any sign that her stupid mother had shown up either, but there *had* been something that looked almost like a sludgy footprint on the bottom of the porch stairs. But she had convinced herself it was nothing, that her mind had *made* her see it, by the time she got to school.

And, in school, there was a different kind of monster for her to worry about.

12:32 P.M.

Carmen was thinking about those scratching noises from the front porch when she shoved her Algebra book into her locker; the sound was very similar, only with a metallic sort of edge to it. It sent a little chill up her spine.

As she was about to close the door, something hurled over her head and clattered against the metal. It was an empty milk carton, the same kind the cafeteria distributed for school lunches.

"Fill 'er up, bitch!"

Carmen didn't even need to turn around to know who it was. Behind this comment came a chorus of moos and boisterous laughter. She sank her shoulders, closed the door, and slowly turned around.

"I said, *fill 'er up!*" Tess Todd's voice echoed through the hallways.

Tess was one of the girls who had started the whole farm-based ribbing. And because Tess was incredibly popular at Somerdale, everyone had basically fallen in line. Five kids stood behind her—three girls and two boys. The boys were dating two of the girls in the group—or whatever served as their opinion of dating in this town. Neither of them was dating Tess though. Carmen figured it was because Tess thought she was far too good to be sullied by anyone at Somerdale High. She was the sort that, at first, seemed like a prim and proper debutant, almost like how people would describe the girl next door but all it took was a single look through her expressive eyes to see the real Tess. She was vindictive … perhaps for the sake of keeping her tidy, little small-town throne in place.

"What's wrong?" Tess asked. "Teats all dried up?"

More laughter—which was sort of stupid because they weren't even funny jokes.

Living in a place like Somerdale, the farm-based jokes were sort of lame and boring. But Carmen knew if she tried to defend herself, it would only get worse, so she did what she knew how, she lowered her head, never making eye contact, and ignored it. She wished she were naïve enough to wonder why they were picking on her. But she was seventeen. She knew. They were picking on her because she was the new kid in a rural community that didn't take well to outsiders. She was also not very pretty … not compared to the Barbie-like figure of Tess Todd and her little army of wannabes. She was homely, odd-looking, and extremely introverted. And, at this age, anything other kids could do to establish themselves as superior was important. She got it; she just hated that she was the one they claimed superiority over.

Carmen was used to their kind. There had been a few groups of them in Bristol too. But because they had all grown up together, Carmen had not always been the one at the other end of their torture. Apparently, though, they were the same no matter where she went. They were the sort who were always leaning against their lockers like they were posing for the cover of *America's Best Bitch* magazine, checking their makeup in their compact mirrors, ensuring they were perfect, twirling their hair on their fingers, making small banana curls that framed their faces, nothing out of place, not a wrinkle on their shirts, or a seam on their jeans. They almost looked plastic, these popular girls, the pretty ones with great hair, perfect tits, nice clothes. The leering eyes of every boy in school weren't enough; they also needed the attention and envy of all the girls too. If they had to take down a few souls in the process, so be it.

Carmen scanned the hallway, clinched the strap on her bookbag, lowered her head, and started walking away.

"Sorry, everyone," Tess belted out behind her. "The milking station is closed today!"

The laughter was deafening, some of them breaking into exaggerated mooing noises. It was absolutely embarrassing, but what alarmed Carmen the most was when she stifled a cry and the tears flowed down her cheek. In a panic, she lowered her head even farther as she felt more tears stinging the corners of her eyes. She'd never been overly emotional, so this was new territory for her. With the chorus of barnyard sounds behind her, Carmen walked faster, wondering where the teachers were to help her. To protect her. Did no one hear them? Did no one care? Or were they just as intoxicated on Tess's personality as the students?

She took a right at the next intersection in the hallway. She passed numerous students, most not bothering to acknowledge her, a snickering here and there. Gagging noises, barnyard mooing, and comments of *Pigstead* and screams of *Pigslut* followed as she headed towards the girl's bathroom near the gym. There, she would feel safe. Normal. Hiding like she always did. After only a week in this school, Carmen figured out that no one ever went into the bathrooms near the gym. She always knew that. It was the same in most schools. Those restrooms reeked of piss and dirty gym socks and was left for girls like Carmen, concealing themselves, praying for a moment of peace.

Carmen entered, dropped her book bag, and leaned against the wall. She finally let loose, allowing the tears to roll freely down her cheeks. She hated that it felt good to do so, but it did.

Just what in the hell am I supposed to do? I can't live like this ...

She didn't want to complain to her dad, because he had enough going on, trying to get settled into the new house, new job, and getting used to life without her mom. Plus, he would just say it was the same no matter where they went. She figured she could maybe go to a school counselor, but that would probably open a whole new level of problems. If she saw a guidance counselor and someone found out about it, Tess Todd and her minions would start calling her a snitch, and the teasing would only get worse. Maybe even unbearable.

So what? Someone has to help me. I can't do this anymore.

Oddly enough, she thought of something her mom used to tell her. Back in middle school, when some of her grade school friends had started excluding her and calling her names, Nancy Winstead had said, *"Everything will be better someday Carmen. You'll see. When people make fun of you, it's because they're jealous of you and want what you have. Just ignore them. In ten years, you'll be in college, away from all of this, and it won't even cross your mind."*

Yeah, well, you're not here now, are you, Mom? Get out of my head and shut up. You ran, so you have no idea what I'm going through.

Things weren't better now; they were worse, and it wasn't just because her mother was gone. It had been like this back in Bristol; but not as bad. She'd known those kids almost since birth, she'd sometimes had a spine. When they came after her, making fun of her clothes, her hair, or just being downright insulting, Carmen would fire back with witty banter or a well-timed middle finger. Here, though, it was—well ... different. Vile. She sometimes wondered if that's why they mov—

"So, what's your story?" The voice seemed to come from no-where and nearly made Carmen scream.

She stepped away from the wall and watched as one of the stall doors open.

A girl exited and eyed Carmen suspiciously.

Carmen remembered seeing her a few times in the crowd. This girl had never bothered to join to insult her, that was for sure. She always passed by, never making eye contact with anyone which is a definite check on the plus side, as far as Carmen was concerned.

The first thing Carmen noticed was the overly large army boots as she stopped in front of the mirror to stare curiously at herself. Her long skirt swayed slightly as she turned to face Car-men. She was dressed in all black, her face somewhat fair with light freckles that made her fiery hair braided down on each side shimmer a vibrant crimson in the dull bathroom light. Carmen decided the girl was pretty but not textbook, Tess Todd-pretty. It was in a way that was hard to define.

"What?" Carmen asked stupidly, caught off guard.

"What's your story? What's wrong with you?"

Carmen idly twisted her hair and tucked it behind her ears.

The girl approached, those black boots clunking along the grubby tiled floor.

"Nothing. I don't have a story."

"Well, something is wrong, or you wouldn't be hiding in the bathroom, crying."

Carmen did her best not to feel frightened, she didn't want to appear like a frumpy ole bitch hiding in a bathroom. Give an-other reason for someone to pick on her about. "I'm not crying." It was another stupid comment. Of course, she had been crying. Her eyes were still bleary, and her cheeks were still wet with tears. She wiped them away with her coat sleeve and sniffled to clear her nose.

"Hey," the girl said, slowly raising her hands. "I'm not judging. It's not like I've never used a bathroom to escape into." She hesitated a moment and tilted her head, inspecting Carmen as if she were a monkey at the zoo. "You okay?"

"I will be."

The girl frowned, as if she knew this was a lie. She shrugged and offered her a delicate hand. "I'm Willa. Willa Dalton."

Carmen noticed the silver rings on each finger. One was an upside-down cross, at least the way it faced her, which made Carmen's pulse skitter. "Willa?" Carmen felt the traces of what might be a smile touch her lips. "That's a ... strange name."

"Says the crying girl in the bathroom. No offense, sweet cheeks, but I don't think you're in any position to make fun of someone."

"I-I'm not making fun. I think it's pretty. *Strange* is a compliment."

"Ah, you do seem like that type. Also, I would have been offended to be insulted by a girl walking around with a crude note taped to her back."

"Note?"

Willa approached her and reached around her back.

Carmen's gaze followed the gesture, wondering but already half-knowing what Willa was doing. When she brought her hand away, holding a sheet of paper with a piece of tape at the top, her fears were confirmed. Two words were written in black marker: PIG SLUT.

"Charming," Willa said. "Any idea how long that's been there? But more important, what the hell does it mean? PIG-SLUT?"

Shaking her head in a somewhat nervous tick, "no idea." Carmen took the paper, balled it up, and tossed it across the restroom. *Real mature, people.* "Thanks for that. By the way, I'm Carmen. Carmen Winstead."

"Oh, I know." Willa dug a pack of Kool's from her skirt pocket, expertly plucked one out, and lit it up.

"You do?"

"Yeah. Everyone knows who you are."

"Oh god."

"Well, it does seem like Tess Todd has selected you for her most recent shitlist. And when you get on that list, your name tends to go around a bit. Besides, I pretty much know everything that goes on in this godforsaken town. More than most." Willa gave Carmen a fiendish stare.

Carmen walked to the sink and saw the reflection staring back at her of someone she almost did not recognize. Frail and tired. Disgusting and defeated. Her hands trembled as she turned on the water. It flowed from the faucet like a cascade slushing a mountainside, overflowing the porcelain basin, landing on her shoes. Perfect. Ignoring it, she cuffed her hands and felt the cool water splash against her skin, washing away the tears. Better.

But it wouldn't be for long. She knew that. She couldn't stay in this sanctuary forever. Eventually, she'd have to go back out. At that thought, her breath burned as it filled her lungs. A ball of panic developed in her throat, growing bigger and bigger. The more she tried to swallow it away, the more she felt as though it might coil around her throat and she might choke.

By the time she looked past her reflection in the mirror, Willa was right beside her. Although her eyes were enlarged with dark shadow and her lips lined with a deep scarlet, she looked kind, and that was something Carmen needed in that moment.

Willa had already taken a brown paper towel from the little box above the sink and was offering it to her.

"I just don't know why she'd chose me. New girl, sure. Ugly, okay. Weird, I'll admit... but what threat am I to her?"

"Oh honey, there doesn't need to be a reason. The *why* doesn't matter to her. It's just the way she is. And sadder than that, she has that little army who adores her. So, if she hates you, they'll hate you too. No questions asked." Willa took a long drag on her cigarette and slowly puffed out.

Carmen never noticed how most people smoked before, but she thought something seemed very sexy about the way she did it. Almost intoxicating. Willa was *definitely* a different sort of pretty—mainly because she didn't seem to care.

"Sounds like you're on this shitlist too."

"Of course, I am," Willa said with a smile. "Just look at me. Listen, I've known Tess and some of her little gang since elementary school. This crap started years ago, and it's been building and building every year since, like, fourth grade. Just think, ten years ago, Tess Todd and I colored a fucking caterpillar together for a project in science class. It's a weird world, isn't it?"

"I-I guess." That comment, *weird*, made Carmen instantly remember the noises outside her front door, and she suppressed a chill. *Weirder than you think.*

Willa took another long drag of her cigarette and checked her watch. "Gotta split. But, if it means anything, if Tess has something against you, then you're cool as shit in my book. You got a friend in me, Carmen Winstead." She chuckled and nodded to the crumpled ball of paper in the corner of the restroom. "Even if you *are* a pig slut. Whatever the hell that means." Willa Dalton gave a little salute, tossed her Kool into the closest sink, and left the restroom.

Carmen waited a moment, took a deep breath, and a slight smile arched her lips as she headed for the door as well. *Willa*, she thought. It was the first time since being at Somerdale she felt like maybe, she had a friend. But the thought rushed out of her like a train when she made it exactly four steps out of the bathroom before Tess Todd stepped directly in front of her.

Two other girls followed close behind.

Tess wore a vile expression, like a snake that had just cornered the mouse it wanted to devour. "Aww, look girls, it's the weirdo. What is it? Pig Slut? Is that what they're calling you these days?"

Maybe it was because of Willa, because she finally knew she had someone on her side, but Carmen found her voice. "Tess, please."

"Tess, please," she mimicked. "Please Tess ... please *what* ... you skank."

"Tess ..."

"*T-Tess.*" Mimicking her again.

The other girls laughed.

"Get my name out of your mouth, farmgirl."

"Ooh, another farm name. Clever," Carmen whispered, but it was out of her mouth before she could stop it. At first, she was surprised at how good it felt to let loose. She relished the flash of defeat in Tess's eyes, but it didn't last long, and, by then, there was already a boiling sort of regret in her stomach. She'd made a mistake. This wasn't like things back home in Bristol. This was new territory.

The two girls stepped alongside Tess. The one on the right, with the gorgeous blue eyes, was named Miriam George.

"What did you say to me?" Tess said.

"No-Nothing. I'm sorry."

Tess stepped forward, and, for a moment, Carmen thought they would attack her. Instead, Tess and Miriam worked together in quick succession and wrenched Carmen's bookbag off her shoulders. The other girl, Cassie Hollins, just stood there, laughing as they unzipped it. Tess dumped everything on the floor: books, pens, her calculator, a hairbrush, a few notebooks.

Carmen watched as her pencils rolled across the hallway and under a locker with a red balloon taped to it.

"Look at that!" Tess screamed. "Nasty girl has a nasty bookbag. What do you know?"

Tears built in Carmen's eyes once again. Her stomach felt cold and frantic. A burning sensation entered her throat, and she had an overwhelming feeling to vomit—just another thing for Tess to attack her for. She pinched her lips together, inhaling through her nostrils, holding it in. She swallowed the fiery, bitter taste of bile, feeling it slide down her throat and bottom out in her stomach. She could do nothing as Tess and the others kicked the contents of her bookbag all over the hallway, spitting at her shoes, and laughing.

"Hey, what's this?" Miriam bent down and grabbed one of the books that had come out—Carmen's journal.

"Please, don't. Give it to me," Carmen murmured, her head down and her hair hanging in oily strings over her face.

"Moo for it, and it's yours." Tess took the journal from Miriam, opened it, and scanned the first page.

"Tess, please don't…" Carmen said, hating how weak she sounded.

"Jesus, this is classic," Tess said as a small crowd gathered.

Carmen snatched for it but was too slow. The moment she missed; Tess read aloud. Carmen hoped she'd make up something, maybe something rife with more farm jokes, but no … it was worse. She read what was actually written there.

"Dear Diary, I miss my mom, but I hate her too. Why did she have to leave?" Tess whined in a baby voice.

People laughed all around them.

"Why did she leave?" Tess asked, holding the diary to her chest. "Do you even have to ask that? I can tell you. She left because you're ugly, and she couldn't bring herself to love you. I mean, just look at you. Do you ever wash your hair? I mean, maybe she wanted you to kill yourself. Did you ever try to kill yourself, farmgirl? Maybe she knew you were too stupid to do that, so she left."

A single tear-stained Carmen's cheek as she glared at Tess. Her head cocked with pure hatred radiating from her eyes.

Miriam and the other girl laughed, and, just like the sheep they were, several other students did too. Laughter seemed to be coming from everywhere, laced with obscenities and punctuated by Tess Todd's cackling. In the midst of it all, a whispered voice broke through. "Yo, here comes Mr. Thompson."

The crowd dispersed, and Tess gave one final kick to the bookbag on the ground before she also turned to leave.

The laughter lingered as Carmen crawled around, gathering her things. She found her pencil, pens, and calculator. Her hairbrush had been kicked three lockers down, and pages of her math book were torn out, scattered across the floor. No one bothered to help.

By the time she was done shoving in the final book, Mr. Thompson, the Phys Ed teacher, had arrived. "You okay?"

Still shaking, Carmen nodded and gave a strained, "Yeah. Thanks."

Mr. Thompson looked like he was about to say something else, but he checked his watch, grunted something unintelligible, and strode toward the gym.

Carmen got to her feet and checked her books as the bell rang overhead. When she reached the end of her inventory, she checked again and again her heart thumping faster and faster. Something was missing.

Her diary. Her diary was gone.

And the last place she had seen it was in Tess's hands.

"Shit," Carmen said, lowering her head as another surge of tears came on. But they were not tears of despair this time. These were tears of fear because she knew what was coming. A vile ribbing of her deepest secrets, her inner thoughts, and details about her life. She also knew Tess would take them all and use them against her. She didn't want to cry, but the tears pushed through and Carmen felt a wave of fear slither from her gut and strangle her throat. It tightened around her, coiling, she knew what was coming and all she could do is wait.

4:22 P.M.

When Carmen got home that afternoon, she was surprised to see her father sitting at the kitchen table. She'd been expecting him to be held up in his office, drowning in work. She really had no idea what he did—something to do with technological solutions for small businesses—but whatever it was, it kept him online and behind his computer most of the day. This time though, he wasn't in his office, but she wished he was. She just wanted to be alone.

Carmen stomped into the kitchen, dropped her bookbag on the floor, and went straight to the fridge for a Yoo-hoo.

"Rough day?" her father asked.

"They're all rough, Dad."

"Sorry, kiddo. High school can be a rough ride. Especially when you're the new kid."

"Thanks for the pep talk." She unscrewed the top to her Yoo-hoo and took a swig.

"All jokes aside, anything I can do? Need me to call there and file some complaints? Need me to beat up some parents? You need kickboxing lessons?"

If she wasn't in such a foul mood, Carmen would've chuckled at the image of her scrawny father beating anyone up. It was almost as funny as her doing anything resembling exercise. "No, I don't think it's come to that yet."

"Sorry you're having to go through this, kiddo. And I'm sorry you got stuck with the more passive parent."

"Yeah, but I got the better one." She sat at the table as he smiled at her.

He sighed deeply. His job had always been stressful, and she was sure it wasn't easy for him to be in a new place either. Of course, it had been his idea to come way the hell out here to the middle of nowhere, so it was his own fault. But she also knew he did it to protect her but here—it wasn't any better—it was worse.

"Got much homework?"

"Some."

"Want to watch a movie tonight? I got some oven pizzas at the grocery store today. Could make a night of it."

"Sure, Dad. Just … no action crap. If I have to see Bruce Willis jump off that building one more time …"

"Fine, fine," he said and finished his beer. "Get to that homework, then. I've got some work stuff I need to wrap up. We'll do dinner in about an hour or so. Sound good?"

She nodded, sipping her Yoo-hoo. She watched her father leave the kitchen and powerwalk down the hallway to his office—a man who loved his work and was happy to get to it. Her father had, for the most part, always been a happy sort of man. Even when his life started to derail, he'd remained optimistic and hopeful. Carmen often thought he'd behaved that way for her, to ensure she had always kept her own spirits up. Sometimes when she looked at him, sadness engulfed her. She could always see the sorrow in his eyes—maybe solitary, she wasn't sure—she just knew something was there, something that didn't equal happiness anyway.

She found herself thinking about her mom. A little over a year ago, on Carmen's sixteenth birthday, she'd come home with expectations of spending that afternoon just like every birthday before it—with a trip to Poppy's Pizza, followed by her mother's homemade chocolate cake with strawberry frosting. Her mother took birthdays quite seriously and even decorated a new banner every year. Carmen had been thinking about that year's banner as she ran into the house.

Right away, she had felt the silence. Her mother, usually at home when she arrived, was not there. In fact, nothing was there. The house wasn't filled with the smell of her freshly baked birthday cake and there were no purple balloons—another staple of her usual birthday celebrations. Instead, she had found a quiet house. Dark and empty. Her mother had packed up and had just left. No note, nothing. Just gone.

It had taken her father—who had arrived ten minutes later—to explain it to her. Nancy Winstead had called him at work, told him of her plans, and that had been that.

To this day, Carmen had never got any sort of true explanation. According to her father, her mother had simply tired of married life. In the year or so that followed, Carmen always wondered if it was the banner or the cake that had broken her mother and had made her realize she was tired of the domestic life. Or maybe it was just Carmen herself.

"Bitch," she muttered as she took another gulp of her Yoohoo.

The absence of her mother was one thing Carmen had hoped to keep from the cruel kids at school. But that little secret was out now. *Great*, she thought as she collected her bookbag and sauntered to her room.

When no midnight winds were whistling through her room's busted window frame, it wasn't so bad. The sunlight poured through her window, making it comfortably warm, setting it in a homey, cheery pink glow. She sat on her bed—she'd never had a desk—and did her homework. She only got through one algebra problem before she thought of Tess. Right now, she was probably sitting with her friends, combing through her journal, laughing over Carmen's deepest, darkest secrets.

Carmen cringed but refused to cry again. If she could hold onto one thing, after all was said and done, it would be her refusal to break over Tess Todd's teasing. It wasn't the most reassuring of anchors, but it would have to do.

THURSDAY, OCT. 20, 2008

7:42 A.M.

The following day, the missing journal was all Carmen could think about. Every time she thought of something she had written in it, she tried to imagine Tess reading it and laughing with everyone at school. She had some very private stuff in there—her inner thoughts, inner feelings. There were ruminations on her mother and why she had left, far too detailed descriptions of crushes she had on boys, and quite a few passages about how she hated the way her body looked and had trouble pleasuring herself because of it. That, in turn, led to some pretty unapologetic thoughts on sex.

Oh god, she thought as she approached the school's front doors. *This will be brutal.*

The misery of it was almost enough to make Carmen go to the principal to report the journal stolen. But that would make her a snitch, and it wasn't like Tess and her troop needed even more of a reason to hate her.

Carmen thought the assault would begin in Mr. Carlton's class. But Tess, didn't even look at her. Tess sat two rows over and a few seats ahead. Carmen watched her, waiting for the other shoe to drop, wondering what it must be like to be beautiful and adored by everyone. Sure, Carmen had met pretty girls before who weren't complete bitches, but there was something about the bitchy type of gorgeous girl that Carmen had always secretly envied. There was something about an overly confident, beautiful girl that was profoundly sexy—to be gorgeous and in control, to get whatever you wanted whenever you wanted it. Carmen couldn't even start to imagine what that might be like.

She was so ensnared in that fantasy that she wasn't aware Tess Todd had turned to stare at her. Tess's smirk, bordered by curls, widened. "I told you not to look at me, Pigstead!" she sneered. She didn't shout it, but she didn't whisper it either.

Half the students chuckled, a few so loudly that Mr. Carlton turned from where he was jotting something about Mary Shelley on the whiteboard. "I'd suggest everyone stop laughing right now."

It took a few moments, but the class finally simmered down, and Mr. Carlton resumed writing.

With his back once again turned, Tess tilted her head upward and used her index finger to pull up her nose. She made a small oinking noise and gave Carmen a coquettish smile.

Carmen looked away, her cheeks flushing. It would be different if Tess was just being mean. But no, this one, Carmen felt, was all her fault. She'd been staring at Tess, envious of her life, to want to be Tess Todd; maybe Carmen deserved the ridicule.

Carmen stared at the clock for the remainder of the class. The day was only half over, but it would likely only get worse.

Finally, the bell rang. She took her time getting out of her desk, not wanting to be stuck in the push of bodies trying to get out the door. When everyone else was nearly gone, she grabbed her bookbag and tried to make a speedy exit.

Before she could reach the door, Mr. Carlton called, "Carmen, hold up a second."

She cringed—not only because she hated it when teachers tried to sound cool but because she had not been singled out by any teachers yet. Surely some of them had to know the other students were mocking and ridiculing her. Would this be the first attempt to ensure she was adjusting okay, to see if she needed any additional help? She knew it would come eventually, it always did but she hadn't expected it this soon, or from Mr. Carlton. Mr. Carlton seemed the type not to get to involved in the stereo-typical side of teenagers and the high school banter. If it didn't have anything to do with literature, or the poetry club, he seemed immune to the situation.

Still, she stopped and slowly turned around.

Mr. Carlton was sitting on the edge of his desk, embodying that hip, I'm-your-buddy pose that teachers never got quite right.

"Yeah?" she asked.

"You don't smile much, you know that?" Mr. Carlton said, peering worriedly at her, brushing back his thinning hair.

"I guess."

"Having a hard time adjusting?"

A hard time? She repeated to herself. *Of course, I am.* "No, not really."

"If you are, you can tell me. I'm here to listen. So are the guidance counselors. Carmen ... I moved three times between seventh and twelfth grade. I know how hard it can be. I know how mean kids can be to the new person. You sure you're good?"

"I guess ..." She bit her bottom lip and headed for the door before the situation could worsen.

"Let me know if you ever need to talk!"

Carmen barely heard this as she sailed into the hallway. But now, the halls were almost empty. And that is what she hoped for. And if she were lucky, she would escape to her next class before Tess and her gang would even see her. If they didn't see her—they couldn't pick on her. But if they did, she would do what she always did. She would duck her head, tighten a grip around her bookbag, and push through the crowd to safety.

1:10 P.M.

She managed to make it through lunch unscathed. She sat strategically by herself at the end of a table directly beside the table the faculty and staff sometimes sat at, eating quickly under the bored eyes of a few teachers, and then escaped to the library where she sat alone until the next bell rang.

Her next class was Phys Ed. She liked a few sports, but not in the presence of girls like Tess Todd. And PE was yet another class she shared with Tess. Naturally, Tess Todd wore a pair of shorts that came dangerously close to violating school guidelines, accentuating her sculpted ass and allowing as much of her legs as possible to show. Even Carmen found it hard to look away—not out of attraction but at the absurdity of perfection.

As she waited in line to try pull-ups, a few chuckles and sneers were sent in her direction. When it was Carmen's turn, she gave minimal effort just to get away. When she sat to attempt the V-sit reach, making a V of her legs, one of Tess's friends—a short, wiry girl named Virgie Vaughan—said quite loudly, "Whew … someone smell bacon?"

Carmen did her best to ignore it. Her emotions were waging war, unable to decide if she wanted to be angry or humiliated.

When the class ended in a game of pick-up basketball, Carmen opted to sit in the bleachers and read Mr. Carlton's latest assignment, which was to read Shirley Jackson's "The Lottery" and write a two-page paper on how some of its themes were present in modern society. Honestly, it wasn't that hard to do, Carmen thought, when verbal rocks were being thrown at her all day.

She saw the class barreling toward the locker room before she heard the whistle blow. Carmen had also planned this out. At the end of class, she used the same approach as in Mr. Carlton's class; she attempted to be the last one in the locker room so everyone else was already engaged in conversation, likely missing the fact she was even there.

Inside the stuffy room, which smelled like sweat and baby powder, Carmen instantly went to her locker. What might it be like to not have to rush through changing, to worry someone would see what she called the xylophones—the shapeless line of her ribs against her skin? It could be worse; she could be overweight, giving Tess and company even more things to make fun of. She wasn't *to* upset by her gaunt frame, but it would've been nice to have perky breasts instead of nubs, or a defined rear. For a moment, her plan worked. No one noticed her. The locker room was filled with shouts and laughter, as well as the pleasant ambient sound of adequate showers splashing onto the tile floor. Carmen noticed the usual suspects were either already under the water or stripping out of their PE uniforms to get in. For those girls, showering after gym was no big deal. They laughed, traded shampoos, complimented each other's breasts, and discussed boys.

The girls stretched and enjoyed the hot water, laughing and flicking it toward each other. Chatter echoed against the tiles as hot water dripped down their breasts and nipples. Carmen knew she wasn't gay—she'd had far too many crushes on boys for this to be true—but she envied the bodies of other girls. Tess Todd might have been a heinous and evil human being, but she seemed flawless. It was made even more obvious as she washed her hair under the jets, back slightly arched to tilt her perfect breasts into the spotlight. The water flowed over every sublime curve.

She stared at the image in front of her until the girls became a blur. She finally snapped out of it when Tess and her friends turned off the water and grabbed their towels. Carmen hurriedly, reached into her locker for her school clothes, she cursed herself. What the hell had she been doing staring at Tess like that? Now the chances of her getting out of here unseen were almost slim.

She managed to kick her thin legs from her gym shorts. For the split second her plain white panties were exposed, she felt humiliated, even though no one had noticed her yet. Her hands landed on her gym bag, and she instantly felt something wet. Confused, she retrieved her bag, unzipped it, and stared, trying to make sense of the sight in front of her.

Her clothes were soaked. She removed her pants out and found them drenched. Her shirt came next, soaking wet. They had, of course, all been dry when she had changed. Tears stung the corners of her eyes. She wiped them away as laughing erupted behind her.

"What's wrong, Pigstead?" Tess asked. "Something happen to your clothes. Maybe someone finally washed them. You know, to help you out."

Carmen turned to face her. Only, it wasn't just Tess. It was Tess and five others. Now six, then seven. They were closing in on her. Carmen dropped her wet clothes, realizing they would do her no good. She reached for the gym shorts she had just discarded, hoping to cover herself. But her heart sank when Miriam George swooped in and got them first.

When she did, she held her shorts at arm's length and made an exaggerated *ewww* sound.

"Aww, what's the matter, Pigstead?" Virgie Vaughan asked. She was pretty too, like all of them, even with her mouth twisted in such an ugly way.

"Did you have an accident?" This came from Cassie—a girl Carmen had always thought was quiet and impartial. The comment, coming from someone so unassuming, somehow hurt worse than any of Tess's barbs.

Tess stepped closer. Her crisp, white cardigan buttoned to her breasts was just short enough to bare the ruby belly ring on her taut stomach. Black capri pants and red heels clicked across the tile as she pulled a small book from her bag and flipped through the pages.

Her diary.

Tess grinned sadistically. "Some of us have already read this. Pretty juicy stuff, Pigstead. I have to say I didn't expect it to be so ... what is the word?" Tess eyed the other girls, laughing and smiling diabolically. "Dirty." Tess laughed again. "You are a nasty whore, aren't you?"

Carmen wanted to escape, to make a run for it and tell Mr. Thompson what was happening. Maybe he would help her like he did when she started faking her headaches or when he saved her the day prior when Tess took her journal. She wasn't sure but she remained hopeful that he would.

But before she could move, Miri George and another girl stepped between her and the exit.

"*Why did my mom leave me?*" Tess began in a dramatic whine then ripped several pages from the diary and tossed them into the air.

The girls laughed and leaped for the pages as if they were snowflakes descending from the sky.

"*My mom left me ... I'm bored ... I hate my life ... I want to go back to Bristol ... Why are kids at school mean to me?*" Tess read, continuing to tear the pages.

Raucous laughter assaulted Carmen's ears.

"*I want to feel a boy's hands on me. I want to be wanted, loved, kissed. I want to feel fingers in me, hands on my waist, sort of hard and rough ...*"

A chorus of gagging noises filled the locker room.

Tess stopped, tore out more pages, and took another step forward to shove Carmen.

She stumbled against the wall, striking it hard enough to rattle her skull. When she rebounded, someone slapped her on the backside. The popping noise was loud and meaty, initiating another bout of laughter. Carmen barely felt it at all. Some part of her was going numb, breaking.

The laughter was like the drone of a storm from within the locker room, an ambient noise, like thunder rumbling in Carmen's head.

And through it all, Tess did not stop. She bent to Carmen's ear and whispered, "You put my name in your journal, bitch."

"What?" It was the only word Carmen could produce in that moment.

"You heard me! You wrote about me in your nasty book! A nasty whore, with a nasty book."

"Does she want *you* to touch her and kiss her too?" Virgie asked.

Again, more laughter.

"Why is my name in your book? You jealous of me? You hate me? You have dreams of going down on me? Eat me out? Huh, carpet muncher."

Even if Carmen had wanted, she could not speak. Every fiber of her body was frozen in embarrassment and panic.

"Let me see it!" Virgie snatched it from Tess and read.

Miriam and Cassie joined, taking the journal and reading portions of it at random. "*Monday, November eighth. I just want to be loved, kissed. Wanted.*"

The sounds of exaggerated sucking and kissing sounds filled Carmen's ears. Her jaw clenching, she tried to shut out the sounds, but it was like wildfire ricocheting off the lips of all the girls in the locker room.

"Good luck finding someone to do it," Tess said, grinning at her. "Who the hell would want to even touch you? Look at you!"

"Maybe it's Willa," Virgie screamed.

"Oh my god, that's right," Cassie responded.

"I guess you didn't know I was in one of the stalls, huh?" Virgie said. "I heard you and Willa yesterday. You made a little friend, didn't you?"

"I bet it didn't stop there," Tess said. "I bet Willa came by your house last night. Maybe she climbed through the window and finger-banged you. Did it feel good when she licked your clit?"

Now the exaggerated sounds were of the girls pretending to vomit.

Carmen felt dizzy. Her heart pounded so hard she thought, at one point, it would explode out of her chest, and her stomach was a pit of boiling lava. She feared she might actually lose control of herself. Her knees buckled and she felt herself giving way.

The locker room door opened.

Tess grabbed the diary from Cassie and shoved it into her bag. She fixed her hair and tugged the bottom of her sweater, smoothing out her pants.

The girls scattered like flies.

Carmen didn't think she'd ever been so happy to see a teacher in her life.

Only, the person who came through the door was not a teacher. It was Willa. She smirked at the crowd of girls and tilted her head curiously at Carmen. Then she refocused on the girls. "This is like eight-on-one. You girls afraid the farmgirl might beat your asses if you made it a fair fight, Tess?"

"Get lost, Willa," Tess said.

"Yeah, you aren't even in this class!" Cassie pointed at her, standing behind Tess.

"Shows what you know. I am. But I have asthma. I stay in the library while you idiots are playing kickball and running the mile. Looking like complete asses."

"Sure, you are," Tess said. "I bet you spend this period under the bleachers, giving blowjobs to whoever comes by." Tess looked around to the others, egging them on, "right girls?"

"Shit, you found me out!" Willa snapped her fingers. "Was it your dad who told you? He *is* my biggest customer. Says your mom apparently forgot what a cock is for."

Virgie stepped forward and eyed Tess, as if to see if she would respond.

"Back down, Virgie," Willa said. "Head honcho there is pretty slow on the uptake. Might take her another few minutes before she understands."

"Shut up, you dyke witch," Tess said.

Willa held her hand at lip level, palm open, and pretended to blow something toward Tess. Then she shoved Virgie backward.

Virgie stumbled into Cassie, who was standing directly behind her.

Willa's eyes remained locked with Tess's. "Go on, Tess. Do something. I mean you're quick to pick on people that don't defend themselves. Come at me. You know you want to." She even offered her cheek, craning her neck closer.

Carmen watched it all, stunned, as Tess backed down while dramatically tossing her hair.

"Come on, girls," she said. "I'm tired of these dykes. God only knows what diseases they have, and I don't want to catch them."

On her way toward the door, she kicked some of the torn pages from Carmen's diary.

"Just herpes!" Willa called out as Tess and the others left. "And I got it from your nasty father. You stupid cunt!"

Carmen managed a smile at this. Still, she didn't dare move until the last girl was out of the locker room. Finally, Carmen allowed herself to breathe normally, to unhinge her knees and her jaw. She grabbed her gym shorts and slipped them on, then sighed at the state of her clothes.

"You okay?" Willa asked.

"Yeah. They soaked my clothes."

"Ah yeah, that's a good one. I got that a time or two."

"But not anymore?"

Willa shrugged. "Not for a while. They don't mess with me, they know better." She tucked a lock of hair behind her ear and looked earnestly at Carmen. "For real, how are you?"

"Embarrassed. Angry. Pissed. And shocked."

"Shocked?"

"Yeah. No one has ever stood up for me like that."

"Oh, sweetie, don't flatter yourself. That wasn't just for you. God, I love to get under that girl's skin. And ... I'm so good at it."

Carmen tilted her head and smirked. "Yeah, I see that. Sorry, but I have to ask. Are you?"

"Am I what?"

"Gay. They keep calling you a dyke."

Willa burst out laughing, cutting her bright eyes toward Carmen. She cleared her throat and tried to take on a serious approach. "Oh, Carmen Winstead. Is that all you got out of that? And besides, what if I am?"

"Oh-no, I wouldn't care. You just saved my ass. As far as I'm concerned, you're my best friend. Actually, my only friend, but I just wanted to make sure you didn't expect to climb through my window and—"

"First of all, no, I'm not. But if I were, I wouldn't have to sneak in through your window. I'd just come through the door."

"But *I'm* not gay."

"So?" She playfully blew Carmen a kiss, chuckled, and pulled a cigarette pack from her back pocket.

"You can't smoke in here, Willa."

Willa removed her lighter. "Why not?"

"Um, because you can get caught. And, you know, your asthma."

Willa lit the cigarette and took a long drag. "Yeah, that asthma's a bitch. Look, I don't know if I can be your friend if you're going to be a constant stick in the mud. You aren't a goody-goody, are you?"

"No, no ..." Carmen's hands were still shaking. "I don't think so."

"You don't think so?" Willa took another long drag of her cigarette. "Let's test that theory."

"How?"

"Ditch the rest of the day. Come hang at my place for a while."

"Are your parents' home?"

"No clue. My folks ditched me when I was three. I don't know where their home is, much less if they're there. Or alive, for that matter. I live with my Aunt True, and she's pretty fucking cool. So, come on, let's blow this place."

Carmen's first reaction was to say no. While not opposed to breaking the rules, it might've been a little too early at a new school to start cutting classes. Then again, Willa was the only person who seemed to care about her. She'd shown more compassion for Carmen than anyone else since she'd arrived in Somerdale—including her father. Besides, if she got home at her regular time, her father would never know. "Okay."

Willa nodded, took another drag of her cigarette, and clapped Carmen's back. "There might be hope for you yet, Carmen Winstead!"

2:35 P.M.

Willa drove an old Chevy Cavalier. The bumpers were covered in faded stickers adorned with the bands she listened to: The Cure, Nine Inch Nails, Rammstein, and Deftones. Carmen recognized only a few of them and had no idea what Willa had blaring through her busted speakers as they drove to Willa's house. It was loud and aggressive, a combination that seemed to suit Willa perfectly.

Willa lived in an area that seemed just as rural as the farmland Carmen and her father lived on. It was about six miles from the school and down a long, paved driveway. The house itself was quite basic—a one-story white house with a small porch.

"There's one thing you might want to know about my Aunt True," Willa said as they got out of the car.

"What's that?" Carmen asked, still a little stirred up from the incident in the locker room and the thrill of skipping class.

"Well ... she's a witch."

Carmen made a *pfff* sound and waved away the comment. "Yeah, okay."

"Okay, maybe not a witch, but she *is* Wiccan. And around here, you can guess what that equates to in the eyes of the ignorant."

"Witch," Carmen said, fully understanding.

"Bingo."

"Wiccan, huh? That's sort of cool. I guess. I don't really even know what that is or what they believe."

"Nothing too dark and weird. It's mostly nature worship. Like trees and stuff. But it's more than that."

"What do you mean?"

"Well, there's a mother goddess and she loves communing with some of the deities and spirits of the world. Or something like that. She's tried to get me into it, but it sort of bores me. Seems a little too New-Age-y. But she takes it very seriously. Anyway, just a heads up."

"Got it."

As Carmen followed Willa onto the porch, a little thrill passed through her. She found the idea of worshipping nature somewhat romantic.

When she entered, she felt slightly disappointed. She wasn't sure what she had been expecting—maybe black curtains, stuffed ravens, healing crystals, and wooden totems. Instead, it looked like something out of one of those interior design magazines she sometimes saw at the checkout aisle in the supermarket. Everything was very angular and minimal, well-polished, and clean. *Boring.*

Oh my god, she thought to herself. *You really are ignorant. With stereotypes like that, you're no better than anyone else.*

"Aunt True!" Willa called out. "It's me! I have a friend here!"

A distant "What?" came from the other end of the house, followed by a series of hurried footsteps, and, within a few seconds, a woman appeared in the hallway. Willa's aunt looked flustered but happy. Her appearance *did* somewhat match what Carmen had envisioned—long, riotous curls, mostly gray, a flowing white peasant dress with sleeves big enough to fit five arms and a pentacle charm lay securely around her neck. Willa smiled mischievously, running her gaze over Carmen.

"And who is your friend?"

Willa tapped Carmen on the shoulder, as if willing her to speak. "Carmen," she finally said. "Carmen Winstead."

"Well, I'm happy to have you, Carmen. But do your folks know you're skipping school?"

Carmen only shook her head.

True responded with a shrug.

"I told you she's cool," Willa whispered.

"That's flattering," True said. "But it doesn't negate the fact that I have strict rules about having guests over on weekdays."

"You do?"

"Yes, Willa."

"How did I not know this?"

"Because we never have company on weekdays. Or ever, for that matter," True said with a smirk. She stretched and dug a fist into the small of her back.

"Your back hurting again?" Willa asked.

"A bit. Mainly because I've been cleaning the bathroom you insist on keeping like some sort of art gallery." She eyed and winked. "Did you know her hair isn't really red?"

"Aunt True! What the hell." Willa exclaimed with a slight giggle in her tone.

"My back does hurt," True said, ignoring her. "But pain is only the devil's work trying to slow me down."

"Want some help?" Willa asked.

But True waved her away. "Not right now. Entertain your friend." She said walking near Carmen and staring curiously.

"You heard her," Willa said, taking Carmen by the arm. "Come be entertained."

"Well, it was nice to meet you." True leaned in and gently hugged Carmen, and her body tensed. She released Carmen very quickly, and, when she stepped away, Carmen noticed her eyes were wide. Her hands seemed to shake a bit as she shoved them into the pockets of her dress. True gave Carmen a stiff nod as Willa dragged Carmen down the hall and into her bedroom.

As Carmen slipped inside the room, the last thing she saw was True staring after her, her lips moving but no words coming out. *Odd,* she thought as she turned her back to the door and surveyed Willa's room. It was much larger than Carmen's bedroom but, unlike the rest of the house, was something of a mess. Posters on the walls featured some of the same bands covering the back of Willa's car. Piles of black tattered clothes sat here and there, and the bed was unmade. It looked like it hadn't been made in quite some time.

"Alright, Winstead," Willa said. "Who goes first? You or me?"

"Huh?"

"The gay stuff. Like Tess said. Who drops their pants first?"

"But I … I don't …"

"It's a joke, Carmen. Take it easy, will ya."

"I wish I could. I've never been the best at letting stuff like that slide off my back. I don't know why."

"Was it like this at your old school?"

"Sort of. Just not this bad. I never really fit in. I've never fit in anywhere … I guess."

"Same here. I grew up in this hole. Never fit in and knew by seventh grade, when I never got invited to birthday parties or sleep overs that I never would. So, I stopped trying. Stopped caring."

"Is that why you color your hair and wear dark make-up?"

"Sort of. Why? You don't like it?"

"Oh, no, I meant ... well ... forget it."

"Damn Winstead. There you go again. Ease up. And that secret stays with you by the way. It's all blond under this, I decided blond was the most boring and generic hair color for girls around here. Tess Todd is proof. Sweet tits and no brains, that's all she's got going for her."

Carmen eyed Willa. A nervous smile cracked her lips as she began chewing the skin on her nailbeds. "You handled them like a champ though. Why are they so scared of you?"

Willa fished through her stacks of clothes for something. "Because of my Aunt True. I'm not kidding when I said everyone around here associates Wicca with being a witch. They think I'm evil, that I might hocus-pocus them or something, make them grow warts or have their tits fall off. It's crazy really. When I realized that, I decided to use it to my advantage. I mean why not, right?

"I guess."

"You know what I did once?" Willa said, her fiery braid now loose, tousled in her face. Last year, I planted a copy of the Satanic bible in my locker and *accidentally* dropped it when Tess and Cassie walked by."

Carmen found herself smiling so wide she felt a slight pain radiate from her cheeks. *It was nice to smile*, she thought, something she had not done in a long time. "That's awesome."

"It sort of was." Willa tossed Carmen a tee shirt and a pair of jeans. "You look about as skinny as me. Those should do unless you want to go home wearing your gym stuff."

"No. Thanks."

"Anyway, when Cassie saw the book fall, she shit herself. It was great. Cassie believes in this holy roller bullshit. I am sure Mr. Hollins wanted to homeschool her after that. He probably thought the devil was alive and well in Somerdale." Willa looked at Carmen and smiled. "Well, it actually is."

"Yeah, it just doesn't have horns."

"Good one Winstead." Willa snickered.

Carmen couldn't contain her smile as she slipped into the clothes, which smelled like faint flowery perfume and the ghost of cigarette smoke. She couldn't remember the last time anyone had been so kind to her. "Is that why you're helping me? "Because they used to tease you too?"

"Maybe. I'm not sure. But if your enemy hates someone, then that someone must be pretty fucking great, right?"

"I don't know about that."

"Also, let's be real here. I need someone to hang with at the corn festival. I don't want to go by myself. What would that look like?"

"The ... what?"

Willa gave a playfully shocked look. "You mean you haven't heard?"

"No. But *corn* and *festival.* Those words together sound miserable."

"Oh, it is. The town holds it every year. Sort of a last hurrah before winter rolls around and starts freezing everything. It gets cold here, FYI."

"Good. I like the cold."

"I figured. If you're anything like me, you like hiding in big, thick sweaters, right?"

"Hoodies in particular."

Willa nodded in agreement. "Anyway, it's sort of cheesy, as you'd expect. But there's kettle corn and hot chocolate. Who can pass that up? Also, Tess Todd always goes, so there's the bonus of knowing my presence irritates the hell out of her."

"See, that'd be reason enough for me to stay away."

"Oh, no. You can't! Carmen, you can't let girls like this get the better of you. You must stand up for yourself or they'll keep at it. See, for me, my goal is to one day make her crack in a public place and lose her shit in front of everyone. That way, everyone will know what a miserable cunt she is."

Carmen could not tell if Willa was being for real or not, so she just smiled and nodded. "And you expect me to go with you to this thing?"

"Absolutely. It will be alright; I will be there. She won't have the balls, believe me. Plus, I'd like to see how Tess handles having more than one person to pick on. If her little retreat from the locker room today was any indication, I think it might be fun."

Carmen usually tried to avoid confrontations, but something about the way Willa looked as she explained herself was alluring. And Tess had made her life a living hell. "Okay … consider me in, then. I think."

"You a cheap date?"

"Don't know. Never been on one." She was trying to be funny, but it came out flat.

Willa gave a frown and an effortless shrug. "You're not missing much."

"No?"

"Not based on my experience. I've been on two. I think I scared the first one. The second one left me on the side of the road when I wouldn't blow him in his car. Dick. Believe me, Somerdale boys aren't exactly knights in shining armor."

"At my rate, I don't even need a knight. He could be like a squire."

"As long as he knows how to use his sword, right?" Willa laughed as she headed for her bedroom door. "Sorry. I'm not the best host, I guess. You want a soda or anything?"

"Yeah, that would be great."

She waved for Carmen to follow her. "Come take your pick."

As they traipsed to the kitchen, Carmen felt a sort of warmth spreading inside. It was strange and unfamiliar, but, as she took a Coke from Willa, she understood what it was. It was the feeling of having a friend—something she had not experienced in a long, long time, and it felt good.

4:16 P.M.

Joe Winstead was at the kitchen table yet again, drinking a beer. He had never been a heavy drinker, so seeing him drinking so early two days in a row raised a red flag in Carmen's head. The confused and concerned look on his face did not help matters either. "Hey, kiddo."

"Hey, Dad." Carmen tossed her bookbag on the couch, went to the fridge to grab a Yoo-hoo, and joined him at the table. "Everything okay?" She tried not to look directly at the beer as she asked or his eyes for that matter. *Guilt* was written all over her face.

"Yeah, I'm great. Though I should ask you the same."

"What do you mean?"

Joe ran his thumb across the mouth of his beer bottle, obviously thinking of how to word what he wanted to say next. "I got a call from one of your counselors from school, Mr. Fleming. "Well, he claimed you were not in one of your classes."

"Oh." Carmen had never really been in trouble at school. One instance, in the eighth grade, they found her hiding under the bleachers during Phys Ed. avoiding her teacher and classmates. That had landed her in detention for three days, but other than that, trouble was foreign to the Winsteads. She had no idea what to expect from her father as he eyed her over the rim of his beer bottle.

"Did you skip or something?"

"Yeah. Dad I did." Carmen said lowering her head.

"Where did you go?"

"My friend Willa's house."

He raised an eyebrow, the corners of his mouth curling into a grin. "A friend?"

"Yes. Is that so hard to believe?"

"No. But ... well, I got the impression that some of the staff at the school are worried about you. Why would that be?"

"Because I'm the new girl, Dad. That's all."

"Maybe. But ... are you getting teased or something? The man I spoke to was one of the guidance counselors. He said certain girls at your school can be ... well, really mean. That's pretty much how he put it anyway."

"He's right about that."

"So, you *are* getting teased? Teased again, Carmen? Really? When is this going to stop?"

She hesitated. Her father had set it right there on the table. She could complain and even cry about the horrible things that were happening, about how Tess Todd seemed to have some sort of vendetta against her and how the other girls were following her lead. But he didn't need the extra worry. She always tried to be strong for him—no whining, no complaining.

"Of course, I am," she finally answered. "I'm an alien to them. It's going to happen."

"Damn. It happens everywhere we go. I mean that's why we moved here. You know ... small town and all. Thought it would be different. But you're okay, right?"

Carmen lowered her head. The last thing she wanted was to make her dad feel like it was another futile attempt. "I'm fine, Dad." Carmen raised her head and the room fell silent.

"Well, what about this Willa girl? Is she as interesting as her name makes her sound?"

Carmen dazed off for a moment and thought about Willa. A small smile cracked the corner of her lips. "Yeah, she is. She's pretty cool."

"All the same, let's try not to skip class with her anymore, okay?"

"Sure, yeah okay."

"You're welcome to invite her over for dinner or something if you want."

"Maybe one day."

Joe took a swig of his beer and clapped his hands. "Oh! So, I almost forgot. I hate to reward you skipping class, but I do have some pretty good news. I had the internet guys come out today. We have an actual working connection now."

"Awesome. That *is* good news."

"And even better news is waiting for you on your bed."

She gave him a curious look but wasted no time. She ran from the kitchen, up the stairs, and into her small room. In the middle of her bed sat a white box with a very well-known logo on it—an apple with a bite in it. It was the laptop she'd been dropping hints about. She'd accidentally busted her old one in the move.

She almost squealed with delight. When she whirled to thank him, she found him leaning against the door frame, arms crossed and smiling smugly. "Dad, are you serious? How? I mean, can we afford this?"

"We can. Another reason we moved here was because the cost of living is cheaper. And you know I got a raise with the re-location and the new job. You deserve this, Carmen. You've been an absolute trooper ever since your mom left."

As she approached him to give him a hug, Carmen noticed for the first time just how much her father was showing his age. He wasn't old by any means—he'd just celebrated his forty-fifth birthday two months ago—but the deepening wrinkles in his face told of the hardship they'd faced since her mother left. But his big, beautiful hazel eyes always seemed to contain a sparkle of joy and hope.

"Dad, are you sure we can afford this? I know things are tight right now. Well, I know they are always tight, but you know what I mean. How will we pay for this?"

"Didn't I just answer that?" he said, grinning at her. "Besides, I don't want you to worry about such things; that's my job."

"Yeah, but still …"

Joe looked around and frowned at the absolute lack of furniture in her room. There was Carmen's bed, her dresser, and a small bedside table; that was it. "I guess the next thing on the list will be a desk, huh?"

"God, Dad. The computer is enough. I'll use the floor as a desk if I have to."

Joe only shrugged. "We'll see. Now, the only thing I ask in return for the computer is you accompany me to dinner."

"Really? Where around here is there to go?"

Joe adopted the voice of a haughty Englishman and extended the crook of his elbow to her. "Well, as I understand it, the pizza at Bobby's is *quite* greasy and delicious. And we must simply try the corndogs at Jenkin's Mini-Mart."

Carmen laughed deeply and heartily, and, for just a moment, she forgot about what had occurred in the locker room earlier and all the torment that had come before it. "You're the best dad, I want you to know that."

"I try, kiddo, I really do."

She took her father's arm and as he escorted her from the room, for a moment, she heard the scratching again coming from inside her walls. Then wondered if he had heard it too.

10:56 P.M.

Filled on corndogs and grape slushies, Carmen felt bloated and borderline sick as she went to her bedroom. Upon returning from dinner, Joe resigned himself to activating their Netflix account, and Carmen, visited a few social media pages, now that the internet was actually working.

Just as she hunkered onto the bed with the laptop, her phone buzzed. Surprised, she checked it to see a series of short texts from an unfamiliar number with the Somerdale area code: *Hey there, sexy. Do you happen to have Tess Todd's phone number? I'd sure like to do lesbian stuff to her. Did I say "lesbian?" I meant, "lurid and violent. Maybe punch her in the fucking head."*

Carmen laughed out loud. It was a strange feeling to be so happy, so filled with the need to laugh. It was the first time she'd felt such a way since they had moved to Somerdale. She replied quickly and a little disappointed in herself that it did not feel good to trash a girl who had been tormenting her. That behavior was just not who Carmen was. *Don't have her number. Sorry, Willa.*

Willa's response came seconds later. *Just as well. I know at least one of her holes always has either a stick or her own head shoved up it.*

Through guilt for laughing, Carmen wrote back, *that's disgusting.*

She spent the next half an hour texting with Willa. Carmen shared the story about the laptop and corndogs, feeling like a normal teenager with a somewhat normal life.

Jenkins' corndogs are the best, Willa commented. *Hope you're ready to spend about three hours blowing up the toilet though. WOAH!*

The conversation was so much fun and so natural that Carmen was shocked when she realized it was 11:35. She got out of bed, poked her head out the door, and heard her father's light snoring from the couch. Carmen crept from her room and tiptoed down the stairs.

He had started watching a documentary—something on global warming.

Carmen shut off the television, laid her father down comfortably, covered him with a blanket, and kissed his forehead. When she returned to her room, she had another text from Willa.

Getting late. Gotta go to bed. See ya at school tomorrow. FRI-DAY! Praise the baby Jesus. And don't forget ... you and me, corn festival on Saturday.

Carmen smiled and responded, *It's a date!* She put down the phone, tinkered with the computer for a bit longer, setting up some social media sites then got ready for bed. She hummed a little as she brushed her teeth and combed her hair in the upstairs bathroom.

She settled down to sleep, her cheeks hurting from all the smiling and laughing she'd been enjoying for the last six hours. When she pulled the covers to her neck, she felt secure and safe and for the first time in her life, happy. She slowly started to drift off, sleep tugging her away. Then, just as she was on the brink of slumber, she heard something. A tapping, very close to her head.

Her eyes shot open, and she stared into the darkness of her room. She waited a moment to see if the noise had been a dream or something in her imagination—maybe everything was beginning to take its toll on her. She listened quietly and the silence stretched on.

But then ... there it was again.

Tap. Tap.

It was coming from her window.

Her first instinct was to sit upright in bed, to peer into the darkness. But that was much easier said than done. Fear gripping her, all she could do was lie motionless. The sound continued, the light tapping, similar to the noises she'd heard before—low, menacing. And, as the sounds continued, something else accompanied it. She did everything she could to convince herself it was just the wind whipping around the corners of the house, but she knew this was not true. Whatever she was hearing was not the wind. It was a voice —a long, coarse moan of agony.

Carmen's heart raced in her chest. Blood drained from her face, and her skin went cold and numb. She wanted to scream, but she could not draw a deep enough breath, and it suddenly seemed impossible to open her mouth.

Tap. Tap. And then the moaning voice, whispering something she could not decipher. The rational part of her mind told her there were easily a hundred different natural occurrences that could be causing this commotion. But the *irrational* part of her, the part that took over right then, was certain something evil was out there waiting ... waiting patiently for her.

Finally, Carmen exhaled a faint moan. That tiny sound was enough to give her a bit of confidence, allowing her to sit upright in bed. She spied the butterfly lamp on her side table and nearly knocked it off as she reached for the pull string.

The room flooded with soft light. For a moment, Carmen thought she saw something at the window, something dark and fleeting and moving like liquid. Maybe it was her own reflection at the edges of the glass. But maybe it wasn't. Maybe something was in the darkness, staring at her, watching her. Waiting. She tore off the blanket and stepped out of bed. The coolness of the room slid across Carmen's skin like silk, leaving remnants of goose bumps all over her body. Ignoring them, she shambled toward the window and peered into the darkness, straining her eyes, searching, wondering.

She tasted something in her throat—something with a sort of metallic tinge that made her wonder if absolute horror could actually have a taste. She studied the window. Nothing, of course, was out there, only her own reflection staring back at her. But it was not her normal reflection; it was distorted. It appeared as if her face was melting away, like her skin was being ripped from her bones. Carmen inhaled quickly. The sight startled her as she closed her eyes, willing it away. When she opened them again, it was gone. Just her lucid reflection stared back. She exhaled a sigh of relief as she slowly stepped from the window and padded to her bed.

Leaving the butterfly lamp on, she fell against the pillow and willed herself to be calm. After a while, she heard the very faint sounds of her father snoring on the couch. It was enough to make her feel safe again. She felt the warmth of her wool blanket as she curled her fingers around the edges, securing it. Subconsciously, she regarded it as some sort of invisibility cloak. Her hair fell on the pillow, and the images of the window came to the forefront of her mind again. Carmen tried to will away the images and told herself to concentrate on the comforting rhythm of her father's snoring, and, after a few minutes, the sound finally engulfed her as she felt herself being pulled hesitantly into a deep sleep.

FRIDAY, OCTOBER 21, 2008

6:32 A.M.

Carmen woke to the morning sun radiating through her room. She lay in bed for a long time until the terrifying noises from the night before dripped into her mind. She rolled over, drawing her knees to her stomach, and stared toward her window. She sat up quickly, dangling her legs on the side of her bed, and got up. Feeling quite safe in the morning glow, she approached her window and stared out. She searched around and saw nothing on the glass or in the frost-crowned yard. But she had fallen asleep last night thinking about what she had heard, what she had seen, and, as she woke this morning, the thoughts remained. Trickling in the back of her mind.

Her lingering thoughts were interrupted by a sudden *ding*—a notification that someone had sent a message. Carmen timidly approached her bed with widen eyes and opened the screen. Another *ding*, then another. Before she could open the first message, her inbox flooded. Carmen clicked the first message. *Die bitch.* Then another, *Got milk.* And another, *Pigstead.* Her eyes clouded with fear as she slammed her laptop and whispered to herself, "breathe."

Her dad was pouring coffee into a thermos in the kitchen when she finally pulled herself together enough to make it downstairs. He was dressed in a button-down shirt and khakis rather than his usual around-the-house attire of a hoodie and jeans.

She nearly told him about what she'd heard the night before but decided against it. He would tell her it was just the changing weather, the wind, the house settling, or whatever he could concoct in his mind to make her feel better. And he would probably be right. She also wanted to tell him about the laptop as well but decided against it. So, she left it alone.

"All dressed up, I see," Carmen commented.

"Yeah. I got a text from my supervisor this morning. There's an emergency meeting they need me in the office for. And I hate speaking in front of people. You are like me in that sense, at least you got it honestly. So, wish me luck, would you?"

"Yeah sure, Dad. Good luck."

But Joe Winstead wasn't sure if she was being honest or insufferably sarcastic. "Depending on how the meeting goes, I might be a little late getting home. I'll call you. Maybe I can bring dinner."

"Or I could cook something. I'm aware of how much that laptop costs, Dad. Let me cook and save us some money."

"Fair enough." Joe grabbed his bag and kissed her on the forehead.

Carmen watched as he walked out the door. She thought he seemed a little nervous but also somewhat excited. But she was happy to see him like that. It had taken him far too long to realize he could have a life outside the wretched woman he had married. Carmen wasn't sure, but she thought her father was the type of man who had always feared being alone. Maybe he was finally coming around to the idea that he could start over here in Somerdale. And hopefully his starting over would go much smoother than her own.

Carmen ate some oatmeal and had half a cup of coffee—something her father frowned upon but had not outright banned. She dreaded going back to school. Each day was like being presented a gift from a stranger and not knowing if a pile of shit or a nail bomb was inside the box. And now with the messages on her computer, Carmen felt like she was being attacked from all sides. She almost felt extremely anxious. So, to pull it together, she did her best to remember the fun she'd had last night with her father and while texting Willa as she grabbed her coat and bundled up for the cool morning waiting for her outside. *Round two*, she thought as she hurried out the door.

As Carmen stepped onto the porch, she felt the frigid wind roaring by her. It brought to mind the moaning she'd heard outside her window last night, so she tossed her coat's hood over her head to block the wind. She stepped out, her feet crunching the little sheet of frost that had gathered on the grass overnight. She walked down the driveway to where the bus had been picking her up. She hated that she was still riding the bus, but she hadn't taken the driver's test yet, and besides, she did not expect her father to buy her a car. Once they got settled and life wasn't such hell for her here in Somerdale, she planned to get a job and save to buy her own. Idly, she wondered if Willa would be willing to pick her up in the mornings. It would certainly serve to make her days a little better, or at least until she stepped foot in the hallways of school where everyone was waiting … like a plague—ready to devour her at any moment.

8:10 A.M.

The quiet of Carmen's morning was broken when the bus pulled into one of the allotted parking spots in front of the school.

Somerdale High loomed in front of her like a nightmare, and her anxiety instantly resumed as she stepped onto the pavement.

She kept her head down as soon as she entered, like she always did, trying not to be seen as she headed for her locker. She dialed in her combination, opened it to get her book for first period Algebra, and saw a folded sheet of paper propped against the side that had not been there the day before, which made her think someone had slid it through the little vented portion along the top of the locker door.

She opened it and saw a photocopied page from her journal. She skimmed it to see which entry it was, and her face flushed. It was a pretty explicit section describing a sexual and borderline violent dream she'd had about a boy she'd had a crush on in Bristol. At the top of the page, written in red magic marker, was: *HAHA YOU HORNY PIG!*

It was clearly a message from Tess Todd. Stomach knotting, Carmen balled up the paper, shoved it into her bookbag, and headed for class. On the way, someone made an oink sound, but she dared not look to see who it was as she slipped through the door. She slunk into her seat, letting her hair hang around her face like blinders.

Algebra was not the problem though. It was Mr. Carlton's English class where Tess Todd seemed to be at her worst. Before class started, she pulled out her phone and texted Willa. *I don't suppose you want to skip fifth period, do you?*

The response from Willa came back pretty quickly. *Would love to but can't. Got a test, and I'm FAILING. Let's do lunch though!*

Carmen sighed and stowed her phone. Maybe having lunch with Willa would give her the strength to endure Tess's taunts. Maybe she could find strength she never knew she had. But deep-down, Carmen knew that she didn't. As Mrs. Hunt, a tall woman with beady eyes—probably long past retirement, pulled stacks of papers out of her bag, Carmen slumped lower and lower in her seat. But as she did, a girl, three rows over with long brown hair made an oinking sound. Carmen looked up with a startled wince, expecting a deeper blow. Carmen's eyes closed. Veins pulsated. She felt her breath grow thick with horror. *No more please god,* she thought, and waited for fear to devour her. But Mrs. Hunt made a *shoosh* sound towards the class and the room fell silent. Carmen, overcome with an indescribable sigh of relief— like a giant bolder had been lifted off her shoulders relaxed. But in her mind, she knew it wasn't over. She knew that soon the whispers would start, and the laughter would be deafening.

12:02 P.M.

The lunchroom was like any other American high school cafeteria: full of chatter, cliques divided by tables—the jocks and the cheerleaders snuggled up near the windows that lined the school, science club academics on the outskirts—then there were the upper cuts strategically placed by the lunch line, like the sun that other planets had to revolve around. That was Tess Todd's group—the perfect ones, the Café Society. That's where everyone wanted to sit, where most high school girls only dreamed of fitting in. And as for the boys, they can always hark back their time when they got their first chub. Give credit to Tess Todd, and she would surely take it. But at the tables by the door, in deep space and perfectly happy about it, were Carmen and Willa. The outcasts. Exiled. The freaks.

As Tess and her little troop entered to get their food, they broke out into their oinks and kissing noises.

Carmen just looked at the table.

Willa, however, had no problem giving them back what they gave. She raised her right hand and flashed them her middle finger.

"You wish, bitch!" Tess said as she walked by, smiling because all eyes were on her. It made her feel flawless, valued, in control.

Willa nodded enthusiastically. "Every night."

Tess rolled her eyes and walked away.

"How do you do that?" Carmen asked.

"Do what?"

"Take their ridicule like that."

"Because I could give two shits and a fuck what Tess Todd thinks about me. That's why. Plus, all those gay jokes she makes about me and you, you know she's going to end up being a bull dyke in the end, right? Or maybe one of those housewives who becomes nothing more than a fuckbag for her old man and ends up gray and lonely by her early forties. Part of some lonely wives' club, meeting some loser in a rat bag hotel just to get her rocks off. Hell, I'm just trying to get her there faster. Trying to help her out." Willa threw her juice carton on the table. "Listen Winstead, if you take all this shit from that little dweeb, this world, the one out there, will eat you alive my friend. Think about that."

"I know. I have. It's just I'm used to it … I guess."

"Don't let that bitch get to you. She suffers from a disease, you know that, right?"

"No, I didn't know that. What is wrong with her?"

"Cunt-titus. It's a very rare disease, but Tess has it. It has spread through her whole body. And now it's eating her fucking brain." Willa leaned into Carmen and laughed.

Carmen noticed Willa's green eyes had a little sparkle to them but also knew there was a dark side too. Even though they both laughed about this, it did not ease Carmen's anxiety about Mr. Carlton's class.

When lunchtime ended, her stomach churned like butter as she shambled to class and took her seat. The bell rang, class started, and Carmen simply waited for the torture to begin. She was waiting for farm jokes or something being thrown around class about her diary. She was nervous, even scared, but, to Carmen's surprise, the class passed without a single comment—not even a mean look from Tess, or anyone for that matter.

Tess spent all class applying makeup and secretly texting while Mr. Carlton discussed Mary Shelley and the myths that had followed her after *Frankenstein*.

After a while, Carmen relaxed. She watched the clock tick away the seconds, making her think about the noises in her room last night.

Tap ... tap ...

3:02 P.M.

The day was nearly over. She'd survived, with no tense interactions with Tess or any of her friends. As Carmen maneuvered to her locker for the final time that week, she felt a surge of excitement for the coming weekend. She never been invited to anything much less a festival and she figured her, and Willa would do their best to have a great time. Something that in her mind—she needed.

As she approached her locker, the exaggerated sound of shuffling papers greeted her ears. It was loud enough to be heard over the murmur and thrum of the crowd of students shifting through the hallways. She noticed Virgie holding a large stack of paper, grinning sadistically at her. *Oh, no. Here it comes.*

"Have fun with this," Virgie whispered and tossed the stack of papers into the air. Some of them fell right away, but about half of them caught a breeze and fluttered down the hall. The sound they made was oddly frightening, as the papers rained upon the rush of students. Virgie bumped Carmen's shoulder hard as she passed. "Have a lovely weekend, Pigstead."

Carmen snatched one of the sheets of paper from the air as it fluttered down. Just as she set eyes on it, laughter erupted around her. Carmen's stomach roiled, her cheeks flushed, and her heart felt like it had stopped.

Someone had done a rather good Photoshop job on a picture of a lesbian couple engaged in the sixty-nine position. There was nothing subtle about it; legs were spread wide, leaving nothing to the imagination. Only, the faces had been swapped for the faces of Carmen and Willa. The word PIG had been placed under Carmen. WITCH had been placed under Willa.

As Carmen stared at the sheet of paper, a guy approached and clapped her back. "Hot. Pig on witch, I'm into that!" he whispered as laughter filled Carmen's ears.

She felt her cheeks heating as a single tear moistened her skin. Suddenly, she felt a hard pinch on her backside.

Another guy had grabbed her ass, made an oinking sound, and ran to join a group of his cackling friends.

The entire hallway erupted in laughter as Carmen quickly escaped toward the front doors. But more papers floated down like a blizzard. Carmen looked at the second-level stairwell and saw Miri George standing there, leaning over the banister, papers showering from her hands like a flood.

Another face appeared, and Tess Todd stepped alongside her, arms crossed, staring at Carmen and laughing. Cruelly.

Carmen barely glanced down and noticed the back of the papers had the same photocopied page that had been slipped into her locker that morning—her journal entry. "Oh my god," Carmen said, the wind coming right out of her as she ran for the doors, through the jeering students. As she ran, Carmen thought of that journal entry in her handwriting now in the hands of the entire student body.

... just to feel a guy's mouth on me and not necessarily on my lips ... because sometimes I do dream of it, of begging a guy to put it in my mouth ... and there are far too many dirty things I'd do to him and probably nothing I'd say no to ... and when my fingers are in there, I try to think it's him—his cock, his fingers, his tongue, his ANYTHING ...

She exploded outside, blinking in the bright daylight. She'd hoped the fresh air would have helped, but somehow it only made it worse. Something like this, there was no escape from. There was no coming back.

Carmen's body trembled as she stood helpless on the curb. Tears surged down her cheeks, and nausea tangled her gut. Cold sweat beaded on her temples, but there was nowhere to run. Her bus was nowhere in sight. As a group of boys—a few she noticed from Tess Todd's group, surrounded her, taunting her, repeating, *Pigstead, Pigstead*, and clapping. Carmen cuffed her ears with her hands, willing it away. Tears flowed her cheeks, and she knew, it would never be over. Ever. As the group snaked in closer, forming a tight circle she heard something.

"Carmen!" Her name rose above the cruel laughter from a familiar and friendly voice she had not heard since lunch.

She scanned the crowd and heard it again.

"Carmen! Over here!" Willa appeared through the crowd of students waiting for the bus. She looked quite upset, which was alarming because Carmen had never seen her anything other than calm and chill.

A boy whistled at her and showed her one of the sheets of paper.

Willa rewarded him with an elbow to his chest. "Come on," Willa said, tugging her sleeve. Pulling Carmen from the crowd.

"I have to get on the bus," Carmen said, not realizing how close she was to a complete meltdown until she spoke. "I have to get home … I just wanna go home." Her bottom lip quivered, and saliva dripped down her chin.

"I'll take you. Come on. Let's get out of here. Come on." Willa took her by the arm and yanked her away from the curb.

As they hurried toward the student parking lot, the jeers continued.

"Round two!" someone yelled. "Let me watch!"

"Come on, girls, take a break!"

"Hey, can I come too?"

"Hot pig!"

It was a blur. Somewhere between Willa grabbing her arm and finally reaching the parking lot, she'd given in, allowing her head to hang as low as it would go. It was impossible to remember how happy she'd been the night before. Had she dreamed it all? Or was this the world's way of reminding her that she was *Carmen Pigstead—a disgusting loser* and was not allowed to be happy?

She felt like she was simply being pushed along by the breeze as she slid into Willa's passenger seat. When the door closed, she took a series of deep breaths to get control of herself. She wiped away some stray tears and watched Willa crank the car. "Sorry .... Willa. I-I sort of lost it."

"No need to apologize. When I saw these papers, I went looking for Tess. I wanted to kill that bitch. Luckily, I didn't see her, or I would be on my way to prison or some firing squad or something. So, I'd say you're doing a lot better than me. Plus, I'm not really worried about me—I'm used to their stupid bullshit—but you, Winstead, I worry about."

"Me? Why only me?"

"Because you're my friend, Carmen, and I don't like it when people hurt my friends. That's why. Plus, with this—Tess went too far." Carmen stared at Willa.

Even though she felt like she was on the losing end of a barroom brawl, Willa's words made her feel somewhat normal. "So, they upset you too?"

"Of course. I am human." Willa pulled a folded sheet from her jacket's front pocket, held it up, and smiled. "A little."

"Ah, shit," Carmen said, wincing at the sight. "Did you read it?"

"I did. And I don't know what you're ashamed about. This is good stuff. And it's normal."

"Don't try to cheer me up. Look what they did."

"Fine, then." Willa flipped the paper to the picture of the two women enjoying one another. "Let's look at this, then."

"I'd rather not."

"No seriously, look at this! This is supposed to be *me*? Really? Look at the tits on this woman! If I looked like this, I might just stay at home and do this sort of thing to myself all day!"

Carmen couldn't help but laugh. And when she started, Willa started too. It made it easier to ignore the catcalls and laughter outside. But she knew it was only temporary. Eventually, she'd return the bleakness she knew so well. And maybe this was the last straw. Maybe this was the thing that would break her. Because even though she was laughing, she felt like something inside her had broken, and no matter how hard she tried, she might never manage to repair it.

6:02 P.M.

At dinner, Carmen had no appetite. Every now and then, she would catch her father staring at her in a way that was somewhere between appreciation and wonder. She liked the attention of it, because he was one of the few people who looked at her like she was valuable, but it also made her feel a little uncomfortable, because she knew what he was doing, what he was *seeing*. He had told her countless times just how much she resembled her mother, and she could see traces of her every time she looked in the mirror.

She had her mother's eyes, sunken into the sockets, so pale it looked as if someone had colored them with pastel dust. In Bristol, as early as fifth grade, some of the girls would call her Soulless Carmen, because her eyes sometime looked as if there was no color in them at all. But her dad called her Angel Eyes and would sometimes ask her when she would fly away.

I wish I could, Dad. You have no idea, she thought as she watched him eat hot dogs and instant mac and cheese across the kitchen table.

"How was your day, Dad?" she asked, breaking the silence.

"Not too bad. I think once I sort of get the feel for the ins and outs of the bureaucratic side of things, this job should be a cake walk. A cake walk that ensures at least a one-point-five percent raise every year, mind you." He wolfed down the rest of his mac and cheese and nodded toward her. "How about you? Things any better at school? What's wrong? You're not hungry?"

"No, I'm good. Why?"

"You're playing with your food like it's some kind of puzzle you're putting together."

She nearly laughed out loud but didn't want to open up a discussion. The last thing she wanted to do was have him pry into the situation. If he did, he'd likely find her intimate diary entry, and she'd never recover from the mortification of that. "I guess I'm not," she finally said.

"Is it school?"

"No. Everything is fine. But, you know, it's high school. It's just miserable."

"Made any friends yet?"

"Yeah, Dad. I told you about her yesterday, remember?"

He sighed and frowned. "You're right. Girl with a weird name. Willow, right?"

"Willa."

"That's right. And she's … what? Popular? An outcast? An alien?"

"Alien isn't too far off," Carmen said proudly. "Willa is … well, she's strange."

"And you aren't?"

"Ouch, Dad. That hurt."

"You know I meant that as a compliment."

Carmen smiled, giving him a cunning glare. "I know, Dad. Just giving you a hard time. But Willa's cool."

"Well, I know how hard it can be to make new friends in a new school. If you ever want to have this friend over, just let me know."

"You said that yesterday too. Work distracting you much?"

"It is. I'm sorry. I'll do a better job of paying attention." Carmen flipped at her mac and cheese again. She knew he was lying. He would never pry too much. Just enough for it to matter. To make him feel like he is prominent in her life. Something Carmen was used to and honestly, it was just the way she liked it.

Yet it was another reason not to let him in on the Tess situation. Besides, she had Willa now. And the idea of having Willa over was a good one. Her dad had always been nice and would never purposefully embarrass her. So what if school was a living hell? She had her dad in her corner and a new friend; things could be a lot worse. In only a year, everything would be different. She would be attending college, and maybe she wouldn't be the outcast forever. Maybe things would be different then, and just maybe her mom had been right all along. Maybe her mom had left her with something: hope.

"Have you heard about this big corn festival tomorrow?" Joe asked as he stood from the table to take his dirty dishes to the sink.

"I have."

"Any interest in going? Me, I have to go. It'll be me and three other guys from the new job handing out useless crap like pens and those stupid nylon wristbands."

"I don't know. Willa and I had talked about it, but it seems lame, right?"

"It does. So is Willa this new friend of yours?" He grinned at her, letting her know he was just joking. "It could be fun. Maybe head out and give it a try."

"Yeah, maybe." What she, naturally, did not tell him was they had already decided to go. But Tess's little prank today would make it much harder for her to show her face somewhere like that. She figured Willa would understand. Hell, Willa probably wouldn't want to go either. *Yeah, right. This is just one more reason for Willa to go, just to rub it in Tess's face, to let her know she won't ever truly win, that her petty little pranks are just a waste of her time.*

"I'd consider it. Seems like a big deal around here. Corn." He snickered. "My god, why did we move here, to a place that celebrates … corn?"

Carmen laughed and shrugged. "I don't know. But if we ever see kids with machetes and pitchforks coming out of the stalks, we need to move, okay?"

"Huh?"

"*Children of the Corn.* Dad, please tell me you've seen it."

He frowned and shook his head. "Nope. Can't say I have. Wait … when did *you* see it?"

"Please. I was like ten when I saw that."

"That explains so much."

She smirked, broke off the end of her hotdog, and chucked it at his face.

Laughing, he swatted it away.

For the second night in a row, Carmen Winstead laughed. And while it was not enough to forget everything, it did remind her life existed beyond the pain.

10:15 P.M.

As Carmen was walking from her bathroom, something chimed. Her heart sank as she cast a glance at her computer screen sitting on her bed. But it was black. Something chimed again and Carmen realized it was just her phone, it was Willa. The last thing she needed was a replay of the messages she received this morning.

She couldn't handle anything else today—she walked to her bed, grabbed her computer and stowed it away in her top drawer for the night. She grabbed her phone off the side table and stared curious at the screen.

Hope you're wearing something slutty tomorrow. This picture Tess made of us is getting me all hot.

Chortling, Carmen responded, *Sorry. No hot clothes in my wardrobe. Got a tee shirt with a few holes in the back, tho.*

So, when do you want me to pick you up? Willa replied.

Carmen studied her phone. Being made fun of at school or on her computer was one thing, but what if they did it in front of her dad? What if he saw the pictures? She got into bed, pulled the sheets over her body, and shuddered at the thought.

I don't know if I want to go anymore, Carmen admitted.

Of course, you do. You really gonna let that byatch get to you like that?

Yes. Over something like this, I think I am. For a while, anyway.

Then she wins. She's under your skin, and she wins. Besides ... no way in hell I'm going to let this alone.

My dad will be there. Hang with him.

He hot?

Carmen nearly laughed out loud but held it in. She realized quickly how Willa had a way with words, and she was somewhat envious of that. *He looks good for his age, but I don't think he'd go for weird.*

Weird? Me? Never. Seriously. Don't let that skank win. Come on out with me.

Carmen sank in the darkness, the glow of the cellphone screen illuminating her face as she contemplated it. *Will your Aunt True post bail money if we end up assaulting a certain someone?*

Probably not. She may end up helping assault her and be in jail with us. True isn't exactly a fan of Tess Todd either. That, or she'll cast a spell on her. We're witches, us Daltons. Remember?

Ooh, a spell. Can she make her vag grow mushrooms and mold?

Damn, Winstead. I like the way you think.

Carmen quickly regretted making that comment. She felt bad. Making fun of someone and laughing with Willa made her no better than Tess. Even though, the person she's making fun of has made her life miserable since moving to Somerdale. Part of Carmen knew Tess deserved it but the other part—the simple part felt guilty. An emotion that Carmen was not used to.

So ... when you gonna pick me up?

There was a rare pause in Willa's responses. Carmen wished for a second time that night she hadn't sent a text. Maybe she was making a mistake, but when she got Willa's response, she knew it was too late.

Got some stuff to do with Aunt True in the morning. Pick you up around 12ish?

Carmen picked at her nails, hoping maybe Willa would have changed her mind, but she didn't. When her phone buzzed again, she muttered, "Twelvish, who talks like that?" but texted, *OK!*

She put down the phone, not sure how to feel about it. With Willa by her side, it might be okay. She hoped so, anyway.

She lay in the darkness and closed her eyes, hoping the noises wouldn't come at her tonight. After the day she'd had, she didn't think she could take it. Once, she thought she heard something like a whisper at her window, but a gust of wind followed it, so she chalked it up to the wind cutting around the edges of her house. She hoped anyway.

2:22 A.M.

While sleep was slow to come, the dreams were not. As darkness wrapped around her, Carmen found herself walking through the cornstalks bordering the westside of town. The rows were slightly broken and skewed, as if some sort of carnival had come through, set down its roots, and then disappeared into the night. Empty popcorn boxes, deflated balloons, and half-eaten candied apples littered the ground. As she walked, dried stalks brushed her skin. She realized she was naked. This did not embarrass her she was excited. She felt turned on, wondering if someone might be in the field waiting for her, someone who would appreciate that she was naked and do all the things she wanted him to do …

She reached out and touched the closest cornstalk. When her hand grazed the leaf, she realized it was not a cornstalk at all. Instead, each blossom was a page of the journal entry Tess had blasted through the school.

She tore one from a nearby stalk, and it turned to mud on her hand. She flung it to the ground, and worms wriggled all around it. There were so many writhing bodies that they covered her feet. A strange combination of revulsion and sexual need bloomed in her, so deep it was almost painful. She ran her hand down her stomach, to the heat between her legs. She moaned.

And then she saw the scarecrow directly ahead of her at the end of the row. It was Willa, stripped naked and eviscerated, with a huge gash in her stomach that had been stuffed with straw. Her mouth had also been stuffed with something that looked like moldy bread. Her eyes were gone, plucked out by a raven perched on her slumped shoulder.

Carmen screamed, and Willa's head snapped up from the post she'd been nailed to. She smiled, and the mold dripped from her mouth and plopped on the ground, bursting open. Spiders crawled out. Some rushed for Carmen while others crawled up Willa's bare and bleeding legs.

"She's under your skin, and she wins." Willa hissed.

Overhead, jagged clouds slid over the moon as the night was alive with shadows dancing all around. Carmen tried to scream but as she opened her mouth dark fluid escaped. Just beyond the row, eyes seemed to be watching. Waiting.

Then the whispers began. They came in fast intervals that Carmen could not make out what it was saying. Like cars rushing by on the freeway. Then suddenly, "Carmen," one of the voices whispered. Then silence fell all around.

Run! She had to run, had to escape before the unseen force held her in its grip before the whispering came back. But she was paralyzed, unable to move. She was held tight by the bonds of the cornfield. She was helpless against the forces around her. Then the darkness moved in, twirling, whispering, talking amongst themselves, planning.

Saturday, October 22, 2008

8:32 A.M.

Carmen woke to the sound of her father singing a Dire Straits song downstairs.

Even in the light of morning, the nightmare still clung to her. Also, to her surprise, she'd awoken aroused, her nipples hard, a pulsing between her legs. She quickly got out of bed and, as she threw on a sweatshirt, caught wind the most glorious thing she'd smelled since moving to Somerdale—bacon. Eureka. Her dad couldn't have picked a better day to make her breakfast.

As she entered the kitchen, her dad polished off his coffee and set the mug and his plate in the sink.

"You on your way out?"

"I am. I'm supposed to be there to help set up our booth at nine. Did you decide what you're doing?"

"Yeah, yeah, I'm going. Willa is picking me up at noon."

"Okay. So, we've never crossed this bridge before. I'm trusting your judgement with this Willa person. Is she good people?"

"Maybe the best this pit of a town has to offer."

Joe frowned at her as he gathered a folder and a stack of pamphlets from the edge of the kitchen table. "You hating it that much?"

She shrugged. "It's just … different. It'll be okay. I'll get used to it."

He walked over and kissed her on the forehead. "If it makes you feel any better, I haven't quite gotten used to it myself."

"It does help," she lied, thinking, *But I bet no one at your work has made pornographic pictures of you and your coworker. I bet no one has grabbed your ass and made oinking sounds. Or sent messages wanting you to die.*

Carmen sat at the table with a plate her dad had prepared for her. He ensured her eggs were over easy and her bacon still had remnants of fat, just the way she liked it. As she dug in, she couldn't help feeling a little excited. It was Saturday, and she now had a friend. Plans. Someone to hang out with. Someone to share secrets with and maybe someone she could trust. It was something she had never really had before.

By the time eleven o' clock came around, she was ready to go—not only to get out of the house and spend some time with Willa but to prove to herself that she could be different here. There was life beyond what she was used to. Normally on a Saturday, Carmen would curl up on the couch with a good book, Dan Brown mostly and eat Cheetos all day. But today was different. She felt like part of her tapped into Willa's strength. For that moment, Carmen Winstead felt like she could take on the world, battle her demons, and finally be happy. Something that she deserved.

1:28 P.M.

What surprised Carmen the most about the corn festival was how quaint and pleasant it was. The event was held on the far end of a local family farm. A section with vendor booths were arranged in a square, creating a wide lane of grass to walk down. Branching off that lane and meandering around the booths were various fall-related activities—a pumpkin-carving contest, a corn maze, a little tractor-pulled train for the children, and lots of obstacle courses made from tires and bales of hay.

The only thing Carmen did not care for was the music. At the back end of the festival, staged against the bordering forest, a trio of musicians were playing old-time country and bluegrass at a bandstand. They were clearly talented, but bluegrass had always sounded like the wailing of sick cats to Carmen.

The smell of apple cider, cinnamon, and funnel cakes tantalized her. She felt a twinge of worry as the nightmare threatened to return but quickly squashed it. The weather was so crisp and the atmosphere so cheerful that it was hard to dwell on the bad, especially when she and Willa stopped by the apple cider booth and she got to experience it for the very first time. It was tart and sweet in a way she had not been expecting. She absolutely loved it.

"So, this goes on every year?" Carmen asked as she savored yet another sip of the cider.

She and Willa were maneuvering through the crowds at the various booths and food vendors.

"Yes, ma'am, every October, for as long as I can remember. And the festival always seems to bring that brutal cold weather. Heavy sweaters and hoodies and cold cheeks. I love it. I love fall."

Carmen shushed her with a smile. "People might hear the excitement in your voice."

"Shit, you're right." She made a zipping motion across her lips as they continued down the little lane. "What about you?"

"Fall's okay, but I always liked winter. It might sound weird, but I love the bitter cold of it all. Which is odd because I hate snow."

"You're a strange one, Carmen Winstead."

"So I'm told." But Carmen had to admit the festival could possibly make her switch her favorite season. Fall here was crisp and wonderful, not dreary and rainy like in Bristol. The bordering forests were already taking on the reds and oranges of the season. It was gorgeous.

"Right there," Willa said, nudging Carmen and pointing toward a small red food truck with bright kernels of yellow corn painted on the side. "That vendor, Street Corn on the Cob. You have to try it."

"Street corn? What's that?"

"Not sure. Some Mexican-inspired corn. Trust me. It'll change your life."

Judging by the line outside the window, most of Somerdale shared this opinion. When it was her turn, Carmen ordered two. She took one bite of her corn coated in salt, pepper, cotija cheese, and some sort of little sweet pepper flakes and moaned in delight. It was delicious, a stark contrast to the sweetness of the apple cider.

"Good thing you got two, huh?" Willa said with a nudge.

"No. This one's for my dad." She scanned the booths, rather ashamed that she could not recall the name of his new company. Something-something Solutions. "He should be here, somewhere." As her gaze drifted over the crowd, she noticed several faces she recognized from school.

Most met her gaze and quickly looked away.

Her cheeks reddened, but Carmen finally found her father at a booth with a Synergy Solutions banner. That was it. He was there, handing a woman a pamphlet. It made Carmen quite happy to see her father engaging with other people so openly. She smiled, approaching slowly, waiting until he was done talking. When he was finished, she angled up to her father and offered the corn.

Joe saw her, and his face lit up. "Hey there, sweetie. Glad to see you came out."

"Sure. Glad I did. Otherwise, I wouldn't have seen you flirting with that lady."

"What? That wasn't flirting."

"If you say so. Did you at least get her number?"

"Stop."

Carmen shrugged and looked back to Willa. "Willa, this is my dad. Dad, this is Willa."

"Nice to meet you," Joe said, proffering his hand.

Willa took it, giving a strained smile. "You too. Also, yeah, I think that was flirting Mr. Winstead."

"So now there are two of you?" he said, rolling his eyes. "And call me Joe."

"Hey, I brought you corn."

"I see that. Thanks." He took it and warily nibbled a little of it. "Heck. This is good." "I know, right?"

Not taking a breath as he devoured the corn, he retrieved a dollar bill from his pocket. "Could you do me a huge favor and get me a coffee? As you can see, I'm the only guy at the booth. The other guys are no-shows, so I can't leave."

"Sure," Carmen said, snatching the dollar. "I'll be right back."

"Hey, Carmen?"

"Yeah?" She turned to see him smiling at her.

"I'm really glad you decided to come."

It was a simple statement, but it carried weight. He was telling her that he was proud of her for taking a chance and doing something different. She'd never liked social situations, after all. Even without knowing the torment she had been enduring at school, he had to have known how much she'd been struggling.

"Yeah, me too," she said, smiling back.

She and Willa walked through the hordes of people. The crowd had thickened since they had arrived. Still, despite the crowds, Carmen didn't have to turn back to know her dad was still watching them. It was a good feeling—one that made her feel safe and loved—and Carmen savored it.

1:42 P.M.

As they waited in line for her father's coffee, Carmen listened to Willa explain why she didn't like coffee. Apparently, it made her feel nervous, and her stomach simply couldn't tolerate it. She'd tried several different kinds, but they'd all sent her running to the toilet.

"I have to say," Carmen said, as she stepped to the counter to order, "I've never had a friend who was comfortable enough with me to talk about her irritable bowel syndrome."

"Well, get used to it, baby. We're going deep. By the way, tea also gives me the trots."

Carmen laughed and was about to place the order for her father's coffee when something struck her hard in the side of the head, like a bolt of lightning hitting a tree. Whatever it was thudded to the ground as Carmen reached for her head, stunned. On the ground lay a cleanly stripped corncob. She looked behind her with dread, already knowing what she'd find.

Tess Todd was standing a few feet behind her, surrounded by her usual group of clones—Virgie, Cassie, and Miriam—and Luca Gaines, quarterback of the football team. "Oink, oink, bitch," Tess said.

Carmen froze for a moment, then slowly turned back and ordered her dad's coffee. The words came out garbled as she choked back a sob, wiping a single tear from her eyes. She hated that some people—especially Tess—had such an effect on her—making her feel so helpless and weak.

As the man behind the counter poured the coffee, Carmen sensed Willa stepping away from her and tensed. Carmen wondered how far Willa would take things. She seemed to have no issue with causing a scene—a fact that both terrified and pleased Carmen at the same time.

"Yo, Tess," Willa said, bending to grab the cob. "You sure you're done with this?" She studied the cob, then looked to the boy on Tess's arm. "Sorry, Luca. Looks like you've got some stiff competition."

"Shut your fucking mouth witch," Luca stepped forward.

"Quiet," Tess barked at him. And just like a good dog, like everyone else in her orbit, Luca stepped backward, jaws snapping closed like a whip. "Willa, aren't you tired of standing up for Pigstead?"

Carmen paid the dollar and took the coffee from the vendor's hands, her own shaking. When she turned, Tess was leaning against a stack of nearby hay bales, surrounded by her friends. As usual, she looked absolutely gorgeous. Her hair was radiant and sparkling like gold, and a black lace maxi dress with a sheer eyelash lace top accentuated every curve and her flawless skin—just perfect for a corn festival with hay, barrels, and mud.

"Ah, hell." Willa rolled her eyes at the sparkling object in Tess's hand—a tiara. "Corn Queen again. Second year in a row, right, Tess?"

"Damn straight." Tess smiled proudly.

"So sorry I missed the blessed event," Willa said, rolling her eyes. "Must be some really tight competition, all those teenage girls prancing and preening to be crowned the Queen of Corn."

"So ... that's, like, something people actually want to win?" Carmen asked, astounded.

Tess's smile fell.

"Oh yeah, Corn Queen," Willa said. "Its ... um ... respected, I guess? Better than Whore of Babylon or Local Cum Dumpster, for sure."

"You're just jealous," Miri sneered.

"Oh god, believe me, I'm not." Willa laughed maniacally. "I'm not nearly corny enough."

Tess turned her gaze from Willa and glared at Carmen. "You got something to say, Pigstead?"

Carmen shook her head and exhaled a soft, "No. Jus-just listening."

Tess and her girls laughed. "Listening to what?" Tess asked.

Again, Carmen shook her head. She now wanted to get out of there—go home, hide, and stay as far away from this place as possible. What the hell had she been thinking by coming here? Why would she think anything about her life could be normal?

"Just a guess," Willa said with a shrug. "But maybe she's listening for the apology you're going to give her."

Tess stopped laughing. "You're out of your stupid little mind if you think I'll apologize to you or her. Hell, that pig should be *glad* anyone is paying attention to her at all. You too, you fucking loser. Both of you are nothing but losers a waste of ... well everything."

"Yeah, losers." Miri mimicked pointing her finger towards Carmen, hiding behind Tess.

"Shut up Miri." Focusing back to Tess. "You're paying a lot of attention to us lately," Willa said. "Makes me wonder why."

"Because you don't belong here! You *or* Pigstead. Jesus, Carmen, seems your mother is the only smart one in the family. Hauled ass when she still could. Escaped from her loser daughter and worthless husband. She probably caught you fucking your dad. *Nasty pig.*

Oink-oink bitch.

Instinctively, Carmen stepped closer, her face red, a million hornets stinging her skin and for a moment, she almost felt strong enough—like something pushing her, willing her to strike. But as she raised her hand, she stopped. Instead, she lowered her head not saying a word.

Then she felt Willa reach out and take the cup of coffee from her hand.

"I need that coffee, Carmen. This bitch is tiring me." Willa removed the coffee lid and threw it in Tess's direction, letting it splash all over Tess's dress.

Tess froze, her mouth in a cartoonish *O*.

Willa smiled at the whole group. "Oops. Clumsy me."

Luca stepped forward and pushed Willa into Carmen, who reached out and tried to catch Willa before she could stumble to the ground, but Willa fell anyway. As she helped Willa to her feet, Carmen realized people had gathered around them.

The next few seconds happened in a blur. Before Carmen knew it, Tess brought her hand across Carmen's face, fast and hard. The smack and resulting sting ignited fireworks in Carmen's vision. She fisted her hands, ready to fight back, to defend herself. But the crowd around them was growing, and now the volcano was simmering—the calm right before it blew off the top of the mountain.

Carmen gave Willa an apologetic glance, shifted her stance, and took off running. She didn't care where. And, as she ran with tears falling in hot streams down her cheeks, she heard Tess's laughter behind her, like a monster on her heels.

1:56 P.M.

Carmen didn't know where she was going. She simply ran. When she reached the edge of the field and entered the corn, she barely realized it. The sound of the corn rustling was deafening. Dried husks scratched her skin.

Minutes or a lifetime later, she spun around and realized she'd been swallowed by them.

Husks, their leaves glinting with light in the afternoon sun, were etched against the blue sky and clouds moving overhead. Each direction looked identical. Slowing, she listened, but the sound of the bluegrass music seemed to come from everywhere.

She hurried her step. She hated that she'd left Willa behind, but she didn't want Willa to be her shield anymore. It wasn't fair. Willa was catching the brunt of it all, because she was sticking up for a girl who couldn't stand up for herself.

Running blindly, Carmen finally made it to the end of the field and could barely hear the bluegrass music, and all the delicious smells from the vendors were gone. Ahead of her was a thin strip of field that led into a thin forest. The pines stood stoic and quiet. Twisted roots dipped in and out of the ground. Their distorted branches reached out, fingers grasping the air. Beyond them was a dip to the land and a seemingly random square of concrete.

She approached it slowly, supposing it was some sort of receptacle for the town water or sewage. With her eyes blurred from crying, the cool air burned her lungs as she stepped from the cornfield and walked closer. It stretched farther into the field than she had thought. Just behind that was a massive pipe embedded into the hillside. It was probably big enough to drive a vehicle through. It seemed her original thought was right; it did appear to be some sort of sewage juncture, only it looked as if it was no longer in use. Gazing at that large pipe embedded into the earth, a morbid part of her wanted to walk into it, to explore the dark rusty interior. Maybe get lost in it forever.

She climbed onto the concrete block and stopped at a big manhole. The lid was partially removed, revealing a crescent of darkness below. A series of scratches lined the concrete, she wasn't sure what they were from, maybe from where workers had removed the cover numerous times was her first thought. Something diabolical was her second. Either way, she stood on the edge and peered into the fathomless darkness. She could not see the bottom but could hear the slight rushing of water from somewhere below. Just then, the wind blustered, violently whistling through the pines.

As Carmen spun around, her hair slapped against her cheek, loose, catching in the tears and snot smeared on her face.

Behind the concrete block and tucked between a slight rise in the ground and the huge pipe was a deep pit extending roughly fifty feet back, where a series of pipes were all connected and fed into the ground. Likely, a short hike down that huge copper pipe would lead to smells and darkness no one wanted to face.

Carmen sat on the very edge to catch her breath and stared across the forest and the cornstalks beyond, leaves tossing and rustling in the breeze. The dream she had the night prior danced like a ballerina in her mind. She remembered Willa. Staked to the tall plank like a scarecrow, disemboweled—hissing words at her. *She's under your skin, and she wins.* Carmen lowered her head and knew she had to return to the festival, apologize to her dad. She needed to apologize to Willa too for being such a loser friend. *Maybe Tess was right*, she thought. Carmen Winstead was worthless.

In a minute though, Carmen thought. *Or two.* She closed her eyes and filled her lungs with the crisp air, the smell of damp earth and dead foliage. She slid around and dangled her feet over the side, kicking them idly as they hovered above the darkness, like a small child might do. As she did, she thought about Tess again, then Willa— wondered what they were doing.

A slight shuffling behind her interrupted her thoughts— footsteps padding through the grass.

She scrambled to her feet and turned.

Tess, along with Virgie, Miri, and Cassie, stood just a few feet from her. Tess, of course, was in front. Virgie and Miri flanked her, and Cassie brought up the rear.

Carmen inhaled a surprised gasp.

The girls snickered.

Carmen had to admit, the sudden sight of them *had* frightened her quite badly. And now here they were, cornering her, as if she were their prey.

They moved closer, circling Carmen around the manhole.

Carmen's eyes widened as she glanced down, trying not to get too close to the opening, to ensure her sneakers were still on solid ground. The manhole was a couple feet behind her, yes, but one wrong move, and …

"Find a new home?" Virgie teased.

"Oh no," Tess said. "Even this is too good for her."

In the shadows of the forest, without Willa to save her, Carmen felt defeat wash over her. In that moment, she understood why they hated her, and she honestly didn't blame them. Maybe she *was* pathetic. Maybe she deserved all this.

"Tess … why? Why are you treating me like this? I never did anything to you."

All four girls laughed, circling Carmen.

"Because you're nothing," Tess spat. "And as the nastiest girl at school, you need to be reminded of that."

"Joke's on you," Carmen said, doing everything she could to keep from crying in front of her. "I know I'm nothing. I don't need you to remind me."

Tess stepped closer.

Carmen could practically feel the chasm behind her, beckoning her.

"Carmen, it's okay," Tess said. "I see the way you look at me. I know you're jealous. But it sort of grosses me out. It makes me think you look at me the same way you look at Willa."

"You're beautiful, Tess," Carmen said.

For a moment, Tess's eyes flickered with superiority, as if it were just another compliment she could add to her suit of armor.

"On the outside," Carmen finished. "Because on the inside, you're the ugliest person I've ever met. I mean, what happened in your life that was so awful that you mask it by being cruel to others? To me?"

Tess's face fell. "You really think I care what a nobody like you thinks about me?" Tess sneered.

The girls continued to circle her, closing in.

"Stop it," Carmen said, her heart pounding. She whirled around and faced Miri, then Virgie, then Cassie. "All of you. Please."

"Or what, Pigstead? Willa isn't here to protect you. So, it's just you and us."

"What are you going to do, Tess?" she asked, tears flowing down her cheeks. Maybe they'd start to sympathize if she at least *tried* standing up for herself.

Tess lunged for her.

Carmen flinched, stepping backward. Her feet felt the rim of the manhole. The moment she glanced down; Tess lightly shoved her chest. Her arms windmilled forward, scrabbling for anything she could grip, and her eyes widened as they met Tess's.

Tess smiled, almost triumphantly, and pushed again—not hard, but it was more than enough.

With her foot already flirting with the edge of the manhole, Carmen lost her balance and fell backward. Her left foot went directly into the opened portion of the hole. Her heel struck the cover, which was only covering about a quarter of the rear of the hole. Carmen screamed and reached up for purchase. She slapped for the lip of the hole, but even before her fingers could grip it, the back of her head struck the hard metal. She heard the noise of it—an almost comical, gonglike sound. She grabbed for the edge of the hole, the pads of her fingers digging into the rough concrete. But pain exploded in her head, making everything dim. She hung on for a moment, futilely, her body's strength crumbling. She remained hovering in the mouth of the hole just long enough to hear a voice.

"Jesus, Tess …" Cassie winced.

For a second, she dared to hope someone would reach down, offer a hand, help her. But no one did. She looked up at four heads silhouetted by a pale blue sky.

In the end, you can't depend on anyone else. You must save your-self. She heard her mother's voice.

Collecting every bit of resolve inside her, Carmen groaned and pulled as hard as she could. It felt as though the darkness below her was trying to pull her down. Still, she pulled. She pulled hard enough for her aching head to slowly come up over the rim of the manhole cover, but it sapped all the strength from her.

In the approaching darkness clouding the edges of her vision, someone moved forward. Someone to help. *Thank God,* she dared to hope, letting out a short cry for help.

That was the last thing Carmen saw before her fingers gave out on her and released. Now the world was not only hazy but falling away, growing smaller, darker. She tried to scream again, but her head slammed into something hard. The skin on the side of her face was shredded in the darkness, and something hit her chin. Her teeth splintered with a pain she'd never before felt, a pain that took her breath away.

Carmen, she heard a whisper.

Then her elbow hit the wall behind her. Something in her arm popped and bent backward at an unnatural angle. More pain. So much pain she'd begun to go numb to it. Her head fell faster than the rest of her body, and she nearly made it over in a complete turn. The top of her head stopped her from doing so; it struck something hard, peeling hair and skin back, cracking open her skull.

A terrific splash interrupted the sound of her blood rushing through her ears as she hit the bottom. It was a thick, muddy splash, but it did not block out the sound of several bones breaking.

Darkness seeped in. Before it claimed her completely, Carmen thought she heard someone calling her name. *Willa!* As her eyes widened, she tasted blood, mud, and a foul liquid filling her lungs. Carmen lay there, in the wet sludge of the trench, eighteen feet below the universe from which she had fallen. She could not move. Tears spilling helplessly, she turned her face to the light above her, choking and gasping. The darkness was closing in, swallowing her. And, after a few seconds, she could barely breathe.

In the final moments of her life, she felt dirty water trickling around her head.

Then it slipped away to nothingness.

After that, there was only darkness.

PART 2

TUESDAY, NOVEMBER 1, 2008

2:55 A.M.

Trulia Dalton, known to everyone in Somerdale as True, jerked awake. For a brief moment, she fumbled sleepily to grasp something at the side of her bed. A nightmare, that was all. Only, the more awake she got, the surer she was that it had not been a nightmare at all. It had been more like a vision—a premonition.

She'd seen an endless cornfield splattered with blood, so much blood that it looked as if it had rained from the sky. The gullies between the rows of corn had puddled with it. And somewhere among the corn, she'd had a feeling something very dark was lurking, lying in wait.

Trembling slightly, True got out of bed and checked the clock. She took a sip of the water she always kept on her night table, grabbed the white terry cloth robe that Willa had bought her, wrapped it securely around her shoulders, and walked into the living room.

She wasn't at all surprised to find Willa sleeping on the couch. Willa had not slept in her bed ever since Carmen Winstead had died. True shuddered at the memory of the so-called dream. The spirits of the earth had granted her visions before but never like this.

They had spoken to her quite clearly the first time she had met Carmen Winstead. When she first set eyes on the girl, she'd felt a slight twinge of unease. It was nothing new, really. Over the years, as she'd grown more in tune with the earth, she'd gotten strong first impressions of strangers—and most of those impressions were not good. She'd sometimes get a tug of fear from random people when she went to the grocery store or a bright spark, which indicated a generally positive disposition.

But with Carmen, that first glance had given True an odd, almost queasy feeling. She'd honestly thought nothing of it at first. But then she had actually touched the girl, and something flooded her. Not simply fear. Something darker. Absolute terror. True had had to stifle a cry of surprise and pull away as quickly as possible.

The more she'd thought about it, the more she knew what the feeling was. She'd felt death on Carmen. Death, that was coming fast. There was no way to stop death once it set its eyes on someone. That was something she knew well. Plus, with the spirits around her telling her to release Carmen, what could she have done?

It was hard to believe Willa hadn't felt it. True had gotten a certain vibe from Willa early on. Willa was meant for grand things and would likely become as intuitive and powerful as she was someday. Still, she wondered if she could have dropped some discreet clue to Willa—maybe something she could have said or done that would not cause a disturbance in nature but could also have saved Carmen's life.

Of course, it was too late now. It was over.

Or was it? Even though Carmen was gone, for some reason, True felt something stirring in the air—something malevolent. Something with teeth. It was coming …

It's time, True thought. *I need to teach her more. I must teach her to protect herself, to show her the things I respect and believe have a real bite to them.*

As True watched Willa sleeping on the couch, Willa moaned. She looked distressed for a moment, then fell back into her usual calm. True watched her for a while longer before she padded down the hallway to her bed.

She lay completely still in the darkness of her room. A small yellow light flowed in from the hallway.

Yes, something was coming. *They* were trying to tell her something. It was a sort of communication she knew most Wiccans were not capable of. But she had spent most of her life communing with *them*—though she was still not quite sure who *they* were. Some, she knew, would believe it might be the Divine Couple: Diana, the moon goddess, and Pan, the horned god.

But True got the sense that the presence she felt was the result of some of the other wild-earth deities—the deities who had been here long before human imagination had concocted other gods in their primitive, little brains.

Whatever the force was, True felt it circling her house, cloaking it like a shield and spreading throughout the town. It was a great honor to feel their influence so profoundly, but she could not deny she was also slightly afraid. And while she felt Willa might be spared, she could not shake the feeling that, in due time, Somerdale would never be the same.

3:06 A.M.

Tess bolted from bed and ran to the bathroom. She barely made it in time, dropping to her knees in front of the toilet just before she threw up. There wasn't much, as she'd eaten a very small dinner. She hadn't had much of an appetite for a week or so, and her current situation wasn't helping. She puked a second time and clung to the sides of the toilet. When she realized she had come in so quickly that she had forgotten to turn on the lights, she remedied that right away. She got up, slapped at the light switch, and knelt back by the toilet. It made her feel a little better, though not much.

Ever since she'd watched Carmen fall down that manhole, Tess had been terrified of the dark. Even in her bedroom, she had both of her lamps on. But the light had done nothing to ease her mind when she'd woken thirty seconds ago with a flashing image of Carmen Winstead's face in her mind. Even dead, the girl managed to pop up everywhere.

"Bitch," she moaned against the side of the toilet. As the tears came on, she could not help but wonder if she was referring to Carmen Winstead or herself. She'd wrestled with a lot of internal conflict like that over the past few days.

She slowly rose from the toilet and rinsed her mouth in the sink. When she finished, she turned off the lights and hurried down the hallway to her room, where she fell into bed. She closed her eyes and was met by the same image of Carmen falling down the hole. It was cemented in her brain now. While Tess had not intended to hurt her, it had happened. Did that make her a bad person? It was a question that had awoken her, nauseated, on three occasions since that fateful day of the corn festival.

You're the ugliest person I know. That was Carmen's voice, shaking with fear, that reverberated in her head. *How dare her*, she thought

And even when the memory of Carmen wasn't haunting her, she'd been forced to relive that moment again and again due to the police's incessant questioning. It was like they didn't believe her or something.

She shuddered as an image of that wannabe goth bitch Willa popped into her head, the stare of absolute shock and rage she'd thrown at Tess in the moments after it had happened. Tess had felt something physical in that stare, like some invisible knife sawing at her flesh and worming into her soul. She had no doubt in that moment, if given the opportunity, Willa Dalton would have killed her.

Tess still felt the sting of it, and it creeped into her mind sometimes when she closed her eyes. She wasn't sure if the rumors about Willa being a witch were true, but that look she'd given Tess made it easy to believe. It was her eyes, so full of rage, clinging to her like old, grey cobwebs. *There's always been something slightly off about that bitch,* Tess thought. Her and her weird aunt. *Something very strange.*

Tess lay in the faint light of her room, staring at the ceiling. Sometimes the lights danced through her bedroom from a passing car. She reached down, grabbed her blanket, and folded it up to her chest. She closed her eyes and tried desperately to find sleep, but, even in the safety of her bed, the images of Carmen Winstead still leaked into her mind.

WEDNESDAY, NOVEMBER 2, 2008

1:05 P.M.

Detective Samantha Kerr had big plans for her afternoon. They included getting shit-faced drunk at Stubbies, stumbling to her apartment, then drinking more until she could not keep her eyes open. As far as plans went, it was a simple one. But it was also the best idea she'd ever had. She had to keep telling herself this as she straddled the barstool on Wednesday afternoon and ordered cheese fries, a beer, and a shot of tequila to get her started.

It had to look sad—a twenty-nine-year-old woman drinking alone in the middle of a weekday. It could have been worse, she supposed. She could have actually taken the time to pretty herself up before coming out. As it was, she was simply wearing a long-sleeved tee, ratty jeans, and a pair of Converses. She stared into the mirror behind the bar and tucked her hair behind her ears. The blond streaks lay limply to her shoulders, not having had any special attention in weeks. Her eyes, though crystal blue and usually one of her most striking features, looked hollow and tired.

Oh, Sam, she thought, looking at her reflection. *You've seen better days.* But she didn't care. She had not come out today to pick up men. She'd come to get drunk as quickly as possible.

She barely touched her cheese fries, instead filling her stomach with beer and three more tequila shots. She was about to order her fourth when a familiar voice sounded behind her.

"What's for lunch?"

Sam turned on her stool and glared at Mac Talbot. Sam wasn't quite buzzed enough to miss his look of concern. It annoyed her, but it also made her feel at least a bit better about the last few days of her life. Mac had been Sam's partner for the better part of two years, and they'd become like siblings. Mac was eight years her senior, and though no romantic chemistry existed between them, they did share a sort of magical bond of understanding.

"Cheese fries, apparently," Sam said. "Although right now, I'm more interested in the liquid side of things."

"Want some company?"

"Depends on if I'm going to get a lecture."

"I haven't decided that yet." Mac sat on the barstool next to Sam, waved over the bartender, and ordered a Coke.

"No rum in that?"

"No. I'm working today, remember?

"Ah, must be nice."

Mac nodded dramatically and grinned at her. "So, I see we're in the pity party phase of things."

"We are. And I don't remember inviting you, asshole." She sipped from her beer, enjoying the company but also sort of wishing he'd go away.

"Let me point out, before you get too wasted to remember this conversation, that you haven't been formally suspended."

"Oh, I know. I was just asked to not come in for a few days. Makes it easier for them to talk shit and decide my future."

"Sam, I really don't think it'll be like that. Look, it's pretty much unanimous among the force. Everyone knows what happened."

"Oh, do tell." Sam faced Mac, slamming her hand against the bar.

Mac shrugged as the bartender brought over his Coke. The shrug was one that, to Sam, seemed to say it wasn't even worth discussing. Sam agreed, but still, a part of her needed to hear it, to know exactly what everyone else at the precinct was saying about her.

"Everyone knows Fredricks broke into your house, and it certainly wasn't to make you some cookies or dinner," Mac said. "Fredricks has even admitted that you asked him to leave and that he was being stubborn about it."

"But he's still trying to press charges?"

"Well, you did shoot him."

"Right. So rather than wait with bated breath at home while a bunch of men decide the fate of my career, I thought it might be wiser to come out and have a few drinks with friends."

"A few...with friends?"

Sam shrugged. "Fine. Several."

"Where's the friends? In your damn head?"

"You're an ass, you know that right?"

Mac sighed and eyed his Coke.

Sam could tell he wished there *was* something more in it.

"How long had it been going on?"

"Fredricks or my drinking problem?"

"Fredricks. Jeez, Sam." Mac laughed and stared in the mirror behind the bar.

She did her best to do the math in her increasingly swimmy head. "Four months or so."

"And was it ever anything other than hooking up?"

"No. God, I can't stand to even talk to him. Fredericks is an idiot. But he's a good-looking idiot that's surprisingly good in bed."

"Too much information."

"I mean, really good. That man has some sort of incantation on his tongue or something."

"Are you trying to make me puke?"

"Sorry. I just feel like I need to really explain why I was with him for so long. Four months is a lifetime to have to listen to his shit. I just got tired of it, and I told him that. It was over."

"I say this as a caring partner and nothing more, so don't get all drunk and horny on me. But there's no way in this world that Fredricks deserved you."

She snorted. "If you thought that would make me horny, it makes me worry about your capacity to pick up women."

"I've been worried about that since college."

They shared a laugh and fell into silence.

Mac playfully nudged her. "I think it really will all come out okay, Sam. Sure, maybe you went a little too far in actually pulling the trigger."

"Hey, it was a clean shot that went through his thigh. God, is he still crying about it?"

"No. Right now, I think he might be crying over his wife leaving with their two kids."

"Hmm. Oddly enough, I don't feel sad for him. Not at all."

"I don't think anyone does. This whole thing has brought a lot of people's true feelings toward Fredericks to light."

That wasn't hard. Fredericks had always been the biggest asshole on the force. Stupid her for falling for his ego after a few too many beers and lonely nights. She cringed, thinking of how idiotic she'd been. The second she let him in, he thought he owned her.

"So, what do they have you on today?" Sam asked, not being at all subtle about changing the subject. "Still pinned to that damn Winstead case?"

"Yep. Talking to more kids today. Sorry ... not talking. *Interviewing.* I'm supposed to be very specific about that."

"Still no answers?"

"Zero."

"If you really do think I'll be fine, do me a favor and wrap that one up before I come back. Something about that whole thing gives me the fucking creeps."

"Same here. Well, maybe not the creeps. But I think it's clear someone is lying to us. Or many someones."

"Yeah. It's something about the whole so-called mean girl crowd. I hate those sorts of girls. And that Tess Todd, I want to smack that little bitch whenever I see her."

"You really hate her, don't you?"

"I do—all of them."

"Why?"

"Because they picked on the weak. I can't stand that shit."

"Well, if you don't want that case, I can probably line you up on something else. There's that drug bust from three months ago that we never—"

Sam pressed her index finger against Mac's lips. "Shh. I'm trying to get drunk. Stop talking about work."

"But you asked me what—"

"I know. It was a mistake."

And with that, they sank into silence. Silence had become comfortable for them sometime during their partnership. Sam knew Mac got a ton of grief from the squad room about being paired with the young female detective who was incredibly easy on the eyes. While Sam didn't necessarily consider herself a catch, she's heard the comments and jokes circulating the locker room. She also knew men tended to stare a bit longer than necessary whenever she passed through a room. Truthfully, though, Mac had never treated her with disrespect and had a sort of big brother, protective vibe to him. She appreciated it since she didn't get that from anyone else.

"Gotta head back to work," Mac said, getting to his feet.

"Oh, and we were just starting to have fun."

He reached into his wallet and tossed a fifty-dollar bill on the bar. "My contribution to your self-destruction." He flagged down the bartender. "Two more drinks for her, and then call her a cab, would you?"

The bartender nodded and smiled.

Sam rolled her eyes. "Ain't he just the best?"

"You know it," Mac said and headed toward the door.

Sam watched him go as the bartender brought her another shot. Sam downed it slowly, relishing the burn. When the shot glass was empty, Sam peered into its mouth. It resembled the manhole she and Mac had spent so much time peering into over the past week. Sam sighed and slid away the shot glass.

"Carmen Fucking Winstead," she muttered, shaking her head and trying to ignore the little chill that went down her spine. "What happened to you?"

3:22 P.M.

Joe Winstead felt guilty. Some days he did nothing but sit at the kitchen table and scream about the loss. People had come by the house: do-gooder neighbors wanting to check on him, a couple pastors wanting to recruit him to their parish, the police wanting to question him, and reporters wanting to put his face on the nightly news. But the constant intrusion hadn't mattered.

He'd slept like the dead ever since that night. A part of him had yearned to sleep in Carmen's room, but it made no sense to him. It was a mental pull to check all the boxes on the stages of grief. Weren't that what grieving parents were supposed to do?

He had no idea, because he had been naïve enough to think that nothing like this would ever happen to his daughter. Not to Carmen.

The closest he'd come was standing in her doorway for about an hour, the day of her funeral. He was dressed in the only suit he had, staring at her bed and the new laptop sitting on her bedside table. He tried to conjure images of Carmen in the room, but there were none to be found. He'd been too preoccupied with work and settling into their new home. He'd told himself that once things got settled, he'd make Carmen a priority. None of that ever happened.

The only memories he could bring to the surface were from the day she had died: Willa Dalton running up to him, tears in her eyes; cops standing around the manhole in the woods to the north of the corn festival; three large policemen holding him back as Carmen's body was pulled from the hole an hour later. Some of those same policemen had tried asking about Carmen's school life and any enemies she might have. He'd told them what he could, though it was not much.

All of this churned in his head as he sat at the kitchen table with a beer in his hand. He wasn't even sure what day it was. Tuesday? No, probably Wednesday. That felt right. It was Wednesday, and Carmen had been dead for eleven days—in the ground for five.

He supposed at some point he needed to start thinking about returning to work. He had done everything he could to notify Carmen's mother, but he could not find her anywhere. The best he'd been able to do was to leave the devastating news with her father. The man had attended the funeral, said a total of six words to Joe, then left. As for Carmen's mother, she hadn't even shown up. But the saddest part to Joe was the people that did show. It made him realize how miserable his daughter's life had been. At the end of a life, and no friends to mourn your death was just— well sad.

So now it was him—just Joe, all alone, wondering what he could've done differently. If he'd known more about her, asked more questions about school, would it have helped? When Willa had come rushing to him at the corn festival, he realized he had only seen her for the first time when Carmen had introduced her about an hour earlier. Willa had been the only friend Carmen had, and Joe barely knew her.

As he sat there, surrounded by beer bottles but disconnected from everything, someone knocked at the door.

He got up slowly with a groan. If this was that damned preacher coming back, Joe just might kill him. Or it might be a member of the kindhearted casserole brigade—women from the community he did not know but brought many dishes. He had more food in his fridge than he could ever eat, especially now that he was all alone.

Instead, he found Willa standing there. The last time he'd seen her was at Carmen's funeral. The funeral had been at three, and Willa and an elderly woman were there early. Joe assumed it was her aunt. He remembered Carmen mentioning Willa did not have a mom either. He figured that was one of the reasons they had connected so quickly. At the funeral, she had been dressed in all black, her auburn hair pulled back in a ponytail. She looked much the same today, standing on his porch, tired and rather waifish. She was wearing a Rammstein tee and a pair of ripped jeans. Her mascara was running; her eyes were dull and blood-shot.

"Can I come in?"

He nodded and stepped aside.

She noticed the empty beer bottles on the kitchen table and frowned. "Sorry."

"No need to be sorry. I guess I needed a break. It's not exactly the most effective way to handle grief." He closed the door and stood by it, not sure where this was headed. "What can I do for you, Willa?"

Willa shrugged and gave a little laugh that had absolutely no humor in it. "I don't even know. I just needed to be with someone who knew her. Does that make sense?"

Joe's heart broke for her a little in that moment. In his own grief, he'd not even realized that at least one other person in this town might also be missing her. And she was Carmen's kindred spirit—something of an outcast, not the best with people, and short on friends.

"Maybe I should thank you," Joe said. "The past few months haven't been easy on her. You befriended her when she needed it the most. She'd never been the same since her mother left. I just don't know... I don't know what else I could have done to make things easier on her."

Willa sat on the edge of the couch and slowly shook her head. "We hadn't known each other long. But I know she loved you and respected you. If anyone didn't do enough, it was me. That day at the festival, I pushed Tess too far. And I should have been there, should have gone after Carmen to make sure she was okay. But I was so caught up in my own shit that I—"

"Tess? Who is that?"

"Tess Todd. A bully. She was mean to Carmen. I mean, downright cruel. I think she did something." Willa picked at her nails.

"Willa, that's a serious accusation."

"I know. I know, I just ..." Willa's voice dipped into a low murmur as she felt gravity pulling her head towards the stairs. She heard something ... *Whispers.*

"Did you see it happen? Did you see this girl do anything?" Joe had heard a group of girls had been around the manhole, but the cops had not given him any names. It hadn't seemed to matter, since countless police reports were leaning toward the same conclusion: an accident.

"Willa? Are you okay?"

"Yeah, sorry ... I thought I ... oh nothing. No, Mr. Winstead I didn't see anything but ... the things this girl did to Carmen. It was so wrong. So ..."

Joe shook his head. "Willa, I can't hear that right now. If I do, I'll start placing blame, and I can't do that. Look, you're welcome to stay here for a bit if you need to. But we can't talk like that."

Willa looked a little disappointed but eventually relented. "Can you tell me something about her? Something no one else knew?"

"Sure. You know that really bad rap song, 'Ice, Ice, Baby,' from the nineties?"

"Yeah. Vanilla Ice. Jesus, why?"

"She loved that damned song. Knew every word. Could rap it on command."

"No ..."

Joe nodded and chuckled. "She'd kill me if she knew I told you that." He then choked back a little sob that had a bit of joy to it. "Maybe not. Carmen couldn't hurt a fly, could she?"

Willa laughed. "No, sir, I guess she couldn't." Willa returned to picking her nails.

Joe finally crossed the room and sat in the recliner near the fireplace. "She loved the winter. I was really looking forward to her first winter here, with all of this open land."

"Yeah, she told me how much she liked the cold."

"She broke three fingers in a sledding accident when she was ten. Slammed right into an oak tree in the back yard. I don't know how she didn't bust open her skull ..." He stopped, fell silent when he realized the wording started tugging at his heart. Busting open her skull, that's exactly what had happened. According to the coroner, it had been a pretty instantaneous death. Joe knew it was meant as comfort, but that somehow hurt him worst of all.

Dead was dead, even if the death was a fast one. Yes, he was glad she had likely not suffered much. But his daughter was gone, and no explanations nor silver linings in this miserable world could change that.

"Well, Willa. Thank you for stopping by. You take care out there."

Willa got up from the couch and slowly approached the door. She stopped short when she thought she saw something. A faint shadow that crossed the banister leading upstairs. She felt her skin tighten as she knew there was something there. Willa's nerves crawled and for a moment, she thought about aunt True. *Watch and listen Willa, the earth never guides you wrong. Run!*

Willa shifted her body, and the thought gave way. "Willa. Are you sure you're, okay?" Joe asked as he noticed Willa's eyes seemed wide and panicked. "Yeah, yeah sure." She replied as she turned around, her eyes flooded with tears. She reached up and hugged him.

"Thank you," he said.

Willa's eyes went to slits, she held him tight, whispered, "I'm so sorry," and ran down the steps.

9:00 P.M.

Sam knocked on Mac Talbot's door just after nine o'clock on Friday night. She had a bag of Chinese food in her left hand and a case of Coors in her right. When Mac answered the door, Sam heard Bruce Springsteen coming from somewhere in the house. And not his good, rocking stuff either. No, it was the *Nebraska* album, a real downer.

"Man, you are *really* trying to set the mood, aren't you?" Sam joked as he let her in. "Springsteen whining about his daddy's house isn't going to get these pants off."

"Don't even go there. I'm done with jokes about how you and I are getting it on."

She shrugged. "Hey, I see you as the winner in those rumors."

"Haven't you gotten into enough trouble with that as of late?" Mac said with an evil smile.

"Damn that was harsh. Okay, you win."

Sam had been to Mac's apartment many times in the past, so she did not wait for an invitation to sit. While she did not consider it a home away from home, it *was* comfortable. She parked herself on the couch and instantly went for the Chinese food. She handed Mac his orange chicken and popped the lid off her lo mein.

Mac killed the music and joined her. "Dinner and a movie. Some might call this a date."

"We're about to watch footage of your interrogations of several young girls," Sam said. "What kind of fucked-up date is that?"

He grinned as he set up everything. As of that morning, it was all but official that Sam would be returning to work on Monday. Officer Steven Fredericks had been found guilty of breaking and entering and had just narrowly escaped an assault charge. Also, it had been ruled that Sam was justified in using her firearm.

"Excited about coming back to work at an official capacity?" Mac asked.

"Yes. I am not, however, a fan of those stupid safety training courses that have been recommended. And if they try to stick me with a therapist, I'll go crazy."

"You … in need of a therapist? Never."

"I hate you, Talbot," Sam said, punching him slightly in his arm.

She loved that Mac was lightly ribbing her about the whole thing. It meant they could get past it. He knew how much she could take and when to hold back. Sam was already mortified enough by the whole Fredericks situation, and she'd had enough awkward exchanges with her coworkers. But Mac had never judged her, never would. Working homicide was hard enough, but a partner that always had your back made it a lot easier.

Mac loaded the first video.

"You're not really allowed to take this stuff from the precinct, right?" Sam asked.

"Hey, if they're going fully digital with everything now, this is the risk they take. But honestly, between the two of us, I don't know the chief would even care. He wants this Winstead thing wrapped as quickly as possible."

Sam popped the top on her first beer and nodded toward the television. "Let's get started then."

Mac pulled up the first of his series of interrogations. He started with Tess Todd because, according to Willa Dalton, she would be the most likely to harm Carmen Winstead. There was clearly no love lost between Carmen's only friend, Willa, and the other girls, especially Tess Todd. Even a few of the teachers they had spoken with from the high school had indicated Tess Todd often gave certain girls a hard time. And that was evident when forensics went through Carmen's laptop.

Sam and Mac watched the video, taken from the far-right corner of the ceiling in the station's interrogation room #2. It started as most interrogations usually did. Mac entered the room, sat across from her, and said, "I need you to state your name for the record, please."

"Tess Todd."

Even in saying only her name, Tess sat as rigid as a tree. She was clearly uneasy, from her posture and robotic way of speaking. But an underlying sort of boldness existed there too. She had the sort of tone in her voice that almost *dared* you to come after her.

"Tess, you were there when Carmen Winstead died, correct?"

"There? No. Not when she died. I had been there, by the sewers. But not when she actually died."

"Willa Dalton would disagree with that. She says you were there and that there also might be a chance that you pushed Carmen."

"That's a lie."

"Why would Willa lie about something like that?"

"First of all, because she was friends with Carmen. She's looking for someone to blame. Second, because she's a lying bitch. And she's jealous of me. She always has been. I don't guess she could help it, being raised by a Satan worshipper and all."

"Willa's family is not the issue here," Mac said. "Now, can you give me an example?"

"Of what?" Tess asked, her voice wavering a bit now.

"Of a time when Willa Dalton has been a lying bitch to you."

Tess went quiet here. She stared at the table, then at the walls. It was almost as if she were waiting for someone to come in and break this up—because how dare someone question her in such a way? When she finally spoke again, Mac paused the video at the first word.

"What do you think?" he asked, looking to Sam.

"I think she's very defensive. Then again, I would be too if the police were trying to pin a murder on me. You know, I was dealing with her asshole parents while you were interrogating her. That little holier-than-thou tone comes *directly* from her mother. You know, they have too much money, live in a nice house, and spoil their precious little princess so much she thinks she can do no wrong." She shook her head. "That was actually my final detail before I got my vacation."

Mac shrugged and un-paused the footage.

"Well, I can't think of anything specific …" Tess said.

"That's fine. Let's move on. Now, Tess, tell me exactly what happened, from the moment Willa Dalton threw the coffee on you to when you learned Carmen Winstead was dead."

Tess spent the next six minutes and thirty seconds retelling her story, with Mac breaking in only occasionally to clarify certain points. According to Tess Todd, she and her friends had been looking for Willa to confront her about the incident with the coffee. They ended up finding Carmen first, at the city's sewage gridwork, outside the treatment plant.

"But we just talked smack to her," Tess said. "Sure, you can call me a bully or whatever. But I had second degree burns on my hands from the coffee; she could've permanently disfigured me. And Carmen had just laughed about it. So we called her some names, so what. We even threatened to beat her up. Things like that. But I never touched her! No one did. When we turned and left, the only girl there with her was Willa. She had just gotten there."

"So," Mac said, "then you left the scene when Willa, the girl you were originally out to tell off, arrived."

"Yes. By then … I don't know. I was tired. Wet. I felt gross and I had enough. You know like it was enough, going off on Carmen. No sense in extending the drama."

"Some of your teachers suggest you might have been giving Carmen a hard time. One of them mentioned some very provocative flyers that were circulating around the school the day before Carmen died. Flyers with Willa and Carmen on them. Would you happen to know anything about that?"

"I know what flyers you're talking about, yes. I saw them, sure. But if you're asking me if I know anything about them, no."

Sam snatched the remote from Mac and paused it. "Okay. So, I don't know if she's lying about her involvement with the Winstead murder, but she's lying her ass off about the flyers. Did you catch that?"

"I did. Her posture got more rigid. Her right hand reflexively clutched the side of the table. Did you see that?"

"I'm just surprised *you* caught it."

Sam playfully nudged him and rewound the footage. "By the way, nice restraint, not wanting to smack the shit out of this girl. She almost sounds like it's her God-given right to be a bitch."

"Oh, I wanted to shake her." Mac popped the top off his beer. "I really did."

Sam started the footage again and watched the moment Tess lied about the flyers. Her shoulders sort of turned from Mac in a guarded posture. Her head tilted just slightly; it was the first time her head had moved at all since Mac had entered the room. And, of course, there was the defensive flexing of her hand where she gripped the edge of the table.

"Either she knows who made the flyers or she did it herself," Sam said.

"I've got that in my notes, and, of course, all her friends are backing her story. Just a few days ago, I got shut down by the school's front office. They checked all the printer records, and the only job that had come out of their printers with a quantity that high was a leaflet promoting the corn festival."

"So, the flyers were printed somewhere else."

"Exactly." Mac took the remote back and switched to Virgie Vaughan's testimony. She had been weeping so much that it had been hard for Mac to get much of anything from her. But the little he *did*, backed up the vast majority of Tess's story. It took a while to get to the actual questioning though.

Sam watched as Virgie Vaughan was brought into the interrogation room. The moment the door closed behind her—Virgie broke. She fell to her knees before she even reached the table, crying so loudly it was more like screaming. Sam's eyes widened. "Dramatic much?"

Mac laughed. "Yeah, tell me about it."

"But she wasn't crying over Carmen's death, right?"

"Not from what I heard. She just buckled under the pressure. As soon as she saw the inside of that interrogation room, she lost it. That, I think, was genuine."

They endured the rest of Virgie's sob fest, then Mac switched to footage from the interrogation of Miriam George. Miriam wasn't as well-composed as Tess, but she was better than Virgie. Mac asked the same questions, and Miriam gave responses that parroted Tess. It was almost as if they had rehearsed the story together. The only place where things were even remotely different was in how bad the name calling had gotten.

"I think Tess realized she had gone too far at some point," Miri said. "Carmen started to cry—not full-out bawl, but there were tears, you know? I felt bad."

"And it was just Tess?" Mac asked on the screen. "You didn't do any of the name calling?"

"No, but I made some pig noises. I mean, hello! She wasn't a nice person."

"What? Why would you do that?"

"Because" she said sheepishly, "we had been calling her Carmen Pigstead. Because she lived on a farm. It was just a joke."

Mac lowered his head and continued taking notes and said nothing. He paused the video again, gulped his beer, and looked at Sam. "Can you believe that?"

"High school girls are the absolute worst. Little bitches."

"But anyway, I think the real place to look is this last one." He closed out Miri George's footage and brought up the fourth girl. "Cassie Hollins. She was scared out of her mind, and it showed. The story was the same as the other girls, but I could tell she was really having to think about each answer she gave. It's like she was taking a test. When I was done speaking with her, I was fully expecting to clean up a puddle of piss. She was nervous about something."

"Hollins," Sam said. "Are her parents Trevor and Kim Hollins?"

Mac fumbled through the files on the table in front of him and slipped out one with a tab that read *Hollins*. "Let's see." His eyes searched the document. "Here, yes. Trevor and Kim Hollins."

"Ah, god."

"Yeah, my words exactly."

While neither of them had ever had any trouble with the Hollins family, it was no secret they were both insufferable assholes. Trevor Hollins owned one of the two construction companies in town, and Kim was co-owner of a realty company. They had a lot of money, didn't mind showing it, and looked down on others who didn't. The fact they were holy roller, Bible-thumping Christians was the cherry on top.

"Well, I personally can't think of a better way to spend a Saturday than irritating one of Somerdale's power couples," Sam said.

"I'm thinking we'd better go over in the morning, try to talk to her before the weekend gets underway and Cassie has time to speak with her little friends."

"Hey, I'm not officially back until Monday."

"Well then, let's make this an unofficial visit."

Sam was rather sad the little interrogation session had come to an end. She had been hoping to really burn the midnight oil, digging into the case.

But then Mac stacked the casefiles, tucked them under his arm, and brought them to the kitchen, and looked at the door—her sign to leave.

Great. Now, she'd have to stop by Stubbies and grab a beer or a few shots to help her sleep. But while she shared a lot with Mac, she wasn't ready to tell him she was afraid to go home alone to an empty house—a house where, whenever she shut off the lights, she imagined Steven Fredericks slinking into bed and forcing himself on her.

But there were worse monsters that she would have to deal with. She imagined that Carmen Winstead probably knew that all too well.

SATURDAY, NOVEMBER 5, 2008

10:02 A.M.

When Trevor Hollins answered the door the following morning, he looked irritated.

Sam guessed he had spotted them getting out of their car and hiking up his pretentiously long sidewalk.

With the front door to his large house opened, Trevor made something of a show of standing in the center of the doorway, sort of the opposite of inviting them in. "Good morning, Detectives. Still digging into the Winstead case? I thought that was done."

"We're still investigating, tying up loose ends," Mac said. "We want to shore up a few inconsistencies. You can understand that, considering most of the people we have to question are teen-age girls, right?"

Sam was glad Mac was taking the lead on this. She would have already said something crude and inappropriate—not that Sam's introduction had been all that polite.

"Are you saying my daughter has not been helpful?" Trevor asked, incredulous. "You've spoken with her three times already. I assume you're here for a fourth go round?"

"We are. Is that okay? Is she free for the next fifteen minutes or so?"

"Detective Talbot, this is *four times*. Isn't that bordering on some sort of abuse toward my daughter, maybe harassment?"

"That's ridiculous," Sam said, unable to help herself. "*Abuse* is the way these girls were talking to Carmen Winstead—who is now dead. And we know your daughter was with these girls, even if she wasn't an active participant."

She would've probably gone further, but just then, Mac flashed her a warning look—*Enough.*

"A girl is dead," Mac said, stepping forward. His nylon boot rested on the first step. "A girl Cassie's age. And, if I'm being frank with you, pieces of it don't add up. I think the girls aren't telling the whole story."

"So now you're calling her a liar?" Trevor asked, stepping forward.

An uneasy smile came over Mac's face. He stroked his beard, staring curiously at Trevor Hollins as he climbed the steps. Invited or not, he was going in. Sam had to admire his technique, his calm demeanor.

"No. I would never do that unless I had ample evidence. But I do think your daughter may be covering for one of her friends, out of loyalty. Maybe they didn't have anything to do with the death, but I firmly believe at least one of them knows *something*. And I know somebody is not being, let's say, forthcoming."

"There are four of them," Trevor said. "Why continue to harass my Cassie?"

"Because she's the only one who doesn't seem to be an outright bitch," Sam blurted.

This time, Mac didn't bother to give her the warning.

Trevor's defensive posture seemed to crumble. He sighed and reached for the storm doorknob. "I want to be present."

"That's perfectly fine," Mac said. He started inside, but Trevor blocked him from entering.

"Also, it must be out here on the porch. My wife is sort of done with all this. She damn near had a panic attack a few days ago."

"That's fine too."

Trevor nodded and went back inside.

Sam sat on the porch swing while Mac took one of the four rockers in front of the large bay window. "What do you think?" Sam asked, swinging back and forth.

"I think he's a dick. But I also think you should control your tone with him before he cuts us off from his daughter completely."

She gave him a sheepish look. "It just came out."

"Yeah, I know, Sam, it always does," Mac said in a not-unaffectionate tone as the door opened.

Cassie came out, not looking at either of them as she slumped into the rocker farthest from them and pulled her knees to her chest. The first thing Sam noticed were her nails—the French manicure was peeling, and the ends were bitten to the quick. She looked like a cat trapped between two dogs—somewhere between nervous and doomed. Her eyes were glassy, glistening with unshed tears.

"Hey, Cassie," Mac said. "Thanks for agreeing to speak with us again."

"Do I have a choice?"

Cassie, in Sam's opinion, was easily the prettiest of the four girls who comprised Tess Todd's group. Tess was gorgeous, sure, and she knew it. Cassie, on the other hand, had that sort of fresh-faced, non-assuming innocence about her. She had the look of a girl who'd blossom into one of those classic-movie star types like the innocent images of Barbra Stanwyck in her twenties, while Tess Todd relied on makeup to retain her beauty.

"Hopefully, this will be the last time," Sam said. "But, Cassie, we need you to be one hundred percent honest with us."

"But I *have* been!" She eyed her father and folded her arms, never making eye contact with Mac or Sam.

"Okay then," Mac said. "So, just one more time. I want to hear what happened that afternoon. But I want you to pretend Tess and the other girls weren't even there. I don't want to hear about anything they did or said. I want to *only* hear about you— what you saw, what you did, what you said. Can you do that?"

She looked a little confused at first, then uncertain, her eyes darting nervously back and forth. "I got to the festival and met up with Te— with some friends. We hung out and watched the Corn Queen pageant. After that, I grabbed something to eat and went to where all the stuff for the festival was: the snacks, the music, all the people. When I was there, we ran into Willa and Carmen. Some of us have always had a thing against them, and some words were exchanged. After the thing with the coffee, we ended up looking for Willa but didn't find her. We did find Carmen though. More words were exchanged—name calling and all, you know. And then we left."

"And that's it?" Sam asked.

"Yes."

"What did you and your friends have against Willa? Look, I get the Carmen thing. It's stupid and childish and mean, but I get it. New girl in school, a girl who's a little different, so certain groups choose to give girls like that a hard time. But why Willa?"

Cassie shifted uncomfortably. "I don't know. There are rumors that she's, like, a witch or something. She lives with her aunt, and her aunt is supposed to be, like, a Satanist or something."

"And you believe those rumors?" Mac asked.

"I don't know … I guess."

"You ever met Willa's aunt?"

"No."

"So, in other words, Tess believes it, so everyone else does too?"

"Hold on, now," Trevor said. "That's not exactly fair. My daughter can think for herself. And I forbid Cassie any contact with the Daltons."

"Really. Why is that?"

"Everyone knows Satan is alive and well in Somerdale and Trulia Dalton is to blame. She reads the satanic bible, not the words of our lord and savior."

Mac and Sam exchanged a look but said nothing. After a few seconds, Mac said, "Well, I said I wouldn't take up much of your time, and I'm a man of my word. Cassie, thanks for enduring this again. I think we're good now."

He looked to Trevor and nodded. "Thank you, Mr. Hollins." Mac started down the porch stairs.

Sam followed behind him, but when she reached the bottom step, curiosity got the better of her. She turned. "Cassie, can I ask you one more thing?"

"Sure," she said hesitantly.

"What do *you* think happened to her? You were one of the last people to see her. You knew what she was like in school. If you had to guess, what do you think happened?"

Cassie stared at Sam, her eyes widening. Then she hitched a shoulder. "I don't know," she said softly. "Maybe ... maybe she just jumped down there herself."

"Jumped herself? You mean, suicide?" Sam almost laughed at the insinuation. Out of all the theories, that had to be the most hare-brained. "Serious?"

"I mean, maybe. Why not? She was ... she was a very unhappy girl. And she was hanging around Willa, who is sort of ... I don't know ... *gloomy and weird* anyway. Maybe she just snapped and jumped."

Sam felt herself tense. She wanted to say a million different things—none of them appropriate. Sam was no stranger to bullying. She'd had her nose broken, face slapped, and crotch kicked by bullies all before she even reached high school. Like Carmen

Winstead, Sam had never quite fit in either. She'd toyed with an interest in girls in middle school and had gotten involved in the metal scene while all of the other girls were into boys and nice clothes. So yeah, she knew all about bullies. She knew how they worked and what it took to break them. "She was unhappy?"

"Yeah. Just, like, sad all the time."

"Well, with the most popular girl group in school constantly calling her names and tearing her down, what do you expect?"

"That's enough!" Trevor Hollins snapped from the porch.

Mac tugged Sam's sleeve. "Come on, Sam," he whispered.

Sam winced, knowing she had gone too far. Even worse, she couldn't help but deny that she had enjoyed the look of pain and shock that crossed Cassie's face. She knew Mac would probably tear into her once they reached the car, but this time, she really didn't care.

5:30 P.M.

Virgie Vaughan had a reputation to uphold. She knew that herself and her friends Tess, Cassie, and Miri were considered cock teases by a lot of boys at school. And that was fine with her. She'd rather be a tease than a whore.

That was the unspoken motto among her friends. Tess was still a virgin and wore it almost like a badge. Only, her virginity wasn't what she put on a pedestal but her reputation as someone no one could ever touch. Not even Luca Gaines, who followed Tess around like a lost puppy, could penetrate her armor, though she always led him on, kept him hopeful.

In fact, Virgie was pretty sure Miri was the only one in their group who'd ever had sex. Miri had done it, oh, a year ago now, because she'd thought doing something Tess hadn't done would up her status. It hadn't. Now Miri spent a lot of her time trying to convince the rest of them to go ahead and get it over with since it was no big deal but, so far, none of them had—mostly because the name of the game was to be more like Tess.

Although, to be honest, Virgie had been considering it for quite a while.

That thought was in the back of her mind as she unbuttoned Shane Seamster's pants, her current, sort-of boyfriend. She felt him tense, unsure what to expect. She'd taken off his pants a few times before, teasing him in about every way imaginable. So far though, the only part of herself she'd taken him into was her hand. Her mouth would come next—though not tonight because he was being a little too needy—and then maybe, if he was a good boy, she'd let him have the whole prize.

With his pants unbuttoned, she put her hand around his cock. He was more than ready. It was like gripping a slab of granite, hard and stiff.

He moaned and tilted his head.

She smiled, not because she liked to see him enjoying it but because she knew he'd get nothing more. She loved to be in control.

Her parents were gone, as they usually were. Her father was away on business, and her stupid mother had followed along. This had given them the convenience of using her bedroom. They'd been making out for about half an hour before she removed his pants, taking her time.

She didn't know why, but as she kissed his neck, licking her way toward his chest, her hands working on him down below, her thoughts turned to Carmen Winstead. It was not just a coincidence that she had been with Shane several times since Carmen's death. He was a welcomed distraction from the police, the teachers, the reporters—all of it.

It wasn't even the sight of Carmen tumbling down the manhole that had stuck with her. It was that god-awful, echoing, thudding sound as her body struck some part of the interior of the hole. She heard it at night sometimes just as she fell asleep.

It made her think of the sound a watermelon would make after being thrown to the ground.

Shane moaned. She leaned in closer, pressing her body to his, trying to get the thoughts out of her head.

His right hand fumbled up her shirt.

She usually slapped it away, but she let him have access this time.

When his hand found her breast, he squeezed a bit too hard.

Tears formed in her eyes as she leaned in, felt skin between her teeth, and bit on his ear until he moaned once again. Her grip on Shane's penis tightened as she relived that day, imagining Tess reaching out and shoving. It had been a light tap, but a tap nonetheless and it had been enough. At least, that's what she kept telling herself. It was *barely* a push even. It was an accident, a mistake. But then down Carmen went, into the waiting dark …

"Babe …?"

She didn't hear anything particularly alarming in Shane's remark. She thought it was him getting close. She'd stop in a minute, just when he was at the breaking point—show him who was in control. Any man could be controlled by his cock. That was a given.

She kissed his neck again, sinking her teeth in just a bit because she knew he liked a little pain. Her hand pumped and squeezed. Everything in the room was tense and hot—the air, his breath, their sweat-coated skin.

"Virgie … it's …" He let out a huge gasp and shuddered, his body suddenly going limp.

Shit. Virgie felt him spend himself, felt her hand growing wet and sticky, but she kept going, angry that it had crept up on her and that he'd not given her ample warning. She gave the last few violent strokes, released him, and pulled away before he could entangle her in his arms.

Before addressing the mess currently in her right hand, she looked down at Shane.

He was in the ultimate state of surrender, seconds after orgasm. He looked weak and frail, putty in her hands.

Her anger gave way to satisfaction. But her hand … She didn't even look at it. It was sticky and gross. She pushed Shane from her and dashed to her adjoining bathroom. The only light came from a small nightlight above the sink. Its yellowish glow cast odd shadows over the room. As she turned on the faucet, she had to admit she was proud of what she'd done. So what if it got out at school? So what if Tess didn't approve?

"*Virgie.*"

She jumped away from the sink and scanned the room. At first, she thought Shane had called her, maybe whispering from the doorway. But he was not there. She reached for the light switch and turned it on.

He was still on the bed, unmoved from where she'd left him, staring grimly at the shadows dancing across the ceiling.

Her heart thudded. Beads of sweat collected on the nape of her neck. She'd just imagined it … but she could have sworn. *It was clear*, she thought, *not the whispering of something in my head.* She peered into the sink.

"I could have sworn," she whispered as she stepped backward and gazed around the bathroom. The white lace shower curtain hung perfectly still behind her, the window shut tight, the bathroom clean and tidy, just the way her mother liked it. There was nothing.

But it had sounded so real … and from somewhere close by. It *had* been real, right there beside her.

Virgie returned to the mirror and rolled her eyes. The stress of late was probably just catching up to her. If imagining her name coming from some phantom voice was the worst of it, she could live with that. "Get over it," she murmured to her reflection and flipped off the light.

Virgie gasped.

The image of a rotted corpse, skin peeled from its bones, stood right behind her reflection in the mirror. Black, stringy hair. A leering smile, most of the teeth smashed and broken. An arm, broken in the center and flopping like jelly, somehow reaching for her. The figure smiled, those shattered teeth gleaming under rotted lips.

Just as Virgie opened her mouth to scream, the figure winked out of existence.

She blinked rapidly to ensure her eyes were working. She'd spied the figure for no more than a split second before she could actually focus on it. She spun around. Nothing. No trace of it whatsoever. *Because it wasn't there at all, you stupid ass.*

She knew this was true—it *had* to be true—because she didn't want to admit the thought that had crossed her mind just then that it had looked a little like … she gasped.

Her heart was slamming in her chest, and she tasted burning in the back of her throat, something she was pretty sure came from a sudden rush of fear. Her legs trembled, begging to run, but she could not move. It felt like they were buckling beneath her. She gripped the sides of the sink and lowered her head. She didn't want to look again to see who was standing behind her.

"It couldn't be. It's impossible," she whispered. As she finally got the strength, she stepped slowly from the bathroom and into the shadows dancing across the ceiling.

"What's wrong?" Shane got up and started toward her.

"Nothing." Virgie said, fighting back tears. "I'm fine."

"You look like something's wrong."

"I said I'm fine, and where the hell are you going?" She tried to sound authoritative, not like she was weak and losing her mind.

"To the bathroom."

"Yeah, not yet," she said, shoving him playfully back toward the bed. Virgie unbuttoned her pants and slid them to the floor.

Shane stared at her as if he had just seen a unicorn. His eyes widened with desire, and Virgie drank it all in.

"Now it's my turn," she said, laying on her back.

As his kisses trailed over her breasts, to her stomach, and then farther down, Virgie did her best to enjoy it. But the entire time, thoughts of the image from the bathroom drifted through her head, replaced every so often by the image of Carmen Winstead falling back through the darkness.

Impossible, she thought.

MONDAY NOVEMBER 7, 2008

3:42 P.M.

Tess was accustomed to people looking at her. But not like this. Boys usually leered at her, drinking her in, and girls gazed at her with longing. But when she arrived at school on Monday morning, she noticed people would only give her furtive glances from the corners of their eyes.

Things had *felt* different too since Carmen's death—more tense and somehow brutal. It seemed to follow her around the hallways like a shadow. She'd never felt alienation like this, not ever. Probably because something had finally happened in this shitty little town, and people were suspecting certain things.

She was wearing the shortest skirt she could get away with against the school's dress code, and it still wasn't drawing the attention she was used to. That wasn't what bothered her though; it was that, for the first time in her life, it felt like the rumor mill was churning, and she wasn't holding the crank.

When she sat in Mr. Carlton's class, only half-listening to him explaining why Faulkner was a genius, Tess's gaze drifted to the seat Carmen Winstead had previously occupied. It may as well have been an active bomb sitting in the middle of the room. A few other students also sneaked looks at it, as well as Mr. Carlton. The empty desk was like a giant elephant, and it might as well have been taking one big shit on Tess.

Tess *knew* she was guilty. There was no getting around that. She had gone a step too far, providing that little nudge. That's all it had been—a nudge. Barely a touch. But the bitch of it was it had made all the difference in the world. It *was* just an accident, really. But try telling that to the police. They'd probably ruin college, her future, *everything*. For what? One fucking nudge?

Insane.

But even her friends seemed to be keeping a safe distance. They'd all met by her locker that morning, but their minds were elsewhere, their attention divided by unsaid things. Virgie had been very quiet, her contribution to conversations little more than a series of nods and *uh-huh*s, which was unlike her. They'd also spotted one another in the hallways between classes and gave each other cutesy, little waves—anything to maintain the façade. And they all walked with that same confident strut everyone expected them to have. After all, they had reputations to uphold. If they stepped out of their routine or their attitudes seemed affected in any way, it would only raise suspicion. Tess could not have that—none of them could.

And the stupid cops had already done enough of that. They'd interviewed her two different times. How much more did she have to withstand?

After the last bell rang, the girls met by Tess's locker before heading home. The only one missing was Miri, because she always left early on Mondays and Wednesdays for her afternoon shift at the local sub shop.

As Tess slid her textbooks into her locker, Virgie stepped in close and whispered, "Anyone else sort of done with the way everyone is looking at us?"

"Screw 'em. Let them look. It'll be old news by the time summer gets here, and then I'll be off to college and done with this place, so I could give three shits how these losers look at me."

"But, Tess …" Cassie's voice quivered with uncertainty.

"But, Tess," Tess mocked her. God, if anyone would fuck up things, it'd be Cassie. "Listen, dweeb, grow a pair, will you?"

"Yes, Tess, but I don't know. I don't think this will just pass over."

"Cassie, you're always worrying about things." Tess rolled her eyes. "If you're going to be all neurotic about this, I might have to strangle you."

"I hate to say it, but she might be right," Virgie said, leaning in close. Her voice was hesitant and sort of frail, as if Cassie's disease was catching. "It's sort of creepy, the way everyone looks at us. It's like they know something."

"Of course, they don't know anything," Tess snapped. "The only person who might have seen was Willa. And if you think anyone in this school will believe a single word *she* says, you're out of your mind. Everyone ignores her dumb ass anyway."

Cassie bit her lip. "But what about the police? They came to my house again this weekend, asking questions."

"What?" Tess slammed her locker so suddenly that Cassie and Virgie leaped backward.

Virgie put a hand to her lips, as if to stifle a scream.

Tess had to restrain herself from grabbing Cassie's collar and slamming her head against the hard metal.

"Yeah, on Saturday."

"What did they ask you?"

"The same questions. But they said they feel like we're not being *forthcoming*."

Tess scoffed. "They're bluffing. That's because they don't have anything." She turned to Virgie. "Did they come to you too?"

Virgie shook her head.

Tess sighed. It had crossed her mind to just go ahead and tell the cops about what really happened. After all, it had been an accident. Of course, she did not mean to push the moron down the hole. Yes, she could be a little bitter and even downright vengeful, but actually hurt someone? Never.

"What if they know and are just looking for evidence or something?" Cassie asked.

"What evidence? There *is* none. All they have is our story, which is pretty airtight as long as no one screws it up." She stared down Cassie.

"What if they keep coming though?" Virgie asked.

"Then we keep telling the same story. Seriously, what the hell are you guys so afraid of? Besides, Cassie could just hit them over the head with her stupid bible, right Cass?" Cassie looked down. "I mean that is what you're relying on these days. Right? The stupid bible. I know you are. Hell, everyone does."

Virgie flinched. She looked terrified, as if she was keeping something from them. "What is it, Virgie? Tell me because you look guilty."

"Nothing! It's just … It's getting pretty scary, Tess."

"I'm telling you, another few weeks and this will blow over. The girl fell down a manhole. I'm sure accidents like that happen every day outside Somerdale. The only reason the police are obsessing about it is because nothing interesting ever happens here. The cops will find out they have no case, no evidence, and they'll rule it an accident. As long *as we stick to the fucking story!*" Tess Todd stormed away from her friends, losing herself in the crowd. She felt their eyes on her, sliding across her like slime, but she shook it off. *This will all be over soon.*

And when it was, all these idiots cutting evil eyes at her would get a steaming hot slice of humble pie. She'd make damn sure of that.

8:35 P.M.

Willa awoke with a shuddering breath. She sat upright in bed, as if on a spring. Her heart was pounding; her hands were clammy. As her eyes adjusted, she glimpsed something at the edge of her bed—a cloaked figure maybe, something totally submerged in the darkest shadows of the bedroom.

But as soon as she saw it, it was gone.

She searched the room, but there was nothing—nothing but gloom. Somehow though, it felt different. She had the overwhelming sensation of being watched.

She threw back her blanket and placed her feet on the floor. Suddenly, she felt like she was a child again, wanting desperately to run out of her room, down the hallway, and into her mother's arms. Only this was a different house, and her mother had not been a part of her life for a long time.

Still, she could not shake the feeling that, at any moment, something would reach out from under the bed to grab her feet. At that thought, Willa leaped up from the bed and dashed to the door. Her hand slapped at the light switch, and her eyes traveled to the back edge of her bed, searching.

Nothing.

But even with the bedroom lights on, Willa did not feel comfortable. The chill in the air was biting, and it felt oddly cramped and impersonal. More than that, it felt … occupied. She felt that someone *else* had been here, the weight of another human presence almost tangible.

She stepped away, not yet ready to take her eyes off her bed. She backed through the opened doorway into the hallway. *Something was there.* A ridiculous thought, her brain said, but her heart knew better.

She sighed in relief when she had reached the hallway. She was safe. True always left a small lamp on, as she tended to get up a few times throughout the night. A faint light emanated from the living room. It was something she was used to. Only tonight, something seemed different. It seemed dark.

While the rumors of Willa being a witch weren't necessarily true, they did have roots in the truth. True was a Wiccan, and when she was feeling particularly in tune with nature, she would even use the label of green witch. Of course, True never referred to herself as a witch in the common usage of the word; she did not practice dark magic, she did not worship Satan, and she did not own a magical flying broom. Depending on who she might be talking to, there were times when True even considered the label of witch insulting.

Honestly, even Willa wasn't quite sure what her aunt identified as. She knew her aunt had some sort of power—some obscure ability to connect with nature. From time to time, Willa would feel a stirring of energy in the house that was not frightening but certainly made her feel a bit uneasy.

Willa had always been a bit turned off from it all because sometimes it just seemed like another religion to her, and she wanted nothing to do with that. Why adhere to rules handed down by gods and goddesses you could not physically see when there were plenty of real-world monsters already in place to control and manipulate you?

But there were also times when she saw a sense of peace and belonging in True. Sometimes she would look almost intoxicated, though True never did partake in anything aside from an occasional glass of wine. It made Willa think there might be something to it all.

As Willa crept toward the living room, she peered into the kitchen. True was sitting at the kitchen table, as she had expected. Two candles flickered to both sides of her. Her hands were on the table, palms facing the ceiling.

Assuming her aunt was undergoing one of her so-called meditation sessions, Willa figured she would give her some privacy. She watched her for a moment in admiration from the stillness and concentration of the act, then she reluctantly turned and headed toward her room.

She made it two steps before True called out to her. "Come here, Willa."

Willa hesitated in the doorway. True'd been in such a state of concentration, and it would probably take a while to regain it. "Sorry, Aunt True. I didn't mean to bother you."

"It's not a bother. Would you come sit with me for a bit?"

True's voice was soft and somber, which was odd. True was usually very bright and cheerful, always trying to lift people's spirits with her gifts. And she had never invited Willa into one of her late-night sessions. Sure, she had asked Willa if she wanted to join her in certain practices and rituals here and there, but her nighttime communal sessions were special and usually off limits.

Willa entered the kitchen and sat beside True. She instantly felt cold, as if she were trespassing or stepping onto some sort of sacred ground.

"Couldn't sleep?" True asked, her eyes still focused on the wall in front of her, palms facing the ceiling.

"I don't know. I just woke up feeling creeped out. Maybe it was a bad dream I don't remember." As she said this, she recalled that figure at the foot of her bed and when she was visiting Joe Winstead at Carmen's house.

"I haven't been sleeping well either. And it all started when Carmen died." True broke her concentration and stared at Willa.

Willa noticed her eyes were paler than usual, more tired.

"Or, if I'm being honest, I believe it started when you first brought her into our home."

"What do you mean?"

"I sensed something about her. Something …. yearning. Something unhappy. I barely even knew the girl—I only met her the one time—but something about her troubled me. It only got worse when she died."

"Why are you just now telling me this?" While she did not fully buy into her aunt's beliefs, her ability to read people and situations had always been uncanny.

"Because it was a fleeting feeling, Willa, and I wasn't sure. But I felt something odd when I touched her, and it only strengthened when you told me she had died. It has troubled the force around all things within this town. Something in the air … I don't know. Something is not happy."

"Someone I know died, Aunt True. I'd think the atmosphere around this house is sort of gloomy. You don't think you're just reading too much into it?"

True slowly shook her head. Then, enunciating each word, she said, "Something. Isn't. Happy."

"Her father isn't happy," Willa said bitterly. "I'm not particularly happy for that matter either."

True shook her head again, ignoring the bit of mockery in Willa's tone. "I mean something in nature. Something in the places most people cannot see. Something has awoken."

Willa couldn't ignore the chill that crept up her spine—or how absolutely frigid her room had gone a few minutes ago. She'd never felt anything like it—and she'd felt and experienced some odd things in the past. But this, this was something new, something more powerful and ominous—if she was being honest with herself, something dangerous and dark. "And you think it has something to do with Carmen?"

"I don't know. But the timing seems to suggest so."

"Is it something bad?"

"I don't know. But … something's coming. Willa, I think something dark is on the way, and I want you to try to be ready for it."

Willa looked down, fumbling with her fingers.

"What is it, Willa? What's wrong?"

"You know Carmen, at the corn festival, told me she kept hearing things in her house at night. Like it was pulling at her, calling her. And when I went to see her dad a few days ago, I could've sworn I heard them too. It was weird."

"Willa, you stay away from that house, you hear me. Something is there; it's been there around Carmen, and I need you to be ready."

"Ready for what, exactly?" Whatever it was, True looked shaken by it, and that was a state Willa had never seen her in.

"I don't know what. But I get the sense our house is being … I don't know … *seen*. Targeted, maybe. Even so, I do not feel a huge sense of danger. We should be cautious, yes, but …"

"Aunt True, I love you very much. But what in the hell are you talking about?"

True leveled her eyes at Willa. "I don't know just yet. But I get a feeling—a feeling about you."

"Aunt True, you're creeping me out. Stop, okay?"

True nodded and blinked rapidly, as if coming out of some sort of a daze. "Yes, of course. But one more thing, Willa. In the next few days, if you feel as if something is sort of prying at you, maybe let it in."

Let it in? Willa had heard enough. She silently rose from the table and returned to bed, trying her best to shake the chill that seemed to have crept inside her and had laced itself around her bones. She kept replaying the conversation she'd just had with True.

As Willa lay silently in the darkness of her room, one thing kept bouncing around in her head: the words that spewed off True's tongue, *Let it in.*

"Let what in?" she whispered as she closed her eyes and wished for sleep to find her.

8:47 P.M.

Miriam George liked the way her manager looked at her. Yeah, Jack was nearly fifty years old, and there wasn't much in his life to admire; his life had, after all, led him to the position of afternoon manager at the Sub Station. Still, his leering eyes made her feel sexy. She also felt okay with him ogling her because she knew he'd never try anything. Or, at least, she didn't think he would. They'd never have that moment like something from a porno where he'd take her from behind at the sandwich-making station, banging her while she made a sub on the counter. Jack went to church regularly, had a wife and three kids, and seemed to get flustered whenever she returned his lingering glances.

Still, it was nice to feel wanted.

Jack had just been giving her one of those glances as he wiped down the last of the tables in the dining area. Now, as he headed through the kitchen, removed his apron, and hooked it on the apron stand, he slipped back to his managerial role, as if he had not just been staring at her ass two seconds ago. "You sure you're okay locking up? I don't mind hanging back."

"It's okay," Miri assured him. Jack had mentioned it was his youngest daughter's birthday, and he had some sort of movie night planned, since he'd missed the pizza party. She also knew, because he complained about it all the time, that his wife would behead him if he was late.

"I just feel bad leaving you here by yourself."

"It's okay, Jack. It's a key and a lock. I know how they operate. I also know how to slide a key between the cracks of my fingers if I need to hurt an attacker on the way to my car. I'm fine, I promise. Now get out of here before your wife slits your throat."

He grinned at this. The thought of Miri George punching anyone was as hilarious as anyone trying to jump her on the way to her car. Things like that just didn't happen in Somerdale. As a

matter of fact, the death of Carmen Winstead was the most interesting thing to have happened in this dusty, little town in years.

Jack waved and sauntered out the door.

Miri honestly didn't mind being left alone. All she had left
to do was wrap up the leftover meats, wash a few pans, and cut
out the lights. She would be out of here in about twenty minutes or so, plus she would get home after her mother was asleep.
That in and of itself was something of a mercy. Miri was pretty
much done with her mother coddling her, asking her repeatedly
if she was okay or if she needed someone to talk to. It had been
never-ending ever since Carmen had died. It was almost like her
mother was worried that she *hadn't* broken down into an incon-
solable mess. But why would she? Carmen was a pig.

So, Miri set to work. The place was already closed, and the
main lights were out. She was in no hurry to get home, wanting
to ensure her total exposure time with her mother boiled down to
a knock on her parents' bedroom door to let them know she was
home and nothing more. Also, she wanted to earn more money
before she left for college and showing she could close on her
own *and* ensure the Sub Station was properly cleaned would get
her closer to that goal. Closing the place wasn't exactly rocket science, but it was pretty high on the responsibility rankings as far
as small-town sub shops went.

She was washing one of the vegetable pans, daydreaming of
what college would be like, when she heard something behind
her—a faraway clattering sound, or maybe a shuffling. It was
hard to tell. It could have been a rat scurrying across the floor,
accidentally disturbing some of the cookware.

She wheeled around, wondering if Jack had decided he *could*
risk his marriage for a fling with a high schooler with great tits
and a hard ass. That thought made her giggle. Eww … *gross.*

But no one was there. She eyed the rear of the kitchen area,
shrugged, and resumed cleaning the pans. But it had been *something*, hadn't it? Probably. About two hundred different things

could have made the noise: pans shifting in the sink, something settling in the freezer, supplies falling over in one of the cabinets. But there was no point in investigating; she just wanted to finish up and clock out.

She had nearly put it completely out of her mind when she heard it again. It was unmistakable this time and certainly not the sound of supplies shifting behind a cabinet. No, this time it was much clearer. It was a voice.

"Miri."

The pan slipped from her soapy hands and clattered into the sink with a teeth-jarring sound. She shrieked and turned around, scanning the kitchen. "Who's there?"

No one responded.

Miri shook her head, biting hard on her tongue to stop her teeth from chattering.

Then ... it came again. Her name, whispered in a raspy voice—only it wasn't a voice that she had ever heard before. It seemed ancient, layered with dust, sick. Wrong. Evil.

"Miri ... "

She took a slow step forward, a wave of anxiety growing inside her. Her eyes darted about, but she could not tell where the voice was coming from. One moment, she thought it had come from behind her. Or from the darkened dining area out front. She couldn't remember if she'd locked the door after Jack had left. Maybe someone had wandered in. But that didn't seem right either. No, the voice seemed to have come from nowhere and everywhere at once.

Her first instinct told her to run, to haul ass out of the Sub Station. But that wouldn't get her brownie points with Jack. And what did that make her if she couldn't cut a stupid minimum wage job at the Sub Station? Surely, there was a logical explanation. Maybe Tess was playing a fucked-up joke on her. Or maybe it was Willa, the freak. Either way, she'd get them back, for sure.

"*Miri.*" The tone had changed. It was more demanding, insistent.

She glanced around for shadows, for any sign someone else was in the room with her. She crept to the doorway and peered into the dining area. No one was there. She turned back to the sink, the sound of dripping water making a hollow, tinny sound as it pinged against the stainless steel.

As she moved closer, her name came again, thicker, and more menacing and this time, right at her ear. Right in her face, from behind her from the cusp of darkness.

"*Miriiiiii …*"

She straightened like an arrow as an ice-cold chill spiked its way through her. She slowly backed away from the sink, her eyes on the drain—the black circle, like the dark void Carmen Winstead had fallen into. Was it calling to her? Drawing her in? Hypnotizing her?

Though she thought she'd been backing away, when her hips hit the edge of the sink, she realized she'd been coming closer. Now, the drain was right beneath her.

"*Miri.*"

"Hell-Hello?"

"Hello," the fiendish voice rasped.

Miri gazed at the blackness, voice trembling as she whispered, "Who are you?"

A gurgling voice replied, "You know."

Black sludge—like a darker and thicker mud with the consistency of jelly—bubbled from the hole and swallowed the stainless-silver drain. But the stench was that of something else. It smelled rotten, like the soil from an opened grave.

Miri moaned and stepped backward. Her eyes anchored on the sink as her legs felt weak and useless. She stumbled against the wall as cackling noises filled the room, coming from everywhere, materializing from the air itself, throaty and choked by the foul material emerging from the drain.

Gathering the strength to run, she took off. When she reached the end of the sandwich station, she bolted for the front door. She took the turn so fast she struck the apron stand and toppled it with a clatter. She fumbled for the keys in the door as she dared a glance over her shoulder. For a moment, she saw something in the shadows.

A lurking figure heading for her—a girl, dressed in a filthy white dress, barefoot, head arched down, limp black hair strung over her face like a curtain. Slitted eyes scorched through every strand.

Miri trembled, tasting something foul in the back of her throat—tangy and sort of coppery, almost like blood.

"Miri ..." the figure said, reaching for her.

Miri cried out as she finally yanked the key from the lock. She blasted through the door, lungs exploding. When she turned to lock it from the outside, the figure was closer, at the edge of the sandwich station.

The figure, small-statured and feminine, but it was also something else—amorphous, like jelly or shadows, its edges beyond the comprehension of her terrorized brain.

"God, please help me ..." Miri turned the keys, locked the door, and raced down the sidewalk to the side of the Sub Station where her car waited in the employee parking lot. She cranked her car and peeled onto the street, not bothering to pause at the Stop sign.

Miri was crying and shaking as she drove through Somerdale. *You didn't see that,* she told herself. *No way in hell that was real. It's just ...* "Shit!" she screamed, slapping her steering wheel.

She navigated out of the central part of Somerdale. The little town looked even deader in the darkness of night, with not a single other soul around. She felt like she was stranded in a ghost town with some unnamable creature on her heels. She found herself peering into the rearview mirror to ensure no one was following her.

But the only thing behind her was an empty road, reflecting the glow of the streetlamps. As she drew closer to home, she felt safer, more certain she had not really heard or seen anything, that her guilt-ridden mind had simply been playing tricks on her and that was all.

By the time she turned onto her street, the horror was all but forgotten. The porch light on her house was inferior to the darkness that surrounded her as she pulled into the driveway. Her headlights created a long tail in the darkness, and when she pulled behind her father's truck, all she was thinking about was a nice bath to get the smell of cold cuts and vinegar off her skin.

But a figure stood there, waiting.

At first, she was sure she was seeing things. She blinked, but it only became clearer. It was a human form, slightly transparent, like looking through the cellophane she used to wrap sandwiches at the sub shop. It was dark and somehow fluid, like melting chocolate, chin lowered to its chest, eyes fastened on her beyond its lowered brow.

And even though Miri couldn't discern its mouth, she was pretty sure it was grinning.

Jesus, please help me ...

She jammed on her brakes, closed her eyes, and wished it away. Trembling, she slowly opened her eyes to see it was gone. She hurried into the safety of her house and closed and locked the door behind her, never looking back in the darkness.

She ran down the hallway to her room, grabbed her phone from her pocket, and furiously texted Tess Todd, *We have to come clean. I'm going crazy.*

She shed her work clothes and slipped into pajamas. As she crawled under the covers of her bed, wishing they were a shield to ward off the things she'd seen that night, her phone dinged at her bedside table.

Go crazy then, you stupid bitch. Just keep your ugly mouth shut. Got it?

Miri tossed the phone to the floor. She huddled under the covers, pulling them closer to her chest. She sat there and stared at the ceiling, the walls, and the window, trembling. With the night falling around her, she knew she would not fall asleep for a very long time.

TUESDAY, NOVEMBER 8, 2008

9:00 A.M.

Detectives Samantha Kerr and Mac Talbot parked their car in front of Joe Winstead's house just after nine o'clock on Tuesday morning. Neither of them acted very quickly to get out of the car. They both studied the house for a while, Mac behind the wheel and Sam sipping a cup of coffee in the passenger seat.

"What are we going to do if we can't wrap this thing?" she asked.

"We'll wrap it. We'll call it an accident and go on to the next case, I suppose."

"The girls are lying. You know that."

"Yeah." He seemed so blasé about it.

"Don't you want to see them *pay?*"

He laughed bitterly. "Hold on, Bronco. What I want to see is justice done. I don't know what kind of personal vendetta you might have against the mean girls of the world, but that's personal. If we can't find any evidence to put these girls away, we have to let it go. *You* know that."

She did. All too well. Her woman's intuition that these spoiled girls deserved to be behind bars, as strong as it was, wouldn't hold up in court. She took another sip and nodded to the house. "So, let's see if Joe Winstead can reveal something to us that will give us permission to slap some handcuffs on them."

They finally got out and approached the front porch. They had called ahead yesterday, just to ensure Joe would be there. He had agreed halfheartedly, as if he really didn't give a damn if they came by or not. Couldn't blame him, considering he was likely in the throes of grief.

Mac knocked on the door, and they heard heavy footfalls approaching right away.

Joe Winstead didn't so much answer the door as throw it open and walk away. He got about halfway down the hallway before he turned, leaned against the wall, and motioned vaguely for them to enter.

Sam's heart broke for him. The dark half-circles under his eyes, scraggly growth on his chin, and slumped shoulders told of a man who'd not had an easy couple of weeks.

"Hey, Detectives. Come on in."

They followed Joe inside, where he essentially fell into a recliner in the living room and kicked up his feet.

As Sam sat on the edge of the couch, she noted the coffee cup and bottle of Maker's Mark on the coffee table. He'd probably been relying on the bourbon to get him through. She didn't blame him though; she couldn't imagine his pain. Not many could.

"What can I do for you two?" Joe asked gruffly.

"I won't lie to you," Mac said. "We don't really have anything new. We've questioned everyone more than once. We also had a forensics team comb every inch of that sewer, Carmen's phone and laptop. I know she was bullied. I mean bullied beyond what any person should be." Mac nervously glanced at Sam. But, unless you have any other ideas, at this point, we're about to close it up and chalk it up to an accident."

Joe shook his head. "Jesus. I mean, I should want that right? To put it behind me. But hell, it doesn't seem natural. It feels like we're ... I don't know. Leaving her there. It sure as hell doesn't feel like closure."

"Has anyone from school reached out to you?"

"Yes, actually. One of the guidance counselors called me a few days ago. I thought that was very nice of them. They knew I was new to the area and gave me the numbers of a few counselors."

"Anyone else?"

"No ... well, yes. Willa Dalton came by. I think she was just sad and lonely. Said she wanted to be around someone else who knew Carmen."

Sam noticed at the mention of Carmen, Joe grimaced as if someone had stabbed him in the gut. "How did Willa seem?"

"I don't know. Just sad."

"Did you find it odd that she came here?"

"I did, at first. Sort of floored me out a bit, having her here. But when I saw how sad and broken, she was, no. It seemed almost normal. You know the grieving, so I was glad to be there for her—and the other way around, you know?"

Sam nodded. Willa had spoken of a huge distaste for Tess Todd and her friends. She had not come right out and said she believed Tess and her friends had intentionally killed Carmen, but she had leaned heavily in that direction. So far, they had not told Joe of Willa's strong suspicion, and it appeared that Willa hadn't mentioned it to him either. Good. The last thing the police needed was an aggrieved father blaming four underage girls for his daughter's death.

Maybe it was better if they did just chalk it up to an accident. But Sam knew what Joe meant; it didn't feel like closure.

She wouldn't be comfortable calling it an accident until they had ruled out everything, turned over every stone.

"Mr. Winstead, I wonder if you'd allow me to have a look around Carmen's room?"

Both Joe and Mac looked to her, confused. Mac seemed a little embarrassed too. "Miller did that while you were off."

"I wasn't *off*," she snapped. "I was asked to sit aside for a bit. Also, I'd like to have a look myself. If that's okay, Mr. Winstead?"

"Help yourself," he said in a monotone, as if he honestly didn't care at all. "It's the first room you'll come to upstairs."

Sam excused herself. By the time she reached the stairs, Mac was asking Joe questions again. They were the same questions he'd been asked before, only reworded and restructured.

Sam found Carmen's door already open. The morning sunlight slashed dusty rays through the half-drawn curtain in the window. The room was of modest size and had a small adjoining bathroom with only a toilet and sink. There were no discernable smells, no lingering perfume or powders that seemed to hover in the rooms of most girls her age.

The bed was neatly made, as she figured Carmen had done before going to the festival, with a stuffed bear perched atop of it. The room was clean, aside from a few books stacked by the side of the bed. It was mostly classic lit, probably assigned by her high school teacher. She smiled when she saw Toni Morrison's *Beloved* in the stack. Sam wasn't much of a reader, but *Beloved* had always been a favorite.

She opened the drawer to the bedside table but found nothing out of the ordinary: a hairbrush, some Chapstick, and a few mismatched earrings. She got to her knees and checked under the bed. Again, she saw nothing to raise any alarms: pairs of shoes and a stray sock, a few dust bunnies. But besides that, it seemed clean and organized.

When Sam got back to her feet, she felt a presence behind her. She quickly turned to the door, expecting to see Mac standing there. She was about to tell him she hadn't found anything but realized the doorway was empty. Odd. She shivered a bit, shrugging off the feeling of being watched.

She refocused her attention to the room. She saw the laptop the forensic team mirrored and returned but knew there would be no phone; the coroner had found it in Carmen's pocket when her body had been pulled out of the manhole. It had been scrubbed for any information that might help regarding the case, but there had been very little, other than a text conversation between Willa and Carmen, that had shown how much they disliked Tess and her group.

Sam entered the bathroom and poked around there. There was no medicine cabinet, just a round Victorian-style mirror with frosted glass on the edges and a small shelf beside it, so she only had drawers and a few cabinets to check. Again, nothing was out of the ordinary. There was toilet paper, some feminine hygiene products, and a few sparse containers of makeup.

As Sam stepped out of the bathroom, she got that sense of someone watching her again. She eyed the bedroom doorway. Still no one. In fact, she could still hear Mac and Joe speaking downstairs, their voices faint. She'd just started for the door when she heard something.

The sound came from behind her, muffled and indistinct. A female voice. She turned toward it quickly, wondering if she'd really heard it at all. Still, she was so jarred by the sound that one hand had gone to her side, hovering over the Glock she kept holstered at her hip.

She peered into the bathroom again, her eyes narrowed. Had she really heard it? If she'd heard *anything* at all, had it really been a voice? Now that she thought of it, it might have been more like a humming noise, like a voice on a radio, or even just the sound of the radiator hissing.

Sure enough, the sound came again. This time, there was no mistaking it was indeed a faint female voice. She could not decipher what it was saying or if it was speaking words at all. It sounded almost like someone humming or stifling a laugh.

Sam cocked her head and listened intently. Though it made no real sense, she was pretty sure the noise was coming from the bathroom. Part of her figured it was the house, maybe the pipes. After all, it was one of those old farmhouses with ancient fixtures and piping.

But then it came again. Laughter. A faint, muffled laugh.

A chill ripped up her spine.

She took a deep breath and walked slowly toward the sink. She felt ridiculous as she leaned over and looked into the drain. The only thing she saw was some dried toothpaste right around the rim. She tilted her ear toward the drain, willing the sound to come again.

It didn't.

Sam backed away from the sink, telling herself she had not heard anything. But it was too concrete, too *real*.

She cast one last look toward the bathroom before leaving Carmen Winstead's room behind. She walked toward the sound of real voices—Mac and Joe Winstead, still talking downstairs.

8:16 P.M.

Virgie watched the laptop screen as Shane removed his pants with just enough interest to keep herself entertained and a little aroused. She'd seen it lots of times by this point, and it just didn't turn her on the way it once had. Still, this was yet another way she kept him on a tight leash. And, if she was being honest with herself, all things sex related kept her mind off the Carmen Winstead thing.

"Is that what you wanted to see, baby?" he asked her.

"Mm-hmm," she said, stifling a yawn and trying to sound seductive.

"And what about you?" He had already started stroking himself.

Virgie rolled her eyes internally. God, he was always so freaking eager. She gently removed her shirt to reveal the light-purple-laced bra he liked so much. "This is all you're getting tonight."

"What?"

She gave him a sexy smile. "Take it or leave it."

"Take," he said with a thirsty grin.

"Well, there's this too. But no peeks."

Virgie made a show of shifting a bit and letting him see that her hand was going below her bellybutton, tracing her soft skin under the band of her G-string. She had no intention of doing anything remotely sexual, because, quite frankly, she didn't really feel like it. Using sexual activity as a distraction and a means to keep him under control had kind of taken the physical pleasure out of it.

She leaned forward and did her best acting job, pretending to pleasure herself. She moaned; she had to admit, she was pretty good at faking this part.

Shane bought it and acted accordingly on his end.

Virgie wondered if something might be wrong with her. Shouldn't she be turned on by watching his display on the screen? Or, at the very least, moderately interested? But the only thing that made her hot about the entire situation was that her parents were home, for once. They were still awake in their bedroom just down the hallway while her boyfriend jerked himself off on her laptop screen less than twenty feet away. She figured her mom was probably reading one of her stupid self-help books about girls washing their faces. Her dad was probably binging on *The Matrix* for the umpteenth time.

So, while watching Shane taking matters into his own hands didn't do it for her, the fact she was getting away with such a thing kind of did.

"Talk to me," Shane said, his voice wavering with pleasure and lust.

She knew what he meant. And she didn't mind talking dirty, but she wanted him to beg for it. "You need to ask nicer than th—"

For a brief moment, her laptop screen went dark. There was a little ripple of static, a brief flash of black, and then Shane's crotch was back on the screen.

She frowned. It was a relatively new laptop, and she'd had no problems with it yet. But their wi-fi connection was spotty, the result of having a big house. How many times had she told her parents they needed an extender? She ignored it and carried on with her act, making a few sensual noises to urge Shane on.

The screen flickered again, then cut out completely.

"Ugh," she groaned, running her finger over the tracker to wake it up. "I told my mother ..." She stopped talking when the screen went from black to white, cut back to a still of Shane again, then more flickering. In the flickering, she thought she saw several images: the dark sky from an upward angle, a skittering rat, dark cascading water ...

"What the ...?" Virgie was so mesmerized by the images and her laptop's odd behavior that she laughed. At first, she thought it was a joke Shane was playing on her. Or maybe her wi-fi was somehow channeling a neighbor's television or a closed-circuit security feed. But, as it continued, a slow and looming dread inched its way through her guts.

The fear crashed forward when the flickering images halted and rested on a single, still scene—a dark tunnel with what looked like a concrete path beside it. There was hardly any light, except for a small sliver of it somewhere above the tunnel. And then, in the darkness, there was movement.

"Shane?" she asked, her voice thick with worry. "Shane, are you seeing this?"

But Shane did not respond. In fact, when sounds erupted from the laptop, they were definitely not Shane's. It was something wet, something slithering. The movement in the darkness slowly became clearer: a vague shape, inching forward. She was immobilized for a moment with so much terror she felt her heartbeat behind her eyes.

On the screen, the figure drew closer. Slowly, she could decipher a shape resembling a terrible sea creature breaching the dark surface of the shallow water. The murk dissolved as she discerned the familiar edges and contours. It was a person crawling through the sludge of the darkness.

She saw the long hair first, then the shape along the curve of a neck. It was a woman slightly hunched over and approaching her screen. And then the figure passed in front of the miniscule light source coming from above, and Virgie saw it clearly.

Beaten, battered—only a ghoul of the girl she once knew—but there was no doubt it was Carmen Winstead. The right side of her head was misshapen, like nothing more than a lump of oatmeal, and her left shoulder hung much lower than her right. But it was her—pale, rotting, dead.

Virgie slowly reached out and slammed down the top. In the split second before she did, Carmen's face filled the screen. She grinned widely, revealing cracked teeth and blackened gums.

Virgie screamed louder than she'd had in her entire life. She teetered off the side of the bed. When she hit the floor, her eyes brimmed with tears, and a terrorizing scream escaped her mouth. Virgie continued to scream, and, as her mother pushed open the door, all Virgie could see was that rotted grin permanently seared into her brain.

WEDNESDAY, NOVEMBER 9, 2008

2:05 P.M.

The good news was that Tess was pretty much over the side-eyed glances people were giving her. If people wanted to think she did something to Carmen, fine. If they wanted to think she was the coldest bitch to ever walk God's green Earth, she was fine with that too. The morons of this shitsplat little town had nothing better to do to distract from their sad little lives. And if hating her helped them do that, so be it.

It was yesterday, right after Algebra, when she made this decision. Since then, she'd felt better. Lighter. She *did* have a bit of help to get her through it all though. She walked into the girl's bathroom, locked herself into a stall, and rifled through her bookbag. She removed a small bottle of vanilla vodka—she'd found it in her parents' liquor cabinet covered in a layer of dust, so she knew they wouldn't miss it— and chugged half of it down. Then she twisted the lid tight and returned the bottle to the zipper pocket.

She closed her eyes and savored the burn of it. She knew she had to be careful, so she breathed deeply, steadied herself, and exited the stall.

When she saw Willa Dalton standing at the sink, reapplying black eyeliner, Tess scowled. They had not crossed paths since the day Carmen fell down the stupid manhole. Willa had been absent from all the classes they had together for a few days, probably in mourning. Or maybe she just cut, not having the balls to face Tess. She wasn't sure, but she knew from what the detectives said that Willa had been talking crap about her. So, Tess figured she owed her, big time.

The two girls stared each other down. Tess wanted to say something—a quick dyke barb that might get Willa riled up—something radiated off Willa that Tess didn't like. She couldn't put a finger on it. There was a tension between them—a surge of electricity prickling her skin.

She shook it off as she washed her hands, grabbed some paper towels, and tossed them in the garbage, her eyes never leaving Willa's through the mirror. "What the hell are you looking at, freak?" Tess stepped toward the door, but Willa's response stopped her.

"I'm starting to think I might be looking at someone with a guilty conscience." Willa simply smiled and left the bathroom.

Tess groaned. She had an impulse to chug the rest of the bottle of vodka, but she had to return to class. She walked back to the sink, inspecting herself in the mirror. She brushed her hair back with her fingers and noticed the dark circles around her eyes. Her mascara was smudged too.

She fished her emergency makeup kit from her bookbag. *Get it together Tess,* she thought as the bell for the final class of the day echoed, bouncing off the surrounding walls. She hurriedly crammed everything into her bag and zipped it. She started for the door; aware she would have to rush to make it to Mr. Pearson's humanities class all the way on the other side of the school. She opened the door and heard a soft whisper behind her.

"*Tess …*"

She stopped and turned around. Nothing was scary about the voice, but it had been unexpected enough to startle her. "What?" She supposed some freak was hiding in one of the stalls, watching her, wanting her. She was used to that.

No one answered.

"What?" she asked again, louder.

Again, no answer.

She stepped back into the central area of the restroom, just in front of the sinks, and heard it again—a fragile, broken sort of voice.

"*Te-sss … Tess Todd.*"

Tess scanned the bathroom, peering between the gaps in the stall doors. They didn't appear to be occupied. She stooped a little. No feet. And the voice was weird. It had an echoing quality to it, as if someone were speaking from a distance away, but it also seemed to fill the bathroom somehow, like the fading echo from deep within a cavern. "Who's there, dammit? This is not funny, you freakin losers."

She immediately walked to the nearest stall and kicked open the door. As expected, no one was inside. She checked the other six and found them all empty. She even looked under the sinks, feeling stupid doing so. She was alone. "To hell with this …"

She started for the door again, and this time the voice screamed her name. "*Tess!*"

She felt it in her skull, like a little bomb had gone off in there.

The pipes beneath the sinks rattled slightly with the boom of the voice. A gurgling sound came from somewhere, like a very wet belch and then …cruel laughter.

Tess backed against the wall and watched in horror as something bubbled up from the drain. It looked like blood at first, then like thick mud mixed with something else. And it smelled foul. A moan rose in Tess's throat as she pressed herself against the tiled wall.

Raspy laughter filled the room, like a speaker piped directly into her ear.

Tess swallowed down a scream and bolted from the restroom. To hell with Mr. Pearson's class. Instead, she ran for the front doors and nearly slammed into them before managing to push one open. She sprinted through the exterior breezeway and to her car in the seniors' parking lot. She jumped inside and locked the doors behind her, taking a series of deep breaths.

She saw a flicker of movement in her rearview mirror. She turned slowly to see what was back there. For just a moment, she thought she saw someone—a girl, matted in filth, sitting in her back seat. She blinked. The back of her car was as pristinely clean as it always was.

Taking more deep breaths, Tess rummaged in her bookbag for the rest of the vodka. She downed it all in one huge gulp. She was starting to understand why her father drank so much of it when she'd been a kid. God, it did help calm the nerves.

But the second she put her key in the ignition, she felt it fighting in her throat, coming back up. She barely got her door open before she threw up in the parking lot, nearly falling out of her car with the suddenness of it. When she was done, she sat in her car for a very long time, and, for some reason, only one memory kept replaying in her mind—the moment Carmen Winstead had fallen down the manhole into the darkness beyond.

7:02 P.M.

Cassie went to church with her parents every Sunday morning. She sat through the incredibly boring hymns their little, Baptist church insisted on singing before listening to the preacher.

After the preacher was a painfully boring Sunday school class. For kids Cassie's age—in the fourteen-to-seventeen range—that meant tons of lessons on keeping yourself pure and obeying your parents.

The only part of the entire process Cassie didn't outright loathe was the half an hour the preacher spent talking. She knew this was odd, as she saw others her age zoning out and almost falling asleep when Pastor Reeves took to the pulpit. She liked listening to him, because he dove deep into stories of Jesus Christ, of how he had healed the crippled and had spoken of peace. It was comforting.

Cassie found herself thinking about Jesus a lot in the week or so following Carmen Winstead's death. She assumed, based on what she knew of the Bible, that Carmen was in Heaven. And unless she did some serious soul searching, she was definitely ending up in Hell. Cassie wasn't sure if she believed in either of those places, but she did believe in karma.

It was a Wednesday night when Cassie felt compelled to pull out her Bible. It did not get much use, so, when she opened it, it still smelled new, just like it had when her mother had given it to her after she'd been pressured to get baptized at the age of thirteen. She remembered her father preaching almost every night how an unwashed soul could never get to Heaven. And no daughter of his was going to burn with all the wretched sinners that would not be worthy of his holy presence and will be denied into the holy land. It scared her so badly that she obliged.

She sat on the end of her bed and found the story of the woman washing Jesus's feet with her hair. It seemed a bit much to Cassie. The woman considered herself sinful and believed Jesus could forgive her. And because Jesus considered her faith so beautiful, in that moment, he forgave her sins. It made Cassie wonder why people lived righteous lives to begin with. *After all, Jesus will forgive you anyway.* What was the point, bending over backward to be virtuous and good, if it were that easy?

Sure, she had not been the one who pushed Carmen. But she was pretty sure she was the only one in their little group who had thought it cruel and stupid to taunt the poor girl from the very start. That wasn't Jesus telling her that. It was just common human decency. Of course, she could have just stepped outside the group, distancing herself from them. But to be Tess Todd's enemy was unthinkable.

As Cassie reread the verses, her phone dinged from her bedside table. She figured it was Virgie. She had been blowing up their text thread, getting everyone's opinions on whether she should just go ahead and sleep with Shane. Apparently, she was worried about what it might be like to start college as a virgin.

Cassie grabbed the phone and checked her new text. It was not from Virgie. In fact, it was from an unknown number. The text was short but sent a spike of fear through her: *You're just as guilty as them.*

She wondered if it might be Miri or Virgie playing with her. Miri had always had a sort of darker streak, but this seemed a little morbid, even for her. She also doubted Miri was smart enough to figure out how to block her number.

She was too curious not to respond, though she knew she was opening herself up to a conversation she truly wasn't ready to have. *Who is this?*

A response came almost right away, but, before she could read it, her screen went black. *That's odd, I just charged it,* she thought, pressing the power button.

Suddenly, the screen reappeared to reveal a photograph on the lock screen but not the picture of her and her friends at the corn festival. No, this was something different. Water, dark and stagnant. And the shape of a hand, reaching out, pale, bony fingers splayed, covered in flaps of tattered skin ...

When the hand jerked suddenly, Cassie gasped.

The dark scene disappeared, leaving the lone message on her screen. *You know!*

Fear coiled inside her. "It's not real," she whispered.

But it *was* real. The more she stared at it, wishing it away, the more she felt the odd sensation, like even now in the safety of her bedroom, *she was not alone.* She threw her phone to the other side of the room and shoved herself backward to her headboard, pulling her knees to her chest. She did not realize until she could move no farther that she'd grabbed her Bible and was gripping it like a shield.

"It's just not real," she repeated, digging her fingernails into the leather cover. Though she'd never been a praying person, she whispered a prayer, surprised at how easily the words came to her lips when she truly needed them the most.

9:13 P.M.

Virgie's parents were once again not home, but she didn't let Shane know that. She'd decided she would give herself to him tonight. And, in having made that decision, she was a little surprised at how excited she was about it. *It's time,* she thought as she stared out the window as they drove home from the movie theater in Parker Falls.

Shane was driving, his right hand high on her knee, talking about *Twilight.* Shane was not a fan but had promised Virgie, he would take her for the sneak preview. And she had loved it. Virgie, excited about how well the night was going, leaned over and nibbled at his ear. "My mom and dad are home," she lied. She was trying to sound as disappointed as possible.

"I know. That sucks."

"So, let's go to your grandpa's field."

"I don't know about that. If he finds out, he'll tell my dad, then I'll never hear the end of it."

Shane's grandfather owned a massive plot of land that had once grown tobacco. But, for as long as Virgie could remember, those fields had been desolated, overgrown stretches of nothing. The fields were mostly bordered by forest and accessible by a narrow dirt road. Earlier in their relationship, they had used the field as a make-out spot several times. It was perfect, tucked away in the middle of nowhere, and if they pulled in far enough, the trees would perfectly hide their car from the outside world. But they hadn't been there in a while, choosing instead to take advantage of Virgie's parents' frequent absences.

"Please," she said with a heavy breath into his ear. She reached into the fork of his legs and gave a little squeeze. "I promise I'll make it worth your time."

He groaned against her perseverance. "Yeah, okay …"

God, she loved how easily he caved to her.

He drove the car to the fields, winding around the northern cusp of Somerdale's city limits. The road was bumpy but not terribly so. As they maneuvered down the dirt track, the bare trees crowded in around them. Against the nearly moonless night, their branches looked intimidating, like living things that had not yet decided if they were built for gentle caresses or the tearing of flesh.

After a while, the trees gave way to the overgrown field. The carcass of an ancient tractor sat, stripped and rusted, at the opposite end of the field, keeping silent watch over the broken stalks of old tobacco plants.

Even before he found their usual parking spot, Virgie was kissing his neck and unbuttoning his pants. When he parked, she removed her shirt for him and pulled him awkwardly into the passenger seat. She adjusted the seat, reclined, and soon he was stripping off her bra. He was usually easily distracted by her breasts, but he had other things in mind tonight, heading directly for her pants.

Several minutes later, when he entered her, he was surprisingly gentle. Still, it hurt. She felt something tearing inside her, like a rat trying to squeeze its body through a hole that had been cover in plastic. But it was a different sort of hurt. She cried out, partly wanting to push him away but also urging him on. Was this seriously what she had been holding out for?

"You need me to stop?"

It was so unexpected and sweet that she felt the need to reward him. She shook her head, grabbed his hips, and pushed him in, feigning excitement. Surprisingly, it did start to feel good, a sort of fulfillment she could not find the proper word for.

When it was over, even though she had come nowhere close to getting off, she felt satisfied.

He kissed her passionately before reaching for the door.

Virgie lay absolutely still, like a statue, thinking, *That's it. It's done. It's over. I'm free.*

"I know it's not exactly romantic, but I need to get out and clean up a little. I think I sort of need to pee too."

"You're right," she said with a sultry smile. "That's not romantic at all."

He slid out of the car and walked toward the hood.

Virgie swatted at the mass of insects flying in, attracted to the dashboard light. She reached across to slam the door. When she went to pull up her pants, she heard her phone thud to the floorboard.

She could not wait to tell Cassie and Miri—especially Miri. She thought she was hot shit because she'd already slept with two guys. But the moment Virgie felt for the phone, she heard a vibrating sound coming from under the seat, an incoming text: *Hello.*

She stared at it for a while. Great. Who was playing games with her now? Probably one of Shane's stupid, immature friends. *Umm ... who the hell is this?*

You know.

She was about to text back again, but the screen went black. She pressed the power button, trying to get it to come back on, but the phone did not respond. She shook it, but nothing happened. She threw her head back against the seat. *Great. Phones broken. Now I'll have to wait until I can text Miri.*

Suddenly, a chill descended upon her, almost as if someone had opened the door, and yet, it stayed closed. She sat upright, scanning for Shane, terrified of the darkness engulfing the car from all angles. Even if it meant being swarmed with insects, she reached for the door, anxious for the glare of the dome light. Her fingers fell on the handle, and just before she pulled it open, she focused on the window, searching the darkness for Shane.

A face was pressed against it. The skin was waxy white, and the eyes appeared to be completely black. Clumps of what looked like dark hair clung to the skin, which was swarming with maggots.

And then a hand came up to the window and slapped at it, the colorless lips arched back into a fiendish smile. Something dark and vile oozed out. "Whore!" the figure screeched, tearing through Virgie like a freight train.

The scream that rose in Virgie's throat made the one she'd let out in her bedroom a few nights ago seem like a pep rally cheer. Fractured and broken, it was the sound of absolute terror, the stuff of asylums and the worst possible imagined versions of Hell.

Virgie curled into the fetal position and closed her eyes to the sight, rocking back and forth. Something warm ran down her leg, and an instinctual part of her knew this had nothing to do with Shane taking her virginity. Her bladder had gone loose at the sight.

She felt a hand brush at her skin as warm tears stained her cheeks. She flinched and tried to scream again, but nothing came out.

"V, what is it? My god, what's wrong?"

"Win-Window," she croaked.

There was silence for a moment while his reassuring hand remained on her back. His other hand stroked her hair, pushing it from her face. "Babe, there's nothing there."

"Her … It's her."

"No, V. No one's there. I swear."

She dared a look at the window, moaning as she did so. She sighed when she saw nothing there. Just like the night she had thought she'd seen something on her laptop, something terrifying had momentarily broken into her world and disappeared.

But it would be back. She knew that.

She stared at the night outside. The shapes of trees and all things natural stood silent, stoic, not even a slight shift in the wind disturbed them, like they were waiting for something to come—something from the darkness. *You imagined it. You're feeling guilty, and your mind is tormenting you. Get a fucking grip already.*

"Was it … Did you get freak out because of what we just did?"

"No! I don't know what it was. Can you just take me home?"

Shane nodded and started the car.

Virgie cringed when the headlights came on. She'd fully expected to see that ghastly figure standing directly in front of the car, but there was nothing to see but a scraggly section of field and the forest beyond. Although nothing was there, Virgie kept her eyes peeled on the exact place where she'd seen the face as Shane made a U-turn. She did not trust the darkness outside, not one single bit. She felt something watching her, wanting her, coming for her. And she knew …it would be back.

12:09 A.M

Ever since the incident at the Sub Station, Miri had not been sleeping well. Whenever she got in bed and closed her eyes, she heard that same demonic voice whispering her name, and her mind's eye projected an image of the dark figure lurking in the darkness.

Maybe she knew it right away and just failed to acknowledge it. But, in the few days that passed, she'd become almost certain the figure had been familiar to her. Yes, it was impossible. Yes, it made her feel like she was losing it, but it had kind of looked like …

Tonight, she found herself in the same position, trying to force those impossible, horrific thoughts from her head. She'd stayed up until just after midnight, ensuring she was practically dead on her feet. She'd also popped one of her mom's sleeping pills. So, let the damn whispers come if they wanted; she'd be asleep in about fifteen minutes.

That was the plan, anyway.

But even so, when she slid into bed, the terror gripped her the second her head hit the pillow. She considered keeping her lamp on but knew it would do no good. There were probably more things that could kill in the bright of day rather than in the darkness of night. But there was something about the vulnerability of being asleep in the darkness that made her shudder.

Taking a deep breath to prepare herself, she pulled the string on her bedside lamp.

Every shadow she saw, every play of light on every surface, made her look twice. She was sure that even the most benign shadow would soon morph into the figure that had been standing in front of her house. Her eyes refused to relax, to close, volleying around the room as if in a race. Eventually, her tired eyes could take it no longer, and she pulled her covers over her head.

Just a few more minutes and I'll be asleep. A few more minutes and—

A distinct sound came from the other side of the room—a sweeping sort of sound, something moving or crawling along the hardwood floor.

No. Just your imagination. That's all.

Then it came again. Was it her imagination, or was it closer this time?

Miri clutched her sheets and slowly poked out her head. She knew it would only scare her more if she imagined what the sound might be. She had to see, had to—

She glimpsed a girl standing motionless in the corner of the room, like an innocent piece of furniture—long, matted hair, torn clothes, a gaunt face. Miri blinked, and she was gone. Her eyes darted around the room. Her pulse beat wildly in her ears, drowning out all other sounds and, in the back of her throat, choking her.

She saw the girl again, now in the middle of her room, standing still. Chin to chest, narrow eyes slicing through her veil of hair.

Directed at her.

Smiling sickly.

At her.

Miri closed her eyes, imagining the figure away. *It isn't here. It isn't real. Your mind is playing tricks on you.* And even if it was, maybe if she just pretended she was asleep, like she used to do as a child when she thought clowns and monsters lived under her bed, maybe it would just go away.

But this was a different kind of clown and a different kind of monster. And she wasn't sure if the things she had done as a child would work in the darkness of her room; she wasn't even sure if anything was there. So rather than pull the covers over her head again, Miri laid back and feigned sleep. She kept her eyes shut tightly, willing the figure to disappear or for sleep to claim her. *Anything.* Her heart slammed against her ribcage, her palms leaked sweat, and no matter how hard she tried to stay still, the involuntary chattering of her teeth made it impossible.

The sweeping sound came again, and this time it was accompanied by a foul odor that roiled her stomach. Spoiled meat? Sewage? Drawing breath through her mouth, she kept her eyes shut, willing it all away. But the stench was unbearable, thick, like a living thing, consuming her room. Soon, it'd seep into her bloodstream, poisoning her. A sick feeling engulfed her then.

Maybe that is what it wants.

She pulled up the covers, intending to bury her head under them. But the sheet would not come. She yanked harder. Something pulled them back, resisting her. Against her better judgement, she slowly opened her eyes. "Impossible," she whispered. Her mouth agape, she tried to scream, but nothing could escape her throat.

Sitting at the foot of her bed, holding onto her sheet with bony fingers and dirt-encrusted nails, was Carmen Winstead, staring at her with a savage smile stretched across her face. "Miri," Carmen rasped, her voice was like two moss-covered rocks being scraped together. "Miri."

"I'm so … I'm sorry—" She gathered her legs and used them to shove her way backward, as far from her former classmate as she could possibly be. Her head hit the solid wood headboard, but the pain barely registered. She was trapped.

Miri threw her hands over her eyes. She opened her mouth to scream, praying someone, anyone, would hear and save her. But suffocated by her own terror, nothing came out.

Carmen sprang forward with a terrific speed. She moved like a blur, like a harsh wind battling through trees.

And when she was on top of Miri, all the breath in Miri's body seemed to evaporate. Not only could she not breathe, but it felt as if glass was building up in her lungs.

As panic built, a sob rose in her throat, she wanted to scream but nothing escaped but a soft gulp as she felt her throat constricting. Flailing her arms in front of her, fighting, Carmen was over her, hovering, touching her. Less than an inch apart, Miri stared into her dead eyes, wide and soulless, like coal. The skin on Carmen's face was cracked open, like something was eating her from the inside out. Dark gel oozed from the lesions, like the stuff she had seen coming from the sink at the Sub Station. Even though she couldn't feel hands on her, she felt the pressure, holding her down, immobile.

Blacker bile oozed from Carmen's mouth. It was the smell she'd detected earlier. Before she knew it, she felt Carmen's cold, scaly fingers around her mouth, trying to force it open.

Miri heard the bones of her jaw crack. The skin around her mouth ripped, and she tasted something sour. Then, as the darkness tightened its grip, bile was being forced into her, going down her throat, choking her. That taste, like something scooped from a grave, was the last thing she was aware of before everything went dark.

THURSDAY, NOVEMBER 10, 2008

7:33 A.M.

When Miri wasn't at the breakfast table, her mother started to get worried. It was Thursday, also known in the George household as FTT: French Toast Thursday. Miri always talked about how it was her favorite day of the week, even when school was in. Her mother, forty-six-year-old Helen George, gave Miri's chair a curious glance as she set the heaping stack of French toast on the table.

She looked at her husband, who was pouring himself a cup of coffee. "Well, we almost made it until she went off to college. I think maybe French toast might not be enough to lure her from bed anymore."

"That's crazy talk," Alan George said with a smile. He sipped from his coffee and headed upstairs to get his daughter.

He was glad they had a kid who still enjoyed being around them, partaking in silly things like French Toast Thursday and the occasional Disney weekend movie binge. Sure, Miri had grown distant over the past few months, but he understood it. She'd gotten her college acceptance letter, and her mind had already shifted to the future, when she'd have to be a lot more independent. So, of course, it would be hard for her to focus on home stuff, like French toast, when the shining kingdom of college awaited her. After all, Miri was eighteen years old. She was bound to sleep in, push the snooze button to its limits, and even play hooky from time to time. But judging from the small mountain of food she'd consumed last Thursday; he'd sincerely believed that FTT would be the final thing to go.

Alan approached her closed bedroom door, which was nothing new. Miri had never been able to sleep with her door open. It had been that way ever since she'd been ten or so. Once she'd learned the boogeyman lived in the closets of bad children and the tooth fairy didn't exist, she'd demanded her privacy, and that was exactly what the Georges gave her. He stared at the door sign he'd made for her when she was twelve, a marquee that read, *Miri's Room*, with pink and purple kittens and a chalkboard underneath. She used to leave notes on there about what she was up to, but the last one there, *Hi, Miri!* with heart dotting the I's, had been written by Mrs. George months ago.

He knocked lightly on the door and called her name, figuring she was probably already awake, getting ready for school, and taking her time to get downstairs. "Miri, your mom is starting to think you've suddenly turned against her French toast."

He waited a beat without an answer. He frowned slightly, sipping from the coffee cup he'd brought upstairs with him. He knocked again, a bit louder this time. "Miriam George? You okay in there?"

Again, there was no answer.

Brow raised, he knocked again, growing worried. He pressed his face against the door and reached for the doorknob. "Hey, princess ... Look, I'm going to come in, okay? If you aren't decent, either answer me or cover up."

Alan George felt little tendrils of fear snake up in his spine. He opened the door and instantly saw her unmade bed, yet clearly slept in. He entered the room and looked around. No Miri. He approached her closet, already knowing she would not be there, but he checked it anyway. He headed to the upstairs bathroom. The door was open, and Miri was not there.

Fear blanketed him, guiding him back down the hallway to Miri's room. He shuddered as he braced himself against the doorframe and called for his wife. By the time she reached the room, fear had overwhelmed him. "Could she have possibly left early?"

"She would've told us," Helen George said, going to Miri's bed and lifting her teddy bear. They exchanged worried glances. "Where is she?"

"I don't know but start calling her friends and the school." He grabbed his phone. "I'm calling that detective."

8:04 A.M.

Sam Kerr stood in the exact same place Alan George had stood when he'd started weeping earlier in the morning. That had been exactly thirty-one minutes ago, and while he was no longer crying, Sam sensed he was only one or two words away from losing it. He stood behind her as Mac ensured he did not interfere with her inspection of Miriam George's room. The mother was downstairs, speaking to two more policemen, organizing how the morning would look in terms of finding her daughter.

It was a rather beautiful room, well-kept and clean, but one for a ten-year-old girl maybe—not a woman of eighteen. Hand-painted butterflies and kittens covered her walls. White-laced curtains and a spread to match draped securely over the back of a leather chair by her desk. Besides that, a laptop sat on her bedside table, a few books were stacked on a floating shelf, and a cellphone lay on the floor—the typical trappings of a teenage girl. As she focused on the room, she stayed tuned to Mac and Alan's conversation in the hallway.

"Any arguments or fights lately?" Mac asked.

"None." Alan brushed back his gray, thinning hair. "I can't even remember the last time we had an argument of any kind. We've always gotten along well. My god, where is she?" His voice cracked.

Here it comes, Sam thought.

"We'll find her, Mr. George, but right now, you have to focus."

"Okay, okay."

"No other kids?"

"No, just Miri."

"And when did you see her last?"

"Um, last night as I went to sleep. I stopped by her room and poked my head in. She was on her laptop, working on a paper for English class. She was right here."

Sam listened to it all as she approached Miri's bed. It wasn't made, nor was it in an utter state of messiness. She studied it, taking notes in her head; the sheets were slightly tugged away from being tucked in at the bottom. They were also not tossed to the side, which would indicate someone getting out of bed in a hurry. There didn't seem to be any sign of a struggle.

She walked to the closet and opened it. It was crammed with nice, designer clothes but in a tidy way. On the floor lay several pairs of shoes lined up, a few pairs of sneakers, a pair of Crocs, and several very girlie-looking styles, mostly open-toed. Surveying the shoes, she called out over her shoulder, "Mr. George, do you happen to know which shoes Miri had been wearing as of late?"

"No," he said, an inquisitive tone to his voice. "But Helen might be able to tell you."

Sam nodded, closing the closet door. "Detective Talbot, can I speak with you a moment?"

Mac excused himself from Alan George and entered the room. He gave his partner a curious look since she only called him *Detective Talbot* around others when she needed to speak in private—and it never was about anything good. "What are you thinking?"

"I'm thinking none of this makes sense. The window is locked from the inside. The bed shows no sign of struggle. She also left her cellphone."

"And if she left of her own accord …" Mac started.

"She would have taken the phone with her," Sam finished. "What teenager leaves without her phone? Hell, they take it with them when they piss. Leaving the house of her own accord without it? It just doesn't happen. I didn't want to check it out while her father was watching. Can you take him down with the others and see if you can find out which shoes she's been wearing lately?"

"Yeah, but why would that matter?"

"Because if she left on her own, she would have stopped to grab a pair of shoes. But if she was taken … I'll bet every pair of her shoes is here, present and accounted for."

Mac gave her a gentle pat on the back. "Good thinking."

Sam stood where she was until she heard Mac recommend that he and George head downstairs to join the other officers. When they were gone, she grabbed the cellphone from the floor. The case was pink, and the PopSocket read, *Glamorous!*

She pushed the button on the side, but the phone would not wake up. She held it down to power it up, assuming it had been cut off. When she did, she only got the flashing battery indicator. She grabbed the charger from the bedside table and connected it to an outlet by her bed. Giving up on the room, she headed downstairs to join everyone else.

As she was descending the stairs, Mac met her halfway. "The mother says Miri has been alternating between a pair of boots and New Balance sneakers for the last two weeks or so. Both pairs of shoes are always located downstairs in the mud room."

"Is there a pair missing?" Sam asked. But she was pretty sure she already knew the answer.

"No. They're both there."

"So not only would she have left without her phone, but she would have been barefoot too. But the alternative scenario is looking more likely that she was taken."

Mac nodded and grabbed his phone. "I'll call it in. We'll get as many units looking for her as possible."

"And I'll call the school. I think we need to talk to her three friends as soon as possible," Sam said, feeling uneasy. She didn't want to go down this road again so soon after the Winstead case, but here she was, and it felt like she had been thrown into a barrel of sharks.

9:17 A.M.

Not wanting to cause a scene or raise any eyebrows, Sam and Mac elected to stay in their unmarked sedan rather than take a patrol car to the high school. As an added precaution, they also parked in the staff parking lot out back and entered through the cafeteria doors. When Sam and Mac walked through the door of guidance counselor Mr. Fleming's office—which was made cramped by an overly large desk full of paperwork—Tess, Virgie, and Cassie were already sitting across from him, and two of them cringed.

Cassie, in particular, looked absolutely mortified. Tess, unfazed, was filing her nails, not making eye contact with any of them.

Typical, Sam thought.

"Good morning, detectives," Mr. Fleming said, leaning back in his chair with his hands behind his head. He too looked rather nervous. Sam had told him the gist when she'd called to have the three girls pulled from class. His mouth was a thin line, a sign he was just as tense as the girls.

Sam and Mac shook Mr. Fleming's hand and stood on each side of his desk, facing the girls, who occupied the only seats in the room. "Did you call their parents?" Mac asked Mr. Fleming.

"Yes. They're on their way."

Sam studied the girls. "I need to know the last time each of you spoke with Miri George."

"Don't you think you should wait for their parents?" Mr. Fleming asked.

"No, I really don't. Time is not on our side. Now, girls, look at me and focus. When's the last time you spoke to Miri?"

The girls remained quiet for a moment. Virgie looked back and forth between her friends, while the other two looked blankly at the floor. Virgie was the first to speak. Her words came out shaky. "I texted with her around seven o'clock last night."

"What about?" Sam asked.

"Just talking about a date I was about to go on. Nothing much."

"What about the rest of you?" Mac asked.

"Last time I spoke to her," Tess said, "was yesterday afternoon. We were in the parking lot, about to head home."

"Did she seem okay when you saw her?"

Tess shrugged. "Same as always. I'm sorry, but what is the point here? I mean, has something happened to her?"

"What about you, Cassie?" Sam asked, ignoring Tess's question.

"Pretty much the same as Tess. I saw her in school. We spoke, but about nothing important. And like Tess said, she seemed fine."

"Oh, of course ... like Tess said," Sam said sarcastically, never taking her eyes off Tess. "So, Virgie, why the text conversation between the two of you?"

"I initiated it. I was asking her some advice for the date."

"And, in the texts, did she seem like herself?"

"Yeah. What's ... I don't understand. What's going on?"

"Girls, Miri wasn't in her bed this morning. So, if any of you know *anything* about where she might be, we need to know right now."

The girls were silent. Cassie's eyes glistened with tears. Virgie's darted back and forth, as if she were expecting some other nasty surprise to come from nowhere. Tess, meanwhile, looked a little confused, as if the news hadn't yet registered with her.

"So, she's *missing?*" Cassie asked.

"That's the best term we can find for it right now," Mac said.

"We have the police scouring Somerdale for her." Sam sat on the edge of the desk, swinging her left foot. "And her parents are calling relatives to see if they know anything. Now, we have no evidence to support any sort of foul play. But, just to convey the seriousness of it, the fact she left without her phone or any shoes or coat does not paint a very good picture. So please, if you know anything at all, we need to know."

Cassie gasped.

The other girls eyed her before Virgie said, "I can't think of anything. It's terrible. I swear she was the same old Miri when I was texting her, giving me a hard time and joking."

"Her parents claimed to have a very good relationship with her. Would you three happen to know any different?"

"That sounds about right, Detective Kerr. She loves her parents." Cassie wiped a tear from her eye. "She talks about her dad all the time."

"I think she might have been a little annoyed with them lately though," Tess said, giving Cassie a look. "Ever since she got into college, she said they've been wanting to spend all this extra time with her. She told me once they were being a real drag."

"She seemed mad about it?" Mac asked.

"No. Just sort of irritated."

"She also said her folks grilled her about the whole Pigst— I mean, Carmen Winstead thing." Tess smirked toward Sam and lowered her head, filing her nails once again.

Sam regarded Mac to see if he had anything else to add.

He cleared his throat. "Girls, listen to me. I mean this, okay? If you hear from her—a phone call, a text, a social media ping, anything—I want you to call me. Here's my card. Just call." Mac pulled a stack of cards from his coat's inside pocket and handed them to each girl. "Also—"

Sam's phone rang, interrupting him. She muted the ringer and checked the caller display. When she saw it was from the station, she quickly glanced at everyone and stepped out of the office, lifting the phone to her ear. "This is Detective Kerr."

"Kerr, we've got some news," Shelly Pearson's familiar voice said. Shelly had worked dispatch for the Somerdale PD for much longer than Sam had been part of the force. She was a cheerful woman most of the time, but something was different, a little off, nothing was cheerful in her voice at all.

Sam's stomach dropped. "What is it, Shelly?"

"We got a call from Floyd Vereen, supervisor at city maintenance. They were doing a routine check by the sewer runoff backups on the Holt property, and when they went down, they found a body. Appears to be a young girl, but no one has made a positive ID yet. You gotta get over there, you and Mac. Cap is flipping his lid over this."

A flare of heat plummeted through her. "Where did he find the body?"

"That's what's weird Sam. He found her in that manhole— the exact place where that Winstead girl died."

10:38 A.M.

"Seriously?" Mac said as they traipsed through the cornfield, swatting the dried stalks that dared to brush his face. "Does anyone even eat corn anymore?"

Sam walked behind him, chuckling. She understood it though. Comical irritability had always been his defense mechanism whenever things got grim and serious. "I believe you're the one who suggested going the scenic route."

"Yeah, next time I have any of my bright ideas, tell me to shut up."

The cornfield was bleak and depressing, full of mud and the rotting stalks. A few stray pieces of litter from the corn festival still lingered here and there—a deflated balloon, some red-and-white striped popcorn bags, the confetti of losing fifty-fifty ticket stubs. The family who owned the land and rented it out for the festivities were the Holts. Garland Holt and his wife Miranda were in their sixties, retired, and leased the land to other farmers.

Sam had heard the Holts had gotten the land for quite cheap in the 1980s, as it was located so close to the town's old sewage runoff. Of course, the runoff had been redirected to another reservoir a little farther outside of Somerdale in the early 2000s, and the facility on the Holts' land had fallen into disuse. That meant they very rarely had to deal with foul odors anymore, which made it the perfect place to hold the annual Somerdale Corn Festival.

As they reached the edge of the field, they neared a thick forest made of mostly pines and bare trees.

"You realize we're likely walking the same path Carmen Winstead did just before she died, right?" Sam asked.

"I do *now*. Tell me, Kerr. Is that morbid streak of yours what makes you such a good snoop rat?"

"Among other things."

A very thin strip of overgrown field separated the cornfield from the forest, which they quickly trekked through. From here, they entered the woods and navigated a slight downward slope. There, the concrete edges of the sewage entry point appeared up ahead. It looked eerie among the dead grass and mostly stripped trees. As they got closer, the small concrete platform with the manhole appeared. After another dip in the ground, they reached the thin ravine that led to the concrete entryway.

Mac stopped just before he stepped onto the concrete platform.

Sam noticed his perplexed expression. "What is it?"

He pointed. "The manhole cover ..."

She followed the direction of his finger, but it took her a few seconds to see what he was pointing out. The manhole cover laid on the ground about eight or nine feet from the platform.

"That thing is heavy," he said. "How'd it get all the way over there?"

"And it was still on the platform the last time we were here, investigating the site. We have to ask if the maintenance crew removed it. But why would they?"

Mac nodded and stepped onto the platform.

Sam joined him, and they walked together to the edge of the uncovered manhole.

"Too dark." He unsnapped the Maglite from his belt, clicked it on, and aimed it into the deep hole.

Sam didn't look. His first comment was all Sam needed to hear.

"Sweet Jesus," Mac said with a long exhale.

Taking a deep breath, Sam looked down and saw a body, though only part of it was visible due to the tunnel's angle at the bottom. A face peered up at them, bloody and broken, only a single eye visible through ruined skin and a crimson mask of blood.

It was Miriam George, looking as if the darkness had partially devoured her.

11:01 A.M.

Less than half an hour later, the field at the rear of the Holt family farm was filled with first responders and emergency vehicles.

As soon as the state police arrived and coordinated with Sam and Mac, the detectives left in their car. With Tess and her remaining two friends already questioned, the next stop seemed pretty obvious to Sam. As Mac drove into Somerdale proper, Sam once again called the high school. For the second time that day, she was transferred to Mr. Fleming's office.

"Sorry to bother you again," Sam said. "But we need to speak with Willa Dalton. Can you have her in your office for us in about twenty minutes? We'd wait until the end of the day, but it's rather pressing."

"Yes, of course. One second, would you …?" She heard him covering the phone and speaking to someone for a moment before coming back on the line. "Did you find Miri?"

"I can't really discuss that at the moment." She cringed when the comment was out of her mouth; it was a comment that all but said, *Yes, and the news isn't good.*

"Oh, I see. Well, if you—" A voice cut in from another line, and Fleming paused before saying, "Sorry, Detective. It seems Willa is absent today."

"Oh, okay. Thank you, Mr. Fleming." She ended the call and frowned as she looked out the window. "Willa Dalton isn't at school today. I'd say that's one hell of a coincidence, don't ya think?"

"I don't like coincidences. So, let's pay her a visit and see what she has to say," Mac said, making an exaggerated loop around a tractor.

They arrived at the Dalton house a little before noon. Trulia Dalton answered the door. Sam knew she'd always gone by True, but she didn't know the woman well enough to use such familiar terms. In fact, she'd only spoken to her once before the Carmen Winstead case, and that had only been a polite "good morning" as she passed her on the street.

Despite the rumors about True being some kind of witch, she had always given off a kind, friendly vibe, and her invitation to enter her home was no exception. She ushered them into the kitchen and went to the stove. "Can I get you some tea?"

"No thank you," Sam said. "We're actually in a bit of a hurry today, so we can't stay long. The reason we're here is because we understand Willa didn't make it to school today."

She pursed her lips. "That's right."

"Anything wrong?" Mac asked.

"Well, to tell you the truth, she's been sort of depressed. Lethargic and in a funk. She's been having a hard time ever since Carmen …" Something must've occurred to her then, because she stopped fiddling with the tea kettle and turned. "Forgive me, but I don't see how being absent from school warrants a visit from a pair of detectives."

"I suppose that *doesn't* make sense. We contacted the school to ask her a few questions about the case but was told she wasn't there. Do you think she'd be okay with speaking to us?"

True shrugged. "You can ask her that. But I think if it might get you closer to finding out exactly what happened and who did it, then she'd be all for it. Have a seat in the living room. I'll get her."

Sam and Mac exchanged glances as True walked down the hallway. They heard a door opening, then a brief murmured conversation. While they waited, Sam peered around the kitchen and into the adjoining living room. The Daltons seemed to live a minimalist life, and she could see no clear indication that the rumors of True being a witch were true. She *did* smell some sort of incense in the air, but that alone was not enough to cause speculation.

The murmur of voices stopped, and True walked toward them.

Willa followed, her auburn hair a mess, eyes bleary. She walked as if True were pulling her by a string, with no energy or purpose to her step.

True sat on one end of the couch as Willa nodded to the detectives, gave them a weak "Hey," then sat on the opposite end from her aunt.

"Willa, your aunt tells us things have been hard for you over the last few days," Mac said. "How are you doing?"

"Fine. Just sad. And I realize how dumb it might seem to you. I didn't even know Carmen all that well, you know. I think it was, like, maybe two weeks … if that. But she was my friend."

"You spoke earlier about feeling guilty," Sam said. "That if you had been with her, maybe things would have been different. Do you still feel that way?"

Willa nodded.

"Willa, there's another reason we're here this morning," Sam said gently. "Something has happened, and we need to ask you some questions about it."

True sat back in her seat, her eyes shifting between the detectives. She didn't seem surprised or anxious about the new development in the least, almost as if she already knew what had happened.

Interesting, Sam noted, before she said, "Willa, this morning we learned that Miriam George had been killed."

Again, True didn't look surprised. But whatever shock her aunt's face lacked was made up for in Willa. The confusion on Willa's face suddenly turned to something that looked like disbelief. Sam wasn't sure, but she thought the girl's expression held a bit of fear too.

"Oh, god. When?" Willa asked, shifting her gaze toward her aunt.

"From what we can gather, she was at home last night, settled in for bed and everything, but then this morning, she was missing. Her body was found about an hour and a half ago … in the sewer system on the Holt farm."

Willa's hand instinctively went to her mouth as a little gasp escaped her throat.

"I'm sorry," Sam said, "but we have to ask you. Willa, can you give us any proof of where you were last night?"

"I was here," she muttered, shaking her head mechanically. She drew a shaky breath and repeated it again. "I was here."

On the heels of her answer, True's welcoming smile disappeared. "You can't seriously think Willa would do something like that!"

"We're not accusing anyone," Mac said quickly. "But we have to start somewhere. Willa was, as you know, Carmen's only real friend. It's the most logical place to start."

"I was here," Willa said for a third time. "The whole night."

Sam eyed True. "Can you verify that?"

"No. I think I went to sleep at ten or so. But what you're even suggesting, it's beyond ridiculous. Willa would never ..."

"Willa, what were you doing at that time? You know, before you went to sleep?" Willa picked at her nails. She looked up and noticed aunt True staring at her.

"Well ... I read a little. Then, I was on my phone. You know, things like that."

"You were on your phone?"

"Yeah, like off and on."

"Doing what?"

"Stuff."

"What kind of ...stuff?"

"Myspace. Read some stuff online. Things like that."

"If it came down to it, would you allow the police to look at your phone?" Sam asked. "If we can get proof that you were on your phone at a certain time, it could really help us."

"Why? To convince you I didn't do anything?" It was the first real emotion she'd shown since coming out of her bedroom.

"Again, we're not accusing you. But—"

"Sure, sure, yeah." Willa stood from the couch and headed for her room.

"Detectives," True said in a low voice, "Willa isn't capable of hurting anyone. I'm not telling you how to do your job, but you're wasting your time on her."

"I hope that's the case," Sam said.

Seconds later, Willa returned to the living room. She handed her phone to Mac and plopped onto the couch.

"Willa, were there any other kids at school who might have not liked Miriam George?" Sam asked.

Willa rolled her eyes to the ceiling. "Yeah. How about, everyone?"

Sam stared at her, waiting for her to elaborate.

She shrugged. "You know. That was their group. They were bullies. And with bullies, the best you can do is try to stay out of their way and hope you're not their next target. I'm sure every single person in that school hated them, but no one had the balls—" She stopped. "The nerve, I mean, to say it."

"No one, except you?" Mac added.

An idea took root in Sam's head just as her phone rang. She checked the caller display and saw it was Deputy Meeks—the first man who had arrived on scene when they'd placed the call about having found Miriam's body. "Excuse me one second." Sam stepped into the adjoined kitchen as she took the call, keeping her voice as low as she could while Mac kept asking True and Willa questions. "This is Detective Kerr."

"Kerr, Meeks here. Look, weird question, but what kind of shoes are you wearing?"

"That *is* a strange question. But if you must know, it's a pair of black Sketchers."

"Size five, womens, right?"

"Um, yeah, but how—"

"And what about Detective Talbot? Rockports, size ten or so?"

Deeply confused, she espied Mac and saw Deputy Meeks was right. "Yes. Did you call just to show that you're some sort of shoe savant?"

"No." He paused and sighed deeply. "I know these things because forensics determined this from the prints we found on the site. There are just a few in the mud around that concrete block."

"Okay …?"

"Well, it's the oddest thing, Kerr. Those are the only prints we found here. You and Talbot. And the ground, while not wet, is malleable enough to keep prints for a while. If someone dragged Miriam George out here, they didn't leave a single print. And neither did the victim, for that matter. It's almost like Miriam George floated out here and dropped herself down this fucking hole."

12:43 P.M.

Sam and Mac headed toward the precinct with Willa's phone in absolute silence. Now one thing was sure: the level of dedication that went into covering tracks and premeditating a copycat scene spoke of a sick sonofabitch who'd probably done this sort of thing before. But in Somerdale? A town that had little crime other than bar fights and breaking up bonfires on a Friday night held by the local Glee club?

It's just not possible, she thought, staring out the passenger side window, her thoughts flipping like a Rolodex. "I just don't even know where to start with this."

"I think we're safe to eliminate Willa from suspicion," Mac said. "Did you see her? Looks like she's wasting away. Makes no sense how Willa would have gotten Miriam's body not only *to* the manhole, but then chucking her down it—especially not without leaving any sort of prints. Willa looks like she might weigh one hundred pounds soaking wet."

"Yeah, and then there was the manhole cover," Sam pointed out. "I doubt Willa could lift it, much less throw it several yards from the hole. And then I think, if they hate each other that much—because I'm telling you, Willa Dalton hates those girls—how did she get the George girl out of her house?"

"So, where the hell does that leave us?"

"I think we have to consider the idea that maybe Miriam went out there on her own. Maybe to meet someone."

"And that answers your question." Mac's fingers tightened around the steering wheel.

"What question?"

"Maybe she met Willa out there."

"No, I don't think so."

"And … there were no prints. And her folks say she was home all night. Shit. What are we missing?" Mac said, flustered.

"Whoever did it must've covered his tracks. And if Miriam went out at two or three in the morning, how the hell would her parents even know? I very seriously doubt she would have told them."

"So, you think maybe we go to her friends again?"

"I doubt three teenage girls so into their looks and reputations would risk going into the cornfield at night. Even if they did, could they do it without leaving prints? I mean Tess Todd is smart but she ain't no goddamn criminal genius."

"Shit," Mac said as his theory disintegrated.

"One way or the other though, we need to talk to Tess, Virgie, and Cassie. Maybe they can provide some answers."

"Well, you know who they'll point to."

"Willa, I know. And Willa will point right back to them. But once we can prove Willa isn't responsible—hopefully by simply checking her phone—the girls'll have to think a little harder."

Mac nodded, and the car went quiet. It was the sort of silence that, to Sam, felt like defeat, because, while she was used to starting a case with no answers, it was quite another situation to be on a case where the further they went, the more confusing and impossible it seemed.

No prints at all. The manhole cover tossed aside like paper.

Yes, this one was starting to seem *very* impossible. But she was determined.

10:06 P.M.

Several hours after nightfall, a new sort of tension blanketed Somerdale. News of Miriam George's death had circulated like wildfire, and now, people were fearing for their safety. The death of two young girls in such a short time had everyone on edge.

In the darkness, if someone had been passing through the outskirts of town near the nicer homes partially hidden in tree-filled enclaves, one might have seen the small gathering of figures on the front porch of the Vaughan house. The three girls met under the cover of night, huddled together under the glow of the porch light.

"Which one of you morbid bitches did it?" The question came from Tess Todd's mouth like a bullet from a gun. And it struck with just as much impact as a bullet would.

Cassie shuddered the most; she seemed to be taking it much harder than anyone else.

Virgie stared at her. To have Tess start their little meeting with such a question was more than a little unnerving. To Virgie, it made Tess, confident, unruffled, but seem just as scared and uncertain as the rest of them.

At first, no one answered. They sat on the porch in the frigid air, staring at each other. Virgie's parents, as usual, weren't home. However, after learning of Miri's murder, Virgie's mother had dropped her work schedule for the week and was currently somewhere in the air between Tulsa and Richmond. Her father would be home from Miami tomorrow afternoon. They both had given

Virgie strict instructions to keep the doors and windows locked and to stay in until they arrived.

Right. Instead, she'd called Tess and Cassie over for a much-needed powwow.

"So, wait," Cassie said. "You mean to tell me you think one of *us* actually killed Miri? Tess, have you lost your fucking mind?"

"Well, what am I supposed to think?" Tess barked. "Ever since that pig died, I've heard the same whining from all of you. *Tess, we need to come clean! Tess, we need to tell the truth! Tess, I'm so scared! Tess, Tess, Tess.* It's bullshit!"

"But why would *we* hurt Miri?" Virgie asked. "Tess, that makes no sense."

"She was … She was scared," Cassie said. "I don't know why exactly, but she'd seemed spooked these last few days."

"She was. I don't know what it was." Virgie folded her hands, laid them in her lap, and stared into the darkness.

"Both of you are giving me your word that neither of you did this?"

Cassie looked like she might start crying at any moment. "No. Of course not."

"She's right," Virgie cut toward Tess. "What about *you?* After all, you're the one who *accidentally* pushed Carmen. You're the one who didn't want to tell anyone what happened. Of the three of us, I think *you'd* be the most likely one to have the most to lose. Right, Cassie?"

Tess stepped closer to Virgie. In the porchlight, her face looked almost waxen. The fury in her eyes was bright, like neon hate. "Don't you even try pinning that on me. That dumb bitch stepped back, and she *fell.* Maybe it wouldn't have happened if we hadn't shown up and given her a hard time, and that's just something we'll all have to live with and wonder about. But to say I *pushed* her … I'll slap you right in your dumb mouth for that. Besides, I did the world a favor."

"Just as long as you don't *push* me, I'm okay with that," Virgie said, unwavering.

The trio of girls stood there, quiet and tense, as if expecting a bomb to explode at any moment.

Tess's body trembled with fury. Slowly, and with what looked like great effort, Tess backed away and leaned against the porch rail. When she looked across the darkened yard, she seemed scared and vulnerable, an expression Virgie wasn't used to. "I bet it was Willa." She turned back to Virgie and Cassie with venom in her gaze. "It would make sense."

"Willa? What are you talking about?" Virgie asked.

"She was that pig's only friend. And even though she didn't actually see Carmen fall, she showed up on the scene soon enough so that she *thought* she knew what had happened. And think about it, she's been awfully quiet. She hasn't really confronted me. We passed one another in the bathroom once, and there wasn't much of anything. She's ... I don't know. It feels like she's planning something, maybe getting her stupid aunt to cast one of those spells or something."

"She's been talking to the police too," Cassie responded.

"Right. She was always leering at us. Hating on us. Maybe jealous," Virgie said.

"Well, we *did* give her reason."

Tess scowled. "Oh, so *now* you're having a change of heart?"

"I don't know. *Miri's* dead!" Cassie cried out, sounding close to tears.

"What if it *was* Willa?" Virgie speculated. "I mean, it's possible, right? I mean she's a fuck-flake anyway. I could see her doing some weird shit like this."

"Well, if it is her, we should just let the police do their jobs," Cassie said. "Stay out of the way and let them figure it out."

"I bet it *was* her," Virgie said. "Jesus, what if all the things we've heard about her and her aunt aren't rumors?"

The comment hung in the night air. It had already been a dark day with news of Miriam's death, so in saying those words, though Virgie doubted they were true, she'd hope she'd feel a bit of comfort. She didn't. Instead, she thought of the face she'd seen in the car window and hugged herself to ward off the chill that seemed to have permanently seeped into her bones. Yet the weight of it all hadn't fully landed on them yet. But as all three of them stared into the darkness, Virgie had a feeling, as if sensing something out there.

TUESDAY, NOVEMBER 15, 2008

11:42 A.M.

I t was the second funeral Cassie had ever attended. In the days following Miri's death, she'd heard her parents talk about how hard it must be for Miri's parents—that they could not imagine having to bury a child. The few times she'd met Miri's folks, they gave the image of one of those perfect 80's sitcom families. She wondered if this sort of tragedy would show what they were really like.

The weather was quite fitting. An early November chill hung in the air. The atmosphere at the graveside was so thick and tense that the rain that fell seemed to be a result of it. Rain tinkled down like glass on black umbrellas, mingling with the sounds of sobs. On occasion, Alan George would make a sound, somewhere between a scream and a high-pitched moan. He had seemed almost fine when he and his wife had been escorted to the open grave, but the moment the preacher started speaking, something inside him broke.

The sounds of sorrow escaping his throat were the worst sounds Cassie had ever heard. She scanned the crowd for Vir-

184 | TRACE MURILLO

gie and Tess and found them mixed among the mourners. Virgie
stared straight ahead toward the casket, unblinking. Tess looked
to the ground, her face crumpling slightly every time Alan George
sputtered one of his ungodly sounds of grief.

Wait … was Tess crying?

Cassie was so busy trying to see if those were raindrops or actual tears that she wasn't really listening to the preacher. She recognized the scripture he was reading, as she'd heard it in church
countless times. It was from Romans, where all God's children
are told that neither death nor life, nor angels nor demons, nor
yadda yadda could ever separate God's children from his love.
Cassie could not hear them as a believer when her friend was
lowered into the ground. Whenever she tried to find comfort in
her beliefs, she recalled the text she had received a week or so ago:
You're just as guilty.

And then, of course, there was the dark imagery pasted to
the walls of her mind. At night, when she closed her eyes, she
thought of Carmen at the bottom of the hole. Sometimes, she'd
see Miri's face in its place.

The thought made a chill spike down her spine as she
scanned the crowd. Tess slowly backed away, flanked by her parents holding matching umbrellas, and Cassie definitely saw a tear
on Tess's flawless cheek.

Cassie wasn't sure how to feel about that. It was good that the
callous girl she'd spoken with five nights ago on Virgie's porch did
indeed have feelings. But, at the same time, Cassie could not help
but feel Tess was the reason they were in this situation. It was Tess
who had always been the ringleader, bullying others to the point
of tears. It had been Tess who had singled out Carmen Winstead
when she had arrived in Somerdale. And it had been Tess who
had, as far back as sixth or seventh grade, publicly lashed out at
anything remotely different or out of the ordinary.

Good, Cassie thought. *Let her cry. Let her mourn. Let her grow
a conscience.*

The funeral ended, and Cassie hoped the terrible moment would be over and things would get better. But after the funeral was the gathering or repast, whatever people called it. Cassie wasn't sure but what she did know is that would not be much easier. To watch people huddled around old pictures of the deceased, drinking, and eating stuffed shrimp, felt even more morbid than the funeral itself.

1:35 P.M.

The gathering was at the George's residence. Cassie's parents had told her on the way to let them know when she was ready to leave. Cassie did not want to attend at all. She thought it would be weird being in Miri's house, knowing she would not be there. But her parents told her she needed to attend no matter what. "It's just a plain and simple sign of respect," her father had told her. "Just put in a short visit. That's all."

So, while her parents spoke to an older couple, George family members Cassie didn't know, she sat in a corner, eating dry apple bars and drinking ginger ale with Virgie. Virgie seemed disconnected but was cordial and polite to everyone who came by to say hello, although, honestly, Virgie had seemed like a different person these last few days. Ever since she'd lost her virginity to Shane, she'd been more reserved, more disconnected, not her usual talkative self. As they sat together at the Georges', Cassie was sure they looked like two lost puppies, not quite sure where they fit into the scene happening around them.

But at least she was with people—real, *living* people. She cringed at the thought of her phone. She hadn't bothered to tell her parents that her phone was dead, because she didn't want another one. In fact, she'd have been happy never to use a phone again.

"It doesn't seem real," Virgie said, speaking in a near whisper as she surveyed the crowd. "Like, how is Miri dead? I think that's why I haven't had a good cry about it yet. It's like my mind won't accept it. My mind thinks it can't be real, you know?"

"I think I've accepted it. And it sucks. But there's something else, something I can't wrap my head around. And it's awful. It's so awful that I can't properly focus on the fact that Miri is gone."

Virgie narrowed her eyes at Cassie. She opened her mouth to speak but held it in while three adults walked by. As they passed, someone whispered that Alan George had passed out on the way back to his house and was currently being taken to the hospital. She shuddered.

Virgie leaned over. "What do you mean? You saw something too, didn't you?"

"*Saw* something? Not really. I just … I got a text from an unknown number. It said I was just as guilty as everyone."

Virgie's eyes widened. "Really? You think it was just a prank? You think Willa—"

Cassie shook her head. "No. Whatever it was, it zapped my phone. It died right after. But I …" She envisioned the image she'd seen on her phone right before the thing went dead. If she told Virgie that, she'd probably be considered as big as a headcase as Willa.

"I saw something." Virgie's eyes widened as she stared at the floor. Her voice was softer than ever now. "Shane and I … we were goofing off on Skype, and something interfered with it. Some static and then a black screen and then this … this weird place appeared. It looked like a tunnel, maybe the tunnel down there."

"Down there?"

"You know, in the manhole."

"Virgie, you're talking crazy," Cassie said in a heavy breath, even though, honestly, after what she'd seen, it didn't sound all that unbelievable.

"I know. But listen. Me and Shane, we were out in his grand-pa's field, messing around. I told you. You know when I lost my V-card, and I saw her …"

"Saw who? Miri?" Cassie's voice was barely a whisper. She wanted to get up, to run away, to stop hearing this, because if Virgie was just trying to spook her, it was working.

"No." Virgie's eyes went to the crowd of people gathering around the food table like vultures. "It was Carmen Winstead."

Cassie nearly dropped her ginger ale. "Virgie, you know it wasn't her. Carmen is dead."

"I know that. I mean, my brain knows it. It's *fact*. But when I saw it right there, in that moment, it was her. I know it was. I know how crazy it sounds but I can't help but wonder …"

Cassie knew where she was going and thought it was ridiculous. Still, a part of her needed to hear it, because deep down, hadn't she thought the same thing too? Cassie trembled with a mixture of panic and curiosity. She wanted to know she wasn't crazy, but now, more than ever, she just wanted to run away. "What?" Cassie asked, urging her to finish.

"I can't help but wonder maybe Willa did something as a witch. Maybe she brought her back."

"Carmen?"

Virgie nodded. "I know it sounds stupid, but, Cassie, I was so scared. I was fucking terrified." She let out a shuddering sigh.

"You know Tess touched her, right? Tess did this. And where is she? She's not even here at this party or gathering or whatever it is. I don't see how these people can eat after a stupid funeral anyway."

Cassie only nodded.

"Hey but *we* were *all* circling around her. Circling like sharks and you know that. It wasn't just Tess. I think in a way, we all pushed her in that stupid hole. And maybe that's why Miri …"

Cassie's stomach dropped. If that was why Miri was dead, then she ... "Oh, my god," Cassie whispered. "Should we tell someone?"

Virgie shrugged. "Who could we tell? Who would believe us? Maybe it's just our own guilt. Maybe were just seeing things, ya know?" But Virgie knew that wasn't true. She knew what she had seen. It was more than her mind playing tricks on her—it was something dark, something evil—and every time she closed her eyes, it was something that replayed inside her mind. It was the darkness that haunted her the most—the darkness and the images of Carmen Winstead.

"You girls need anything?" a pleasantly middle-aged woman asked, leaning into their conversation. "Something else to eat, maybe?"

The two girls stared at her, shell-shocked, as understanding dawned upon them.

"I have to go, Virgie. I have to get out of here. You gonna be okay?"

"Yeah. I just ... just don't know." Cassie stared curiously at Virgie, shaking as she stood and looked for her parents. And when she left the Georges, Cassie felt as if she were carrying something with her—something that incited confusion in her mind. But... also...something else.

8:52 P.M.

Cassie retired to bed early that night. Her parents had done their best to get her to talk about her feelings, but she wasn't ready. They were talking about sorrow, loss, depression. But those things took a major back seat to the emotion currently whirring through her tense nerves.

Fear.

The conversation with Virgie at the gathering after the funeral had really screwed her up. And while she did not believe in ghosts or even the magic power True and Willa Dalton supposedly possessed, she *did* think something odd was going on—something, maybe, *not of this world*.

But at least her parents understood when she told them she was turning in. They said a quick prayer as a family and sent her off with what her dad called his *blessings from God*. Cassie headed upstairs, feeling like she was wearing a bag of bricks on her shoulders. Even though her house was nice and warm, she could still feel the chill of the dreary rain clinging to her.

In her room, the first thing she saw was her Bible lying on her night table where she always kept it. Usually, she found comfort within it, but not tonight; she only felt dread as a Bible verse came to her—Matthew 7:2. *For you will be treated as you treat others. The standard you use in judging is the standard by which you will be judged.*

Her thoughts went to Virgie's story. She'd seen the tunnel or hole on her computer. It must have been a prank. And the person she'd seen in the fields when she was fornicating with Shane, she's going to burn in hell, she thought—had to be a joke too. Shane was a total douchebag, after all. She couldn't put it past him and his immature friends. But what Cassie needed right now was a long, hot bath, something to erase the chill of the day and to ease her tense muscles—time to be alone, to zone out, to shut up her frantic mind.

She took her pajamas to the upstairs bathroom and sat on the edge of the tub as she filled it with hot water. She breathed in the steam, cycling through the day, and doing her best to let her mind go blank. But as soon as she was almost there, the images of the text flooded her mind with panic: *You're just as guilty as Tess.*

Who would even send such a thing? She mentally paged through a list of her friends and acquaintances, people from school, and kept coming back to Willa Dalton. Something about it *did* seem to fit.

With the water completely run and some bubbles and bath salts added to the mix, Cassie stripped and got into the tub. The relief was immediate; all her cares melted into the hazy, hot air. The steam filled her nostrils as she clutched her arms around her knees.

She'd just closed her eyes when a thought came to her. *If those things were just pranks, why is Miri dead?* She breathed deeply, trying to shove aside the thought. Maybe the bath would help clear her mind enough so she could pray and—

The drain gurgled, sending up little bubbles.

Cassie's eyes opened. It had done this many times in the past but never quite this loud. She gave the drain a rueful glance and reclined with her head against the lip of the tub.

The drain gurgled again. This time, it was jarring, sounding like someone was under the water, exhaling a huge breath. A large bubble rolled to the surface. The other bubbles parted as it rolled upward like a small, erupting volcano. The odor that radiated from the bubble was stiffening, foul, dead. It lingered as she stared curiously around the bathroom then to the drain. She shrieked as she realized the drain had apparently expelled something dark.

"Ugh!" She pulled her knees to her chest again. "Dad, what the hell is wrong with the plumbing?" She tried to get out of the tub but froze at the sight of the stuff that seemed to be multiplying among the soft, sweet-smelling bubbles she'd added. It looked like sludge, mingling with her bathwater—not mud or any sort of muck from the drain but something else. Worms and what she thought were maggots floated to the surface. "Oh, god!"

She scrambled faster, feeling vomit rising in her throat as she tried to gain purchase on the slick tile walls. Her feet slipped and skidded on the wet porcelain, and she finally got traction and managed to pull herself up. The water was black now, frothing at the drain, which continued to gurgle and expel more of its detritus—chunks of soft black matter, what could have been rotted wood, bits of refuse, or shit. The smell of decay filled the bathroom, old rotting flesh.

Cassie firmly planted her right foot on the cold, tile floor. As she lifted out her left leg, something tugged on her ankle. Heart thumping, she saw worms and maggots swarming all over her skin. She cried out, pulling hard but still unable to free herself from the darkness beyond the water. Something had her, something in that muck that refused to let go. It was pulling her in.

Her mouth formed the shape of a scream as a thick, brown worm, pulsing all along its body, slithered over her leg and climbed up her flesh. Her fear choked her. All she could manage was a low moan as she swatted it away. She gave her left leg one hard yank, and a pale hand came out of the water and clasped to her ankle with a grip so tight it seemed to be a part of her. She could see its white bones beneath the mottled skin.

As the hand raised out of the water, the rest of the body came with it. Somewhere in that wretched dark water, a human figure had been hiding—gaunt and mangled almost beyond recognition. The top of its head came first, the brow so scraped and torn that she could see glistening white skull underneath. The head that was attached to black hair contained the writhing shapes of worms and maggots. And beneath the fetid hair were a pair of dark, soulless eyes.

"Please," Cassie said, the word coming out in a gasp as fear coursed through her.

The figure emerging from the foul water was unmistakable—Carmen Winstead. When her face was out of the water, Carmen opened her mouth, releasing a horrible sound that was something between a growl and a shriek. More foul water filled with worms, bugs, and bits of trash gushed from her mouth. It brought with it something awful—the smell of dead things, rotting things, forgotten darkness.

With a scream, Cassie pulled her leg away with strength she did not know she had. And when she was finally free, her body was flooded with adrenaline and a survival instinct that had, until now, been dormant inside her. Cassie leaped from the tub and slammed into the sink; her eyes still locked on the tub.

Carmen was getting out of the water, her wet, white tattered dress clinging to her skin. Her flesh had started to rot away, pecked, and nibbled at by countless underground creatures. Deep lesions were etched across her cheeks.

Cassie pressed against the sink, silent—her voice gone, her brain locking down. She pressed her hands to her face, trying to cover her eyes, but it was no use.

Carmen slithered like an eel from the tub, opening her mouth toward Cassie. Black bile leaked from her teeth as she reached for her. Another drop of black bile fell from her lips.

With all her might, Cassie stared into Carmen's dead eyes.

A deafening explosion caused the room to go dark and silent. The door opened, and the last thing Cassie saw was a silhouette standing in the doorway, fading to absolute nothingness.

WEDNESDAY, NOVEMBER 16, 2008

4:15 A.M.

Sam had watched Miriam George's funeral from a distance. She'd parked at the far end of the cemetery—far enough away so all she really saw were the humped shapes of the umbrellas against the gloom and rain but just close enough to see Alan George collapse to the ground at his daughter's coffin.

Oddly enough, she dreamed about the scene that night. Alan George, a man she had only met once, was reaching out but not toward a coffin. Instead, he was reaching for an opened manhole cover. And something was reaching for him in return—something with long, gnarled fingers and something rancid caked under its fingernails.

Sam awoke with a start, her heart pounding in her chest. She was on the very edge of the bed, and when she looked to the other side, she almost wished Fredricks was there. Not too long ago, she'd actually enjoyed waking in the middle of the night to find him beside her. They had taken turns waking one another rather creatively. Those early morning hours when he had shown her what he could do with his tongue had been almost otherworldly. She hated that she missed it. Not that she had ever been in love with the prick. But it was just nice, every now and then, to feel she wasn't absolutely alone, to wake up to pleasure instead of panic.

Thinking of Fredericks, the nightmare subsided. She'd shot the man from that exact same place in the bed. She'd always left her Glock on the bedside table, and he knew it. He'd come in after she told him it was over. What had he been expecting?

She had spackled a spot on the wall during her mandatory week-long leave of absence. It felt foolish now, wanting the familiarity of a man who had nearly raped her, just so she wasn't alone.

Sam stared at the clock, knowing she wouldn't go back to sleep. Just as well, her alarm was set for 5 a.m. So she rolled out of bed, went into the kitchen to brew a pot of coffee, then started her morning routine. She went to the back bedroom, which she had turned into a small gym immediately upon moving in four years ago. She ran through her twenty-minute kettlebell circuit, then did two miles on the elliptical bike. Finally, the aroma of her Café Bustelo finally reached down the hallway, so she went to the kitchen, poured her coffee, and sat on the living room couch.

While she did not buy into prayer or meditation, she did her best to practice what she thought of as the art of mindfulness. She cut on an ambient loop app from her phone and simply sat there, eyes closed, allowing her mind to go blank. She'd been doing it long enough that she could get there remarkably fast. She'd go blank, find her Zen, and just hover there for a moment. She'd heard the effect was similar to those weird isolation tanks people seemed to be buying into—resetting her brain to be more effective at responding to any curve ball that life would throw. She would be ready.

She was nearing the end of her session when the ambient noises from her phone were interrupted by its shuddering and vibration on the table in front of her. She tried to ignore it, but it was barely six o'clock. For a call to be coming in that early, it had to be urgent. She checked the display. It was Mac, just as she'd suspected. "Too early."

"I know. I'm sorry."

"What, you miss me that much?"

"Ha! You wish. I was just wondering if you'd heard about what took place at the Hollins residence last night."

"As in, Cassie Hollins?"

"Yeah."

"Oh god, don't tell me."

"No, nothing like that. But my contact at the hospital clued me in about half an hour ago. She called because she knew we were dealing with the Carmen Winstead case—and, apparently, news is circulating quicker than we'd like."

"Figures. God, I hate the grapevine in this stupid town. Anyway … Cassie. What happened?"

"She came into the hospital last night in a state. I mean, Sam, she was freaking out. Screaming. They had to sedate her, then keep her for a few hours for observation. They finally discharged her about an hour ago."

"Tox screen?"

"Clear."

"Then what was it? What was she scared of?"

"Thought you'd never ask, and, oh, it's a hell of a story. She claims she was taking a bath and Carmen Winstead came after her. Popped right out of the tub among some nasty water. She gave some pretty specific details. Said the water got murky with worms and bugs and fecal matter. Said Carmen came out of the drain somehow, then out of the tub. Her father, who found Cassie sort of spazzing out on the bathroom floor, said there was, of course, nothing there—no ghost, no muck, no nothing. The bathroom was sparkling clean."

The temperature in Sam's house seemed to drop about twenty degrees. "My god. Did you get chills when you heard that too?"

"Too? No …"

Sam rubbed away the goosebumps on her arm. "Oh. Me neither."

"I don't know what to make of this, Sam. I mean … something like that? It's got to be the product of some really serious shit. Guilt maybe?"

"Well, she did just come from her friend's funeral. Maybe she had a reaction to that."

"I don't know. But those girls know something. They're not telling us something, and it's starting to piss me off."

"What about the Dalton girl? You think Willa knows more?"

"I doubt it. But I honestly have no idea what to think anymore."

"I think we have to talk to Cassie. I mean, I hate to go there, but if the guilt is causing her to see things like that—things she believes are *that real*—I don't think it would take much for her to come clean."

"Yeah," Mac said. "But we need to give her at least a day or two. She's too fragile right now. There's no way her parents would let it fly."

"The day after tomorrow then. Her parents might not like it, but I also don't like being lied to."

"Sounds like a plan. Now, what about today? We gotta update Cap; he's breathing down our necks to finish up the Winstead case."

"Oh, really I haven't even noticed," Sam snipped.

"You wouldn't."

"Well, we need to review the forensics reports for the Miriam George scene of death. Maybe interview her parents if the father is up for it. I mean with a sound mind of course."

"You think he's that bad off?"

"Yeah. I watched him have a breakdown at the funeral. He's a mess."

"This whole *thing* is a mess."

"We'll figure it out; Somerdale isn't that damn big. We'll get our break soon enough."

"Yeah," Mac said without much enthusiasm in his voice.

Sam understood Mac's lack of positivity. Because, even as the words had come out of her own mouth, she hadn't really believed it either.

6:35 P.M.

After she'd heard about what happened to Cassie, Virgie wanted to go to her house and visit, but her parents didn't think it was a good idea. She understood their logic; they had a lot going on in their lives. It was clear that the recent deaths in Somerdale were taking their toll. While Virgie herself felt fine—though maybe a bit sad and scared—she supposed her parents were right. Maybe it wasn't the best idea to be around Cassie right now.

Even though she agreed with them on this point, Virgie found it hard to believe her parents knew what was good for her. They were never around and didn't even know her friends' names. The only reason they knew Cassie was because her mother had once been very involved with the church and knew Cassie's parents fairly well.

So, rather than being by Cassie's side, Virgie sat on her bed, playing on her computer as night fell. Miri's death was a hot topic of Myspace, as many students offered their thoughts and prayers on her page. Some concerned parents were even calling for a curfew. Things were getting crazy, something Virgie could sense, even in the confinement of her room.

Outside was a slight drizzle, a holdover from Miri's funeral. Virgie closed her computer and grabbed her phone to scroll through the pictures of her friends. The four of them were always camera ready, something Tess had taught them early on. Tess was always reminding them how to snap a perfect picture, and her camera roll showed as much. She, Miriam, Cassie, and Tess were always posing, always ready. There were pictures of them in the hallways at school, on the sidelines of a football game, at the lake, and in front of the cornfields just before the corn festival.

The corn festival …

Virgie shuddered and set down the phone. She stared through the rain-spattered windowpane and thought of Cassie. She'd been talking to her mere hours before the breakdown, and she'd seemed fine. A little scared, but that was Cassie. What the hell had happened to her?

Weak bitch, she thought, mimicking the comment Tess had made earlier when she'd called to tell Virgie the news.

She forced herself to think of Shane. He'd been extra attentive since that night, calling her, texting her all the time. He probably just wanted round two. But there was an odd relief in it. She had done it and gotten it over with. Part of her already craved it again, despite the pain she had felt. She heard it was supposed to get better, but she had a hard time believing that.

Her thoughts turned to the spectral figure she had seen outside the car that night. She kept trying to tell herself she had not seen it at all—that it had just been a play of shadows mingling with her already overactive mind. But even if that were the case, it did not explain the strange occurrences with her computer or the voice she'd heard somewhere in her bathroom.

So, maybe Cassie had also been experiencing her fair share of things. Only, true to Cassie-form, she'd kept it bottled up. And it had apparently broken her.

Virgie fell back on her pillow, listening to the faint and murmured voices of her parents' downstairs. She was pretty sure her mother was already looking at how soon she could return to work—meeting with some high-profile client somewhere in Florida. As for her father, Virgie had given up on keeping tabs where he was. One week, it was Los Angeles; another week, it was

London; and then maybe Tokyo. And the saddest part of all was that she really didn't care.

It wasn't like they could help her with her problems anyway. Miri was dead. Cassie seemed to be losing her mind. Tess ... well, God only knew what that bitch was thinking. Tess had slipped out of Miri's funeral early, and since then, Virgie hadn't really seen or heard from her that much. It made Virgie wonder if all of this was finally getting to her. *Probably not. The shit that runs through those veins is as cold as the night was long.*

Thinking this, Virgie grabbed her phone again. She opened her text messages and considered texting Cassie. But what would she say? *Hey, hope you're feeling better. So, what do you think is going on with Tess? You think we should come clean, just turn that bitch in?*

No. Her parents were right about that; she needed to give Cassie some more time to sort herself out. Besides, if they came clean now, it would be admitting they had lied. Even though imagining Tess in some awful orange jumpsuit was very appealing, she doubted it'd even come to that. With her luck, she'd be locked up in there with her, joined at the hip for life. Not something that was all that appealing for Virgie.

She skimmed through all the same pictures again, starting last year at Cassie's birthday party. They were all on the back deck, smiling as wide as possible. Then the Spring Fling Dance, then cruising the lake on jet skis, then ... She smiled, feeling a flood of emotion engulf her, when she noticed something.

In a picture of the four of them standing in the hallway the first day of senior year, there, standing in the background, was a shadowy figure. She squinted to look closer. She knew it hadn't been there before. This was a picture she had blown up and put on her night table. She grabbed the frame and stared at it. *Nothing.*

Virgie quickly swiped out of the picture, going to the next. It was just her and Tess, posing sexily in front of Lennie's Ice Cream Parlor with their hips cocked. Virgie was holding a cone of cappuccino swirl, Tess with strawberry. Behind them, at the very edge of the building, stood another figure. Transparent, slender, but human-shaped—it was the same figure from the other photo.

Virgie's first impulse was to throw her phone, but curiosity took hold of her, and she continued to swipe, again and again and again. The figure was lurking in the background of every picture. It was there, as if watching and waiting, behind them in Tess's back yard, at the country club pool, in Miri's bathroom as she and Virgie tested out new bathing suits, in the cornfield, and in the back seat of Tess's car.

Always there. Always watching them.

And in each picture, the figure seemed to be drawing closer. Its face was blurry, the long black hair framing it. In some pictures, the head was tilted, as if thinking. And though no features were present, Virgie knew who it was.

It was Carmen Winstead...watching.

She was in every picture, coming closer and closer to the lens. Virgie swiped maniacally, hoping to somehow erase the reality of it. But as the figure drew so near that it was nearly taking up the entire frame, she realized there was no hope of escaping it.

And when she finally threw her phone across the room, it was too late.

Carmen was there, in her room.

Standing at the end of her bed.

No sooner had Virgie opened her mouth to scream then Carmen's figure flew across her bed. She did not run or jump, not even a glide. She just simply moved, as if projected forward by time and space, right out of some sort of ethereal slingshot. And when Carmen's weight was on Virgie, she could not draw a breath. She was paralyzed.

Carmen had a featureless face, with nothing but coal-black, fathomless eyes and a huge, odious smile. A dark liquid dripped over the lips. The smell of rot and decay wafted across Virgie's face. She felt a ball of vomit rising in her throat.

Something inside Virgie jolted her body. She mewled against the weight of the figure, trying to fight.

Virgie's mouth opened, and that black fluid rushed in, flowing over her tongue and down her throat where it no longer felt wet. Instead, it was something with fingers reaching inside her body, grabbing hold ... and then *squeezing*.

The last thing Virgie Vaughan saw was Carmen Winstead's two black eyes as the dead girl perched upon her chest. And distantly, like the crashing of waves from miles away, the murmur of her parents' voices discussing when they might be able to return to work. Then, nothing but darkness.

THURSDAY, NOVEMBER 17, 2008

9:11 A.M.

S onofabitch." Sam wished a better phrase existed to describe what she was seeing, but she was at a loss for words. In fact, the idea of saying anything else seemed like too much. She was trembling, and something inside her seemed to be shriveling. For one paralyzing moment, she feared she might start crying out of frustration and at the meaningless loss of life before her.

She peered into the manhole again, ensuring she was seeing things correctly. She aimed her flashlight directly at what was down there. As much as she did not want it to be true, her eyes had not deceived her.

Virgie Vaughan was curled in fetal position at the bottom of the hole. The right side of her head looked as if it had been sliced open. Her blood streaked the lip of the manhole, a stark splash of maroon that had not yet dried.

Sam eyed Mac beside her, not wanting to give voice to what she was really thinking: *There's no fucking way this is possible.* Instead, slowly and with great caution, she said, "How does this even happen?"

"I don't know." She was at least a little relieved to hear the edge of fear and doubt in his voice as well.

Sam turned and looked back the way they had come. The rain from the night before had been light but continuous. It had been enough to soak the ground, so the only visible prints belonged to them. Several policemen had gathered along the edge of the woods, but they hadn't come this way.

"Where the hell is forensics?" she shouted. *Goddammit.*

"On their way." Mac crossed his arms and looked skyward, as if there might be an answer there. "We'll need to talk to the Holt family. This whole area needs to be blocked off from public access. Might need to get the county to put some trail cams out here."

"I wonder if we should have done that after we found Miriam George."

"Hindsight is a bitch," he spat. Sam wasn't sure she'd ever seen Mac this upset, this frustrated.

"So is death," Sam retorted. "Especially when it takes three local girls in the same fucking place. Mac, what the hell is going on?"

His silence was answer enough.

They'd gotten the call two hours ago. Virgie Vaughan had not been in her room when her mother had gone in to wake her. When Sam and Mac had arrived at the house, it had been like a step-by-step recreation of the morning they'd found Miri George. One big difference was that Virgie's phone indicated she was involved in a relationship with a local boy named Shane Seamster. Sam and Mac had instantly gone to visit with him, but he hadn't seen her since before the funeral.

The next step had been obvious, if not a bit grim, sending Sam and Mac right back to the manhole that had claimed Carmen Winstead, as well as Miriam George.

And now, Virgie Vaughan.

As Sam peered into the hole, a commotion rose from the woods behind her. She turned to the few gathered cops, including Foster, a twelve-year veteran, trying to ascertain the problem. Sam jumped off the concrete around the manhole and did her best to stay within the muddy tracks she and Mac had already left.

When she reached the edge of the forest, the other cops parted for her, and she sighed. Foster was doing everything he could to restrain Tyson Vaughn from making it the rest of the way to the scene.

"Is she there?" the father was screaming. "Is my baby down there?"

"Mr. Vaughan, you need to calm down," Sam said rigidly. "Please."

"Shoot me if you have to. I don't give a shit. Is it *her?* Is she *down there?*"

Her hesitation was all the answer he needed. He shoved Officer Foster and ran for the yellow tape that surrounded the scene. He slipped on the wet ground, and three other officers grabbed his limp body. Mac was one of them. Tyson Vaughn collapsed at Mac's feet, screaming and wailing.

Mac gently helped Tyson Vaughn to his feet. Mac's face was fierce, but his voice was gentle. Sam couldn't hear what he was saying, but, as he spoke, he closed his eyes briefly and shook his head. Eventually, Tyson hung his head and wept, and Mac put a helpful arm around him. *Damn.* He has always been better at these things than she'd been, in that moment, she was glad he was there.

As Foster led Tyson Vaughan up the hill to his car, Sam and Mac hung their heads in defeat, Sam and Mac looked timid toward each other and trudged up the hill, trying to figure out their next move.

12:07 P.M.

Three hours later, Sam was sitting behind a cheap folding table in the break room at the precinct. While the local Somerdale PD co-ordinated with the state police, Sam and Mac had been given the authority to commandeer the room and use it as a makeshift base of operations until something more suitable could be established. Sam had brought in a dry-erase board from home, and she and Mac were doing their best to make sense of what was happening in Somerdale before the FBI moved in.

The same familiar names were on the board, but none of them seemed to hold any real promise. Tess Todd. Cassie Hollins. Willa Dalton. Dates and times were on the board as well, most of which had been crossed through, as alibis had knocked most of them out.

The room felt stale and smelled of coffee. Sam rubbed at her head, trying to get some sort of thought process going. At this point, *any* ideas would be better than what they had ... which was absolutely nothing.

"So, there was something at Miriam's funeral," Sam said. "I can't be one hundred percent certain, but I'm pretty sure Tess Todd left early, right in the middle of the service before Alan George had his breakdown."

"So? They were close friends. Maybe it was a little too much for her."

"Maybe. But Cassie and Virgie stayed."

"I don't follow."

"You wouldn't. You were not a girl in high school. Those three girls—as well as Miri, when she was still alive—were as thick as thieves. You could see it on your interrogation videos, how their stories all matched up perfectly. But then Miriam was killed. And instead of those three staying together, Tess ducks out? In a moment when they should have been tighter than ever, she split. It makes me wonder if there's more on Tess's mind, something she's not telling us."

"You think things are starting to fall apart for them?" Mac asked, his tone doubtful.

"Yeah. I mean, obviously. Two of them are dead. That'd make anyone crack." She rummaged through the files and papers on the table. Sam came to the preliminary report on Miriam George's autopsy. Because it was being considered a murder case, the results had not yet been made public. In fact, the coroner was being very insistent that the results he'd provided to the police were not complete. But the police had wanted something for reference, so the coroner had complied. "You look at this yet?"

"I did. Nothing in it makes sense. Evidence of strangulation internally but no marks on the outside to suggest exterior pressure."

"There was also evidence of huge amounts of adrenaline in Miriam's body at the time of her death. The coroner even states that she may have had some sort of a miniature heart attack."

"Was that before or after she walked into that manhole without leaving tracks of any kind?" Mac asked.

Sam nodded, sighing, and shoved the coroner's report to the side. "I'm grasping at straws here."

"I know. I think we all are at this point. I also think the next logical steps are talking to Tess and Cassie. And then probably Willa again. Those are our three prime suspects."

"Willa? You know she didn't do it."

"Do I? Do you?" Mac said. "Willa never liked them, yes. Tess and Cassie could be trying to keep their supposed *friends* silent. They all have motive. Anyway, that doesn't mean we can stop being cops and avoid the hard, sad stuff."

"Shit," Sam said, slamming her hand on the table. "I need a coffee. To hell with that. I need a beer."

But neither of them moved. They kept staring at the dry-erase board and sifting through the piles of papers and documents without much enthusiasm. Meanwhile, phones rang outside, and chatter continued at the front of the building. The calls had come with more frequency over the last hour. She'd been a detective long enough to know this news would bring an influx of calls from worried parents. Three teenaged girls killed in under two months, all disposed of in the same location. They had every right to be concerned, especially when Sam and Mac were no closer to solving this case then the day Carmen Winstead had fallen down that hole.

12:07 A.M.

True Dalton heard about Virgie Vaughan's death through one of the few friends she had—Gretchen Heyman, one of the only residents of Somerdale who not only respected True's Wiccan beliefs and practices but also showed a great deal of interest in it. However, Gretchen was also a shameless gossip, so whenever they got together, True let Gretchen do most of the talking.

Still, she had been grateful to hear Gretchen's information about Virgie Vaughan. A tragedy, though as True thought about, she realized it wasn't all that unexpected.

Gretchen Heyman insisted there was a serial killer at work. And to an outsider, True figured that might make sense. According to Gretchen's report from the Somerdale grapevine, those rumors had started swirling as soon as the police had found Miriam George's body. It was possible one of Miriam's friends had killed her, or maybe even Joe Winstead. But now, with Virgie's death, something far more sinister seemed to be taking place.

True already knew that though. She'd felt the stirrings of it for a while, then felt it with an actual physical force when she had met Carmen Winstead. It was a powerful force she'd been in tune with for a very long time—ever since she had first peered beyond the veil of the material world at the age of sixteen. In the decades that had followed, she'd learned to commune with it, to interact with it, to show it the respect it demanded. But she also knew that because of her gifts, some people in town thought she was some sort of hag. Not that she cared. She didn't really care much for the approval of the locals.

And True did not buy into such rumors. The force she listened to was far more reliable than small town gossip. True got her inclinations not from the mouths of bored housewives and retired ladies but from the town itself—the vibrations and energies that thrived within it and the forces that kept it all knitted together.

She was listening to those sources now as she sat at her kitchen table. Candles flickering, palms up, and eyes closed in meditation, she did her best to tap into it. Nature was talking, the wind like a tongue speaking words into her ear. It wasn't too dissimilar to a very small electrical surge, a tingle that started along her forehead and dispersed downward through her body. And despite the lack of words, she could decipher one overarching message: *Careful ...*

There were never any *actual* words. It was more of a feeling. And that's all she needed. She felt it now, very strong, as its force went through her.

She had been sitting silent and still for over an hour, waiting. She pushed away the gossip of Gretchen Heyman, pushed away her own preconceived notions, and let nature claim her mind. The longer she sat there, the clearer it became. And, as the clock on the kitchen wall ticked beyond one o'clock in the morning, True heard what the energy around the town had to say. Yes, there was a warning, but there was something else. And it felt different somehow—larger, sharper, more dangerous.

I am here.

Those three words settled in her head like rocks to the bottom of a sludgy pond. She sat bolt upright in her chair, the words rolling through her like electricity. She squeezed her eyes tighter and leaned forward, sweat beading on her temples. She felt a wave pushing through her, like she was sinking into the force around her, becoming one with it.

She heard it again. *I am here.*

She kept her breathing as calm as she could, even though her pulse shuddered under her skin. The winds and strains of the town and some of the world beyond funneled into her like ethereal tentacles.

"Please go away," True mumbled, almost in prayer.

The response was instant. Her head ached with a sound that rattle through her brain like a freight train. *I. AM. NOT. DONE.*

She felt the venom in the words. It echoed in her head. It was a feminine voice but had a sort of growl to it. The malice echoed all around her.

Willa …

The chair at the table beside True skidded across the floor. True forced her eyes open. She watched as the chair flipped in the air. She shivered as the vengeful force roared again like a sonic boom in her ears.

The cabinet near the stove shook, and pots and pans rattled out onto the floor. Glasses flew from cabinets, shattering shards of glass in its wake. The refrigerator door opened and closed violently, propelling its magnets like bullets across the room, hitting True in the cheek.

A blast of wind blustered through True. She wavered slightly; her hair rustled back as if an ocean breeze was stirring it. As it passed through her, her heart paused, her blood chilled, and a soft whisper echoed in her mind … *I. AM. NOT. DONE.*

People were scared of things they did not understand or could not control. But once True Dalton had learned to become one with nature and all its forces, she had never feared it—not storms, not darkness, not death. But now, as she stood in the gloom of her home among the shards of glass littering the floor, she could *feel* the darkness. Hovering. She could feel it as if it were ᴀ physical presence, simmering like rotted flesh. It was the first time in her life she'd ever been afraid.

1:57 A.M.

Something woke Willa. It wasn't that hard of a feat, considering she hadn't been sleeping well as of late. Willa shivered. Even the inside of her body felt the chill. She wasn't sure if a human heart could actually shudder, but it felt like hers was doing that very thing.

She slowly sat upright in bed, wondering if True was awake. She put her feet on the floor when she heard a sound, like something falling off one of her shelves. Her head swung around, but nothing was there.

The noise came again.

And again.

It was outside. At her window. Willa stood and crept slowly, peering cautiously through the darkness beyond her curtains. A faint shadow moved, and Willa jumped backward. She had felt her heart shudder before, but now it felt like it was leaping and pounding against her chest. She leaned in closer, and this time, the shadow appeared again. Only this time, it stopped. It was a human form, which slowly raised its head, staring at Willa. Eyes dark and empty.

Willa squinted, trying to show herself that this was nothing more than a trick of the eyes or a dream. But the figure suddenly came even closer, impossibly close, as if she could feel its cold breath on her face. Startled, Willa scuttled away from the window, trying without success to make sense of what she'd just seen.

It was Carmen. She was standing outside, staring at her. She looked almost exactly as she had on the day she'd died, only faded, like a ghost. Her eyes were different though; they were two black pits, like the enormous hole that had claimed her.

A scream rose inside Willa's throat, but it fell apart as she shivered in the quiet. The fear was replaced with sadness. Carefully, she approached the window as if she were walking toward an open casket. A single tear slid down her cheek as she raised her hand and rested it on the cold glass. "Carmen ..." Willa whispered; her eyes fixed on the image outside.

Carmen tilted her head slightly. She placed her hand on the window, perfectly aligned to Willa's. Closer, now, Willa noticed the differences in her friend. Her clothes were dirty rags, and decayed skin hung from Carmen's bones.

Willa gasped; a chill raced through her. In it, she felt Carmen's sadness and some of her pain. And something else was lurking too—something dark and *wanting*. It felt like a hunger.

She thought of her Aunt True, who'd tried to explain to her countless times what it felt like to make a connection with the energy of the world, with nature and the unseen forces at play all around them. Her aunt had told her that she had the power too, but until now, she didn't believe it, or didn't *want* to believe it anyway.

Now, she had no choice. It was a feeling she didn't like. She closed her eyes, trying to focus on the energy pulsating from the darkness around Carmen. A flash of light entered her mind, and images appeared, dancing in her brain. It was a horrifying vision of Miri George being dragged through the field of decaying cornstalks by her hair, eyes wide, arms and legs flailing. Carmen was wrenching her into the darkness, and Willa knew exactly where she was taking her.

"Oh god!" Willa cried.

"No god ..." Carmen's voice was soft, like a whisper, but cruel.

Willa kept her hand to the window, the glass the only thing separating them. Willa sensed that if she attempted to pull her hand away, Carmen would not allow it. But all the same, she didn't want to. The forces outside her window were strong, and she felt connected to them, as if, for the moment, they were the same entity.

Something changed.

Willa's eyes widened as a denseness seeped in, blanketing the room and obscuring her vision. Terror sprang into Willa's chest. She had the impulse to run, but it was only an impulse; it felt as though rigging chains ran up her legs, gripping her tightly, paralyzing her.

A great silence consumed the room. Something constricted her throat. She started choking, trying to back slowly away, but she couldn't; she was confined. The force clutched her, dragged her closer to the window. It fastened itself on her lips, its grips forcing her mouth open. She tasted foul, murky water on her tongue, finding its way into her lungs. She choked more, perched forward, blood dripping from her nose. In horror, she realized her feet no longer on the floor. She was levitating in the haze that engulfed her bedroom. Everything blurred, and, for the briefest of moments, she knew she was going to die.

Then suddenly, Willa felt the darkness release her as she crashed to the floor. As quickly as it had come, the fog disappeared. Willa sat upright, eyes darting about, and saw a fiendish smile staring at her through the window.

Then, with faint laughter, Carmen stared empty at Willa for a second, then was gone, descending into the darkness.

PART 3

SATURDAY, NOVEMBER 19, 2008

10:14 P.M.

Sam peered through her car's windshield at the Todd residence. Thanksgiving was right around the corner, and the Todds had certainly gone into overload with the decorations this year. *How many fucking turkeys and haystacks do you need?* she thought as she checked her watch. It was sprinkling—a cold November rain that, at night, was so miserable it seemed morning might never show itself again.

Mac sat in the passenger seat, possibly asleep.

"Hey, Mac?"

He barely stirred. "Yeah?"

"Look. Bigfoot just walked across the yard."

"Awesome," he said without moving his head or even bothering to look. "Get a picture. We'll be famous ... and rich."

"You okay?"

"No. This detail sucks."

Sam nodded. This detail *did* suck. But she also knew it was very necessary.

After Virgie Vaughan, no one could deny it. Someone was coming after the girls in Somerdale. The community was in a tailspin, fearing some deranged serial killer. The mayor had instated a curfew. The FBI had swooped in, taking control of the investigations and resigning Mac and Sam—the detectives who had carried the case so far—to this kind of work. Basically ... babysitting.

While Sam and Mac were watching the Todd household, another pair of cops were watching the Hollins' home. And another pair was parked at the Dalton house. If a killer was going to strike, chances were he'd come for one of those three.

The families did not know they were being watched twenty-four hours a day, though the police had told them that units would be driving by on occasion. All three families had seemed appreciative. As Sam watched the lights go out in the Todd house, she wondered what it was like to know police were watching you, because this could be the very last day of your life. A shudder went through her. Tess might not have been an angel but that was a lot of pressure for *anyone* to be under, much less a seventeen-year-old girl.

"You know," Mac said, finally sitting upright and looking through the window. "Someone who can somehow get these girls out of their beds and into the woods then down that manhole *without leaving tracks* ... how will some detectives sitting in cars really put a stop to him?"

"Is that a legitimate worry, or are you just cranky because you're having to sit in a car with me all night?"

He grinned at her with a playful smolder. "Since the age of sixteen, it has been my life's mission to sit in cars at night, alone, with women like you."

"That's flattering. But let's remember how my last tryst with a coworker went."

"Good point." He glanced at her Glock, then into the darkness and sighed. "Seriously, though, this doesn't make sense. It's like this person is a ghost. The girls' cars were at home on the night they died, so they didn't drive out there. No prints. Nothing. It makes no sense."

It was on the tip of Sam's tongue to tell him about the harrowing moment when she'd been alone in Carmen Winstead's room and heard … something. She had badly tried to dismiss it as nothing more than the house settling or old plumbing, but with his mention of a ghost, it made her wonder.

Sam's phone buzzed in the console between them. It was Mitcham, one of the cops stationed in front of the Hollins' house. She put the call on speaker mode. "Kerr and Talbot here."

"Anything going on over there?" Mitcham asked.

"It's raining," Sam said. "And that's just about the most exciting thing."

"Same here. Every light in the house is off except the one in Cassie's bedroom. This might be the most boring street in this whole damn town."

"I'd challenge you on that," Sam said. "But thanks for checking in."

"Of course."

Sam ended the call and checked the clock—10:35. Their relief unit wasn't due until two in the morning. She knew the two hours between midnight and two would be the longest. Virgie had died two days ago, and she had been in this position twice since then. Those two hours stretched on forever, just like they did on her sleepless nights.

"Go ahead and take a nap. I'll wake you up in a few, and we can switch."

"We are in a parked car." He tilted his head back and closed his eyes. "Want to know how you can wake me up?"

"An elbow to the balls?"

He shook his head, smiling. "Wake me if anything happens."

Sam refocused on the Todd house. She had originally thought all the lights were out, but now she noticed a very faint glow in the upstairs bedroom farthest to the right—Tess Todd's bedroom.

Sam didn't like the girl, but she found herself pitying Tess. The poor girl had to feel as if someone was hunting her as they slowly made their way through her circle of friends. What must that sort of dread feel like? She watched that little sliver of faint light along the window's edge, wondering if Tess was finally feeling even the slightest bit of remorse for her actions.

10:37 P.M.

Tess was walking into the bathroom, preparing to take a shower, when she felt it. Just for a moment, she could have sworn someone was watching her. It was a feeling she had experienced several times following Carmen Winstead's death, but it was more solid this time. Realer.

Ever since the news of Virgie's death, she felt dirty. Maybe because out of everyone, Virgie was her favorite. *My bitch in training,* she'd always called her. She had broken down at least five times since they'd found Virgie in that fucking manhole. She had taken four showers in the past thirty-six hours, and yet she still didn't feel clean.

She undressed in front of the mirror, as she usually did, looking herself over for any signs of getting plump, ensuring her body was as perfect as it could be. She had already accepted that her breasts wouldn't be as big as she wanted and had plans to get implants before college. Her mother had finally agreed. But other than that, and a small birthmark on her inner thigh, she'd always been happy with the way she looked.

But tonight, she barely cared. Instead of looking for imperfections, she looked for grime, dirt, and bugs. God, why did she feel so dirty? She felt as if she had been rolling around in mud, as if insects were crawling all over her, though there was no sign of dirt or grit anywhere.

The hot stream of water sprayed off Tess's chest and flowed down her breasts. She stood in the shower, head back, eyes shut, feeling the strings of water slip down her stomach, thighs, and legs. Where normally it'd feel good to her, relaxing, now the anxiety was too much. She instantly started scrubbing, trying to feel clean. She couldn't even fathom what the next few days would be like. She had not been able to make it through Miriam's funeral, and Virgie's would be ten times worse. She was now starting to wonder if her friends had been right—this *was* getting scary.

It hit her like a punch in the gut, the feeling she was being spied on. Hunted. Stalked. Had Miri and Virgie felt this too? She wondered if that was why she felt so dirty. Maybe it was guilt. But guilty about what? Carmen Winstead? *For the last time, it was an accident.*

She pushed away the thoughts. She'd be fine. In another few weeks, everything would be back to normal. After all, the police were working hard to keep anything from happening to her and Cassie.

A few times, she felt herself wanting to cry—and maybe she was. With the water cascading down her face, it was hard to tell. When she was done washing, she went over her body one more time, just to be sure. The last thing she wanted was to wake at three in the morning, unable to go back to sleep because she felt the filth all over her, crawling on her skin like maggots. The thought of it made her cringe.

As she pushed her face under the stream of water again, she felt something brush against her foot. She wiped the water from her eyes and looked down. Nothing but clean and clear water rushed toward the drain.

Tess tilted her face toward the stream again, closing her eyes and forcing her mind to release those morbid thoughts. She needed to get a grip. Maybe a short stay at the nut bend would help—

or, as her mother called it, the Moonstruck Country Club. Tess remembered visiting her grandmother there a few times as a kid. Stress or something, she never got the straight answer. But either way, that was *not* something she was about to subject herself to. College was just around the corner, and she was almost out of here. Once she left, she'd put this town and all her problems far behind her and never look back. She wasn't going to let something like stress, anxiety, or Carmen fucking Winstead stand in her way.

Just as she began soaping herself again, something ran across her foot. She jumped and saw something moving near the drain.

A gurgling chuckle filled the bathroom. Then a stench of garbage, of rot filled her nostrils, making her gag. The laughter echoed again, and Tess stood in terror as she focused on the drain between her feet. Just an ordinary drain, full of holes, water gurgling down into the black spaces beyond, nothing to see here.

But …

She froze as she peered into the dark recesses and saw it. Something was staring at her—a human eyeball, lid narrowed. Red flecks were scattered across the dark iris and into its sclera.

Tess dropped the soap and blinked. She closed her eyes, wishing it away. Around her, the water fell, as if nothing had changed … except, once again, she felt the grime, the insects, crawling on her skin.

She slowly forced one eye open, not wanting to see, but when she did, it was gone. *That's it. I'm going insane.* She reached for the knob to turn off the water.

Then the gurgling sound came again. This time, louder.

As she stared down, unable to move, her heart throbbing in her chest, a decayed finger pushed up against the drain. The flesh was torn and slightly rotten, the bones like waterlogged sticks. The silver drain cover violently popped out of the hole and rested in front of Tess.

With a massive belch, murky, thick liquid splashed upon the tub's white basin in chunks, coating her skin. More laughter and her name bounced off the bathroom walls, echoing in her mind.

Tess opened her mouth to scream, but nothing would come out but a faint gasp. Her voice was locked—or the scream was so large it was lodged in her throat. She choked, gasping for air, wanting to breathe. Gagging, Tess felt something wedged in her throat—something tangible, thick, something not supposed to be there.

She reached into her mouth and pulled out clumps of long, stringy black hair. In reflex, she doubled over and retched all over her chest.

Knees shaking, she struggled backward to the other end of the shower, knocking over shampoo bottles as she gripped the lace of the shower curtain in her trembling fingers. She turned her head, not wanting to see the black hole opened in the shower floor.

"*Tess,*" a clotted voice echoed, followed by gurgling laughter.

A small squeak of a scream escaped Tess's mouth. Slowly, Tess stepped out of the tub, unable to look away from the shower. In her haste, her still-wet feet slipped, and her gaze finally broke. She fell backward and struck her head on the tile floor.

The water was still running in the shower as little black fireworks ignited in her line of sight. She fought to stay conscious but knew she was going to lose it. She felt everything slipping away, like she was falling fast asleep. As the world went hazy before her eyes, she saw the fuzzy shape of … *something*.

Carmen Winstead stood in front of the tub, her skin had been stripped away leaving decomposing flesh and her black eye sockets gazed downward, staring at her as if she were weak prey.

11:07 P.M.

Tess opened her eyes sometime later to the sound of her mother gently knocking on the door. She bolted upright, scanning the bathroom as her heart thundered, her eyes agape, and tears flowing down her cheeks. But the bathroom was empty. It was a perfectly normal bathroom, steam lingering from the hot water still running in the tub. Tess tried to focus, but her head pounded from the fall, and her vision swam.

"Tess, are you okay?"

"Yeah, yeah I'm fine."

This wasn't true. She had hit her head pretty hard, and she had no idea how long she'd been laying on the floor. What had she seen in the tub, coming up from the drain? Had it just been something her mind conjured from the fall? She slowly tried to rise to her feet but fell back down. She raised her hand and felt the back of her head. Amidst her wet hair was a small bump protruding from her skull, but there was no blood.

A sharp pain ripped across her temples like a slingshot. Her head reeled; she wasn't sure she'd ever had a headache this bad in her life.

"You sure? That water has been going for a while now."

"I know, Mom, jeez. Leave me alone."

Immediately, the sight of that decaying finger came to mind. She quickly scrambled to her feet as the pain in her head pounded like a bass drum. She grabbed the white robe hanging on the back of the door and glanced at the tub. It was clean. The water still beating on the basin was clear. No sign of grime. No mud. No fingers. She studied the drain hole as she reached in and shut off the water, almost expecting to see *something* there ... watching her.

She approached the door and turned the knob, hoping her mother was not still standing there. A story like that would surely get her a weekend stay at Moonstruck Country Club, and Tess was too exhausted to think of another explanation.

She entered her bedroom and was about to close the door when she heard her mom calling her name from the hallway.

"Yes? Damn."

"You need to talk?"

"No, Mom. I don't need to talk," she responded, a snide little bite to her words as she closed the door fully. "I just want to sleep."

She knew her mother was still there, judging from the shadows moving in the sliver under the door. As she waited for her mother to leave, she checked her phone and saw she'd missed a text message. She expected it to be Cassie, but she was wrong.

It's Willa.

Tess stared at the message for a moment, finger hovering over the delete button. *Yeah, not going to respond to you, witch.*

Why would she? What would she and Willa have to talk about? But a second later, curiosity got the best of her. Maybe Willa knew something about what had been going on. In fact, maybe Willa had been behind it all. *What do you want? And how did you get my number?*

We need to meet. Tonight. At the cornfield. It's serious.

Tess trembled as she read the message, and it sent a shiver down her spine. The cornfield? That was convenient. If Willa knew what was going on, and if she was responsible, then this bitch was in for a world of hurt. *Okay, witch. You got my attention. Give me half an hour.*

She quickly opened a text to Cassie. Safety in numbers. Cassie'd probably bitch and moan about how scared she was, but if she knew what was good for her, she'd listen. *Cass, meet me at the Stop N' Save, half an hour.*

A moment later, a text came back. *Are you crazy?*

Tess rolled her eyes and punched in, *if you want to end this once and for all, you'll come.*

A moment later, sufficiently beaten, Cassie replied, *K.*

Tess set down her phone, grimacing at the pain in her head and at the audacity of Willa Dalton. She looked out to the rainy night outside her window, then back to her door. Her mother had finally moved.

She waited a moment and slowly got dressed, slid on her shoes, and looked back to the window. For a moment, she thought she saw a face staring back, watching her. But, of course, it had only been streaks of rain falling down the glass. Watching it made Tess feel sticky … dirty like maggots and throngs of insects were crawling on her. And when she thought of the eye staring at her in the drain, she didn't think she'd ever truly feel clean again.

11:16 P.M.

True had swept the kitchen twice and even vacuumed it, but tiny shards of glass remained pressed against the edges of the counters and cupboards. The memory of some unseen force tearing her kitchen apart was still vivid in her mind, haunting and digging deeper with each passing moment. She had always known the spiritual forces of nature were capable of physical violence when pressed hard enough, but she had never actually experienced it. She was peaceful and pure, but to see and feel a darkness like that …

A shiver ripped up her spine. It all felt different now. She couldn't deny something dark was out there, and it was aware of her openness to it. She feared for Willa most of all. It was stronger than anything she'd experienced. The morning after it had happened, she even thought she might have angered it. Placing that protection around Willa could have disturbed the universe, and now it was seeking her, vengeful. But she also knew if it had wanted to attack her, it would have done so that night.

She had to trust the spirits. She had to believe that whatever part Willa was to play in this, they would protect her. Perhaps they would even open Willa's eyes to her powers.

True peered through the living room window. Nothing moved outside—nothing she could see, anyway—but she could sense something shifting, something on its way. The night was alive out there. She felt it in her bones, on her skin, in every strand of hair. Her scalp tingled softly as the lights in her house dimmed slightly. They flickered at the same time, briefly, but enough for her to notice.

Not wanting Willa to hear, True kept her voice in a soft but trembling whisper. "Please."

The lights behind her flickered again, more severely. The presence was there with her, circling all around.

True breathed deeply, trying to keep her panic at bay. She focused her mind on the forces of nature all around her and gave a mental push to the darkness that surrounded her. She felt the uneasiness leave her at once, a sense of calmness rushing in. Remarkably, she sensed the darkness settling. Rather than a frantic energy circling the place, it now felt like nothing more than another presence in the room, maybe even a friend.

With Willa firmly in her mind, True slowly stepped from the window and walked down the hallway toward Willa's room. She slowly opened the door, not wanting the old, creaking hinges to wake her. She pushed it open, slowly revealing the darkness of the room.

And the empty bed.

True's heart seemed to slam into the floor of her chest. She slapped at the switch on the wall by the door, and the room flooded with light. It revealed the same thing she had seen in the darkness—Willa was gone.

"Willa …?"

She stepped closer, trying to make sense of the sight in front of her. When she looked at the light, it exploded, the filaments snapping within the bulb, casting her in darkness.

"No," True cried out, her eyes volleying around the room. "You can't. She's done nothing! You just can't!"

She nearly started screaming, but some strange emotion settled over her like a blanket. It was veiled and bleak, unpleasant, but it was somehow reassuring. And as it wrapped around her, she thought she heard a whisper spoken from the throat of the night.

She is safe.

True went absolutely still and let those words sink into her. Unable to deny the sense of peace that came in those three words, her muscles relaxed, and her heart sagged in her chest.

She fumbled to the bed, collapsing against the cool sheets, and waited. Calling that detective to report Willa missing would be pointless. They couldn't do anything now. She couldn't do anything either. Whatever was taking place outside was beyond them all.

While it alarmed her that Willa might be a part of it, she hoped it would all be set right by the masculinity of the sun's energy when it rises to cast a new beginning. Until then, she could only wait.

11:32 P.M.

The rain had stopped coming down, but it had left its mark. Everything beyond the windshield looked miserably cold—not quite *wet* but just damp enough to add another bite to the early winter weather. Looking at it nearly made Sam drift off to sleep. While Mac's allotted naptime was over, Sam would not let herself fall into a slumber. It felt irresponsible, especially given how much this case was kicking her ass.

Sam grabbed her phone to find a podcast to help her not doze off, but as soon as she started scrolling, it rang. The name on the display was PARKS. Amy Parks was one of the officers stationed in front of the Dalton property. *Probably just checking in,* Sam thought.

"Hey, Parks," she said, answering the call. "Things slow over th—"

"Willa Dalton is on the move."

It took Sam a moment to figure out what exactly that meant. But the moment she realized the implications, she relaxed the phone on her shoulder while she shook Mac to life.

"Breaking curfew, huh? In a car?"

"No, on foot. She went out her bedroom window, ran across the yard, and slipped into the woods."

"Headed in which direction?"

"Southwest."

Sam took a moment to think this over. As Mac sat upright in his seat, now very much awake, Sam pictured a map of Somerdale in her mind. Southwest from the Dalton property was in the opposite direction of Tess Todd's house. And while it might lead to Cassie Hollins, it really depended on which route Willa took through the woods.

"You're the lead on this; what do I do?" Amy asked.

"If she's going southwest, she'll end up coming to State Road 114. Head there right now and go up and down that stretch, keeping an eye out for her."

"Roger that. And what do you—"

"Shit," Mac said from beside her. "Sam, look."

Sam followed his line of sight to the Todd's front yard and saw Tess walking down the front path toward her car. She got in and sat there for a moment. Parked half a block away behind a neighbor's work truck, Sam and Mac watched as the car slowly crept out of the driveway.

Mac groaned and started the ignition. "Guess curfew means nothing to these people."

"Parks, we've got Tess Todd on the move as well. Let's hang up and switch this to radio." "10-4."

She ended the call and watched the car slowly roll into the street. The car did not look as if it had been cranked yet—no tail-lights, no exhaust—making Sam assume Tess had simply shifted to Neutral and let the car roll, hoping to make a clean getaway.

Once she got a fair distance from the house, Tess finally cranked the car. As she started down the street, Mac slowly pulled away from the curb and lingered behind to ensure he gave Tess enough of a head start.

"Sneaky little bitch." Sam said as her phone rang yet again as Mac switched on the CB radio beneath the dash. It was old school for sure, but they used it quite often. Sam checked her caller display and saw Mitcham's name again. Even before she answered it, Sam had an idea of what Mitcham would tell her.

"Hey, Sam? Cassie just left her house. She's on foot, sprinting down her road. She's— Wait … She just jumped into the woods. Running through the forest …"

"Get on your radio," Sam said. "Willa and Tess are on the move too."

In the brief silence that followed, she and Mac shared an uneasy glance.

"What the hell is going on?"

Sam had no answer.

Mac waited for Tess to turn at the end of the street, then crept along behind her, headlights off, like a ghost.

SUNDAY NOVEMBER 20, 2008

12:14 A.M.

They kept their distance, though when Tess reached the main stretch of Somerdale, there was no way to truly hang back.

"She turned right at the stoplight of Elizabeth Street. Where the hell is she going?" Mac asked, peering through the windshield.

A slight crackling noise sounded from the CB radio. "Kerr, this is Parks. I've been up and down this stretch of State Road 114 and haven't seen any sign of Willa."

"Just keep looking. Mitcham, are you on the line?"

"I'm here, Kerr."

"Any sights on Cassie?"

"Yeah. She came out of the woods near Leander's Farm, ran up about two hundred feet, and went back into the woods. Headed in an eastern direction."

"Okay. We've got eyes on Tess. She just turned right onto Elizabeth Street. If we can all just keep an—" The words froze in her mouth as sudden realization came over her.

Tess was heading in a slightly eastern direction, down Elizabeth Street and to the far end of town. Cassie was also heading east. And depending on what course Willa took through the forests, she'd end up on that same path.

"They're all heading to the sewer reservoir," she said, the words sending a chill through her. "Jesus, they're all headed for the Holt family farm—toward the cornfield."

Parks uttered a curse over the line.

Mitcham's voice came in, rather strained. "You sure about that?"

"Not positive, no. But it certainly looks that way."

"Roger that."

It took everything within Sam not to tell Mac to floor it and pull Tess over right there and then. But the truth of the matter was they had absolutely no idea what was going on. This was not an instance where they could just stop Tess, question her, and put an end to the plan. No, they would have to follow along to see *what* the plan was. Sam could only hope the timing was perfect and they could step in at the right time. There were answers to be had, and Sam intended to have those answers before the night was over.

About five minutes after Tess had turned onto Elizabeth Street, she pulled into the darkened parking lot of the Stop N' Save convenience store.

Mac did his best to remain out of sight, turning a hard right into the nearest spot he could find, a small alleyway that ran between a local diner and the hair salon. Mac turned in his seat, straining his neck.

Sam reclined her seat and did the same, doing her best to see Tess's car. She could see it, but just barely, as she had perhaps knowingly parked in the darkest corner of the lot. "Can you see her any better than I can?"

"I can see her pretty well. She's just sitting there, doing nothing." He reported this over the CB to Mitcham and Parks. When he was done, he stared at Tess's car. "You think she's having second thoughts about whatever she's up to?"

"Maybe," Sam said. "Or maybe she saw us behind her. Maybe she knows we're on to her. If she doesn't move within another five minutes, I think we might go down there and see what she's up to."

Mitcham's voice crackled over the radio. "Cassie just came out on Harper Avenue, heading east, right toward you."

"Got it," Mac said and eyed Sam. "She's meeting with Tess, I bet you."

They sat in silence for three minutes; the only interruption came from Parks, updating them from time to time. Her voice crackled over the airway, sounding as worried as Sam felt. "No clue where Willa went. I swear, it's like the girl just disappeared or something."

"Keep looking." Even if the girl *had* vanished, she was now all but certain this would come to an end in the same place it had started: just past the cornfield at the Holt Farm, right by the old sewage runoff structure.

Mac stared carefully, his eyes peering through the shadows bouncing off the car's hood. He suddenly sat upright, his forehead nearly smacking the windshield. "Right there, right there! Cassie's here."

Sam watched as a shadow dashed across the street. "Is it her?" Sam could hear a little hesitation in Mac's tone.

"Oh yeah. It's her, all right. Look at the side ponytail. It's definitely Cassie Hollins."

Cassie ran directly toward Tess's car.

Tess was moving the car out of the lot before Cassie even had a chance to close her door. When she pulled out, she took a left.

Mac waited for them to get out of sight before he rolled from their hiding place and coasted in the same direction. When he saw Tess's car again, it was turning right, not giving a turn signal.

It was a turn Sam had expected them to take. Likewise, she knew the next turn would come about three miles later; that would take them down a winding road toward the Holt's farm. Knowing where the girls were headed now, Sam told Mac to back off; she did not see the need to tail them. They could keep their distance now, staying well out of sight. The only question was, where was Willa?

"Why do you think they're all meeting? *There,* of all places?"

Sam did not answer right away. No, something didn't add up. "I don't know," she finally said as red taillights brightened the darkness in front of them. Sam watched vigilantly as Tess's car slowed down.

Like a moving speck in the darkness, Tess's car took the turn onto the thin back road known to the locals as Shadow Stretch—a winding, tortuous road that went in for about twenty miles, unmarked in most places, that eventually emptied onto a two-lane in the neighboring county. Sam knew, though, that four miles down, Tess would make a sharp left onto a dirt track that led to the farms. She wasn't sure how they would get to the cornfield, as she was almost certain the Holt family kept a little iron security bar across the road.

The car was silent as they closed in on the cornfield. Mac remained on the CB radio, giving instructions. "We're thirty seconds behind Tess's car. I want both backup units to stop at the corner of Shadow Stretch. The fewer units, the more we can surprise them. Hang back and wait. Once we have them cornered, we'll call for an assist."

Ahead, Tess's brake lights glowed as she turned left onto the dirt road that led to the farm.

Mac slowed a bit to avoid being seen. Once Tess's car was out of sight, hidden by the woods that lined both sides of the drive, he accelerated. The car rocketed forward a bit and, suddenly, shuddered and lurched. The engine puttered and died. All the electronics and dash lights went completely dark.

"What the hell?" Mac groaned, staring at the dashboard. He tried the ignition, and though it turned easily, the engine would not respond. It didn't even *try* to turn over. "Shit," Mac mumbled and grabbed the receiver on the CB radio. He clicked the side button and got out, "Mitcham ... Parks ... we've got a—" before he realized the CB radio was just as dead as the car.

Sam reached for her cellphone and flipped it open but had a feeling it would be useless. Even before she saw its screen and pushed the button on the side to wake it, she knew it would be dead too. She was glad to see Mac looked just as alarmed as her.

He opened his phone, and his eyes searched for hers in the darkness. "Sam, what the hell is going on?"

"Don't know. But we're less than three hundred yards from the road. And if that gate is up, we can still catch up to them."

Mac nodded, but it was clear he was still confused and a little on edge.

It was a feeling Sam understood completely when they stepped from the car. She couldn't put her finger on it, but something felt different. The air felt thick, like miserable humidity, only in winter. She buttoned her peacoat as a chill snaked up the back of her neck. As she took her first steps away from the car, she could swear someone was following her. Watching her. Despite being surrounded by nothing but desolate, bare trees, she felt eyes all over. She glanced back, but, of course, Shadow Stretch was just as dead as everything else around them.

Without saying a word to one another, Sam and Mac ran forward, their soft footfalls like whispers in the night. Sam still felt the sensation of being followed, like someone had known they would be here and was escorting them, delivering them into the darkness.

236 | TRACE MURILLO

12:28 A.M.

Willa had no clue where she was going, but, as she ran through the forest, she could sense something else there with her. When she felt the urge to veer in another direction, an unseen force would turn her, guiding her. It was more than a little voice inside her head, more like a physical sensation—her entire body working like a machine, the nerves and muscles responding to an impulse that was not her own.

A couple of times, when she got winded, she would try to stop to rest, only to be revived by whatever force was moving her along. Her lungs that had been burning ten seconds before would suddenly feel refreshed and ready for her to plunge forward, as if the thing was breathing air into her lungs.

She had no clue where she was going or where she even was. Somewhere in the woods. She leaped over fallen logs and boulders she could not see in the dark. Somehow, the power guiding her was also keeping her out of danger. Her eyes brimmed with tears when she sensed it might be Carmen somewhere in the darkness with her. Maybe it was Carmen *controlling* her, bringing her here.

But it was also familiar. She had sensed it many times before during childhood. She had sensed it on the nights when Aunt True had gotten very deep into her practices. Yes, she had always ignored it and told herself it was hocus-pocus nonsense, but deep down, she'd known there was more to it. Something real. It was here with her now—not just guiding her but inside her, directing her and thinking for her.

And though it was scary, it felt *right*.

Despite the force seeming to take great care with her, she had several cuts and scratches on her face and palms from low-hanging branches. At one point, she glimpsed between the trees and saw a paved back road she was pretty sure was State Road 22, also known as Shadow Stretch. There wasn't much out here, so when she passed that, she shuddered at the thought of where she was headed.

Why? But as soon as the thought went through her head, there was another voice. It was not the voice of whatever was propelling her through the woods, it was a voice she had sensed for most of her life while living with True. *"Keep the darkness out your soul Willa, or it will eat you up like puddin'."* That was True's voice, but it'd never made sense to her until this moment. She remembered True talking about becoming available to the energies and spirits. *"They use us like a pot,"* True would always say. *"We offer them our body and mind when they need it."*

Was the darkness using her now?

She wished True was with her. Maybe then it would make more sense. But when she took another step, her gaze landed on a car parked in front of the iron barrier across the dirt road that led into Holt Family Farm. It was familiar; it was Tess's car.

When she saw it, a little thrill crept inside her. The thing that had pushed her to this spot wanted her to stay, to keep walking forward until she came to the open field. She could feel it inside, urging her forward with a gentle nudge.

So that was exactly what she did. She stepped forward.

She recalled the moments before leaving her house. She had a vague memory of texting Tess. Why? When had the spirits begun to use her? And most importantly, what did they have planned?

Whatever it was, it had worked. Tess had taken her seriously. Tess was here.

Willa let the force guide her out of the tree line and into the large, open expanse of farmland. The field where the corn festival had taken place lay before her. To the left, a bit farther ahead, the tall and now mostly dead stalks of the cornfield poked upward into the night like jagged knives. She could hear soft, murmuring voices coming from that direction, so it was no surprise when she felt her feet taking her there.

After a few seconds, the talking stopped. Two murky shapes came into view, huddled together a few feet from where the cornfield began. The clouds had parted, and the moon was a little more than a quarter full, but it was more than enough light to reveal the figures of Tess and Cassie peering at her in the darkness.

"What do you want, freak?" Tess asked.

Willa heard fear in Tess's words. That was good. Willa wasn't sure if she was pleased to hear it, but the darkness inside her seemed to purr with pleasure. "We can work together and stop this shit," Willa heard her voice say.

"Stop what?" Cassie asked. Willa could hear the frailty in her tone as well.

"*You* did it, didn't you?" Tess intervened. "You and your witch-ass aunt killed Miri and Virgie, didn't you? And now you're … you're *cursing us!*"

"Of course not, that's just stupid."

Willa approached them and stopped no more than five feet away.

Cassie was stepping backward, but Tess held her ground. "I didn't kill her, you know," Tess said. "It was an accident. I didn't kill your stupid friend."

"Maybe it was," Willa said. "But it was an accident that would have never happened if you didn't fear everything you don't understand—everything different than you."

"You don't know what you're—"

"Does it make you feel better to tear down those less than you? Does it make you feel prettier? More powerful?" She could tell the words were cutting into Tess like a blade.

Behind Tess, Cassie was still slowly stepping away, looking legitimately frightened, and, for a moment, Willa wondered if she too could sense the force that had led Willa here. Were they sensing the night breathing all around them, the panting of the earth anticipating what was about to happen?

Tess still held her ground, though Willa had never seen the girl looking so off her game. "The cops have already talked to me. I'm innocent, Willa."

"Are you?"

"Yes!"

Willa was now nearly face to face with Tess, their breaths mingling into a single cloud between them in the frigid air. "Maybe in the eyes of the cops and your stupid parents and friends. But there's someone else you have to answer to, Tess. And she knows the truth. She knows what you did. What you *are* …"

Tess's eyes filled with rage.

Willa felt a hard slap across the face. In the silence of the night, it was as loud as a shotgun blast. Willa staggered backward in surprise, expecting pain, but there was none. She raised her eyes to Tess, completely unfazed.

Tess's eyes widened. "I'm not listening to any more of this bullshit. It was an accident, and I am done talking about that cunt Carmen P-i-g-s-t-e-a-d." Tess cocked her head and rolled her eyes at Willa. "Plus, she's gone. Dead. Maggot food."

"She's not gone, not dead, and you know it."

"You're as crazy as your aunt. She *is* gone. I saw it happen. Okay, so what if I did push her? I didn't think she would fall in the stupid hole." Tess smirked. "But she did … so it was an accident. You called us out here in the middle of the night, and it better not have been to tell us that karma's a bitch, and we have to answer to a dead girl. So, what do you want?"

Willa only smiled.

Tess held her gaze. "So, you did kill Miri? Virgie? Is that what this is? Some kind of revenge plan?" She glanced at Cassie, who now looked scared beyond belief. "It's two against one. You can't do the same to both of us."

Willa shook her head. "I want things to be fair. And it is." She spit directly into Tess's face. "She wants to play with you."

Tess looked around; eyes narrowed. "Play? What are you talking about?"

"You will see." Willa did what she sensed. She looked at Tess and, in a split second, took off into the cornfield, running in the direction of the manhole, where Carmen Winstead met her demons. And where she knew Tess would soon meet hers.

12:40 A.M.

Cassie called out for Tess when she went running into the corn after Willa. They needed to stay together. Obviously. That was the first rule—a rule Tess had just gone and broken.

Even Cassie, as naïve as they sometimes called her, could see it was a setup. Willa wanted Tess to chase her, wanted to separate them, so she could do the same thing to them that she'd done to Virgie and Miri. But Tess either did not hear her or chose to ignore it. Tess tore off and never turned back before disappearing between the rows.

Cassie took three steps into the cornfield, wondering if she should try to keep up. It seemed futile. Tess was already gone, and it was too dark.

While Cassie knew it was artificial to think any type of spirits were at work in the world, she did believe in evil. Something about this field was unholy. She quickly recoiled her foot and froze. Something inside told her to run, but she couldn't. The longer she remained out there, surrounded by a night that somehow seemed to be alive, the more she thought of demons—of the unseen forces of darkness that were forever at work all around her.

She retrieved her cellphone from her pocket, ready to call for help. That was what they should've done from the beginning, what she'd tried to convince Tess of, when she had met her at the market. But Tess had wanted to "teach that bitch a lesson" instead.

The display was black anyway. She pushed frantically on the buttons to wake it up, but nothing happened. It was dead. She pressed the buttons again, hoping, praying, when she heard something scrambling through the cornfield right in front of her.

It wasn't the wind. The wind couldn't make the stalks move like that.

The stalks, brittle and stripped by the winter's chill, were leaning toward her, like skeletal fingers. Not just one or two but, slowly, they all rushed forward, like waves rippling the shoreline. As the stalks seemed to turn toward her, enveloping her, swallowing her, Cassie felt a surge of fear in her throat. She wanted to run, but it was too late. Everything was closing in around her. The fear reached into her bones. The mud sucked at her feet, and the stalks scratched at her skin, ripping her clothes, lashing at her arms, her back, her face. She plunged to her knees, sobbing, reaching out, flailing. Burning pain shot through her. As she fell backward, sprawling, a wail erupted from her throat.

Lying flat on her back in the mud, Cassie's breathing went shallow. She slowly opened her eyes and watched as a soft cloud scudded across the night sky, obscuring the sliver of moon. The heavens looked big to her, bigger than she had ever seen. In a blink though, they darkened. She thought of the day Jesus was crucified, the rumbling black clouds circling his cross, the sin devouring him. And the world around her turned silent.

Pulling in her legs, she stumbled to her feet, the wind gushing violently. She stared across the cornfield as the rustling of the corn moved toward her like a locomotive, the stalks rushing forward, stretching toward her with some sort of unnatural elasticity. The leaves and husks reached for her, slapping her face, before grabbing at her ankles, constricting around her limbs like a snake, tugging her deeper between the rows.

Cassie's back slammed to the ground as she felt another stalk wrap around her other foot. Then, like serpents, the dried shucks wiggled their way up her body, slithering up her skin, spreading

242 | Trace Murillo

and multiplying and growing, cuffing each of her wrists. Breath rushed from her as she was yanked forward, deeper into the field. She tried grabbing some of the nearby stalks, but they were razor-sharp, slicing her palms, working against her. She screamed as it dragged her along the ground, rocks and sticks tearing the flesh from her back. A vine forced its way into her mouth, gagging her, cutting her scream short.

Her breath slowed as grains of dirt moved into her lungs. One stalk ventured up her shirt and clawed at her breasts like fingers while another tickled her thigh, arching its way between her legs, taking away everything pure inside of her. Cassie tried to scream again, but her body was incapable. As the darkness claimed her and pulled her deeper into the corn, Cassie felt herself slipping away. Her eyes filled with tears, and a deep sob grew inside her throat.

"I'm sorry," Cassie whispered as the mist fell all around, devouring her, pulling her deeper into the darkness.

12:44 A.M.

Sam and Mac had just stepped onto the dirt road leading to the Holt property when they heard the first shriek. It was not one of pain but of terror and surprise. It was cut off rather quickly, as if swallowed by the night.

Without missing a beat, Sam glanced at her cellphone. "The damn thing is still dead. It's useless. We're stranded out here."

"Well, maybe if Parks or Mitcham try to radio us and get dead silence, they'll come looking for us."

Sam nodded, but that did nothing to slow her. In fact, as the trees bordering the dirt road thickened and seemed to envelop them, she pushed on faster. The gathering darkness seemed to release an energy in her that she had never felt before. It seemed alive, exhilarating. It was not out of fear or adrenaline but more like a need, a want—maybe even a temptation. She wasn't sure, but she could feel those answers she so desperately sought were out there, close. She wanted to get to the bottom of it. She quickened her step again, a cold stream of sweat rolling down her back as the cool wind braced her, whipping her ponytail across her cheek. She instinctively pulled at her coat as she crunched over the frozen leaves beneath her feet. She periodically looked over her shoulder to ensure Mac was still following close behind.

With his long strides, he was doing a good job keeping up with her, even though she was in better shape. But his right hand was already hovering over his sidearm. He was nervous too.

She didn't blame him though; the shriek they'd heard a few minutes ago had been blood-chilling. But the deeper they got into the woods—and the closer they came to the cornfield—the more certain Sam became that guns would not be much help to them. Not on this night.

It had been eating away at her bones since she had first stepped foot in Carmen Winstead's bedroom, and now, she couldn't shake it. And as the dirt road wound deeper into the woods, the thought felt more and more logical … and terrifying. *Maybe it was possible. Maybe there are things around us we can't see.* The thought made Sam direct her flashlight toward the wooded area that lined the field. Every branch glistened in the light against the dark sky. The shapes of the trees looked like giants standing watch—*protecting.*

Sam's heart pounded, and her lungs begged for a break when she came to a parked car. As she expected, a small iron barricade blocked the road to help keep out trespassers.

"Hold up." Mac panted, resting his hands on his knees. "What's our plan?"

"I don't know. But some strange shit is going on here. Let's move."

Sam and Mac paused for only a moment longer before stepping carefully around the iron bar. As they moved forward again,

Sam glanced over her shoulder. She once again felt like someone was following, watching them. But the only thing she saw behind them was the windshield of Tess's car glistening in the scant moonlight.

12:49 A.M.

If I catch her, I'll kill that bitch … Tess had never been so angry. She was practically blind with rage, imagining just what she would do when she got her hands around Willa's neck. She would strangle her for sure. Or maybe she would crush her head in with a rock. Maybe both.

At one point, she stopped, her heartbeat pounding in her throat, having no idea which direction Willa had headed. Gathering her bearings and listening, she waited until she heard a shriek behind her—a sound that clearly had come from Cassie. Tess was alarmed at first, but then she groaned. *Great. Cassie probably just saw her own shadow.*

Moments after the scream, she heard another sound of something moving ahead of her between the rows, slowly and carefully. She narrowed her eyes, trying to see any sign of Willa in the darkness ahead of her. Of course, just then, the clouds crept across the moon. Now, it was just too dark, and she—

Something rushed past her so close that she felt its wind on her cheek.

She wheeled around, but nothing was there—except a slight movement in the corn as something ran to the left across the rows. *Willa,* she thought and took off after her. "Come on, bitch! What are you, afraid of me?"

Somewhere in the back of her mind, she understood this was foolish. What would she do when she caught her? Beat her up? Kill her? Would she go that far? *Yes,* said the part of her that was still fuming. *Hell yes. She killed my friends. Made my life a living hell. I'll rip her apart.*

So, she ran, her heart pounding and her eyes sharp, peering into the darkness ahead. Leaves and husks smacked her face. Silk from the stalks clung to her like cobwebs. Also, she was sweating, and she *hated* to sweat. She *hated*—

Something growled to her right.

The sound made her freeze, her knees locking in fear. It was not a shriek or any sound she expected a girl to make—even Willa, the freak. As she stopped running, the stalks and leaves no longer slapping at her, the sound still seemed to echo in her ears. Maybe it hadn't been growling but something similar to it—maybe someone clearing their throat or struggling to breathe.

Whatever it was, it vanished into the air and did not come again. She raised her brow and leaned into the darkness, almost willing the sound to return, but a suffocating silence blanketed the field. Everything frozen, unmoving.

She peered ahead and saw it. A shape, darker than the natural darkness of the night, stood a few feet ahead of her. It was waiting, unwavering.

"Willa," Tess said, her voice tight. She slowly pulled out her cellphone, hoping to use it as a flashlight, to put a spotlight on the images standing before her, but the screen was dead. She extended her arm to where Willa was standing, hoping to catch her before she took off running again. "Willa, you bitch."

There was no response. The shadow moved closer, now less than three feet from Tess. It was hunched over. And it leered at Tess with a smile too wide for its face …

Tess didn't like to be wrong. But she was wrong this time. It was not Willa. "C-Carmen …?" The name came from Tess's mouth like a cracked moan.

She knew it was impossible, but the figure standing before her, illuminated harshly by the light, wasn't Willa at all. Carmen stood, wanting, waiting, smiling. She tilted her head, and the emptiness in her eyes reached forward and gripped Tess. The gaze was dead, and yet hostile. *"Tess ... "* She reached for Tess with a hand of rotted skin and visible bone.

Panic rose inside Tess like a coming tidal wave. A horrid cry surged in her throat. She opened her mouth, but nothing came out except a gasp so faint she could not hear it herself. As she tried to find her voice, she realized she could barely breathe. She tried to run, but her feet seemed mired in the mud, like concrete. The cold tightened its grip around her, and she gave a visible, whole-body shiver as Carmen reached her skeletal fingers toward her.

She released what was meant to be a scream but came out instead like the desperate cries of a wounded animal. She dropped her phone in terror, and before she knew it, she was running through the dark cornfield again. She screamed for her life as she heard something moving through the rows behind her, getting closer and closer with every breath.

12:53 A.M.

Cassie finally managed to draw enough breath to scream, but she used it instead to pray. She felt stupid doing it, uttering prayers to a god she only partially believed in while in the presence of something so unmistakably dark, but it was all she could think to do. She uttered a prayer under her breath, keeping her eyes closed. Whatever had her in its grip, she did not want to see it.

"Lord in Heaven, please be with me here and rescue me. Please, God, be the light in this darkness and help me ... please ... *please, God ...*"

Whatever was pulling at her, still hauling her through the cornfield, seemed to respond to her plea. It was irritated, clearly; it increased its speed, and its grip tightened around her ankles. More than that, she felt it sewing its way inside her, sinking through her skin and into her muscle, into her blood.

And then, it stopped. Cassie gasped, finding enough strength to sit upright. Instantly, she felt stinging and aching in her back. She felt the blood trailing down and the burning of torn flesh on her skin. She was sure her back looked like it had been passed through a meat grinder. But when she opened her eyes, the figure was in front of her.

It had the shape of a person—more accurately, of a female. She saw patches of flesh, but it was mostly comprised of darkness. And though Cassie could see no clear features, she knew exactly what she was looking at. She was looking at Carmen Winstead— or, at the very least, some reincarnated version of her who had become joined with the darkness of the cornfield. It made no sense, and though she was terrified of it, Cassie could not come to think of the thing as evil. While it was certainly terrifying, it looked more *lost* than anything else. Maybe even *hurting*.

It stood roughly five feet from her, gathering the darkness to itself. As it moved closer to her, the shape passed *through* the rows in a malicious kind of way.

"Carmen, please. I had no part in it." She wept, trying to speak through tears and the thick layer of dirt that had been pushed in her mouth. "Okay, maybe a little part. I wanted to stop them, I did, but I was … afraid. You know you've never seen me spiteful, never heard me say anything to you or about you!"

They were meager words, and even as she said them, Cassie still felt guilty. She was right. She had never actively said anything against Carmen, never actually *did* anything. But she had been there, right by Tess's side, laughing, but terrified of not fitting in and being an outcast herself because of the reverent faith her parents had instilled in her. She had been there the entire time— knowing it was wrong—and had done nothing about it.

She could recall the moment Tess had given Carmen that shove, sensing even then that things would never be the same. She had known it was all going too far when they'd chased Carmen through the cornfield that day and cornered her at the manhole.

And she'd done nothing.

"Carmen, I'm so sorry."

It came out of her in a wail of sadness. And while she was still scared for her life, her heart shuddered in sorrow with the absolute weight of how much she meant it.

The dark figure responded by rushing at her, and when what served as its hands wrapped around Cassie's throat, she saw into its eyes. They were no doubt Carmen Winstead's sad eyes. There was pain in them, and a rage that felt like fire.

Cassie screamed and thrashed as the handlike thing wrapped around her throat and lifted her off the ground. The entire time, those eyes looked at her, studying her. Judging her.

"Please," she croaked. And then, Cassie was thrown. The air rushed by her, the corn stalks snapping and bending at her back. She wasn't fully aware of what had happened until she hit the ground. Once again, the wind rushed out of her. She could only make a soundless gasp, curling into a ball, as the pain tore through her body. She was sure she was dying, her lungs failing to draw air.

She lay there, not moving. Tears flooded her eyes, and slowly, breath came back, and every muscle ached. Feeling pain meant she was still alive, after all. And she would take the pain. She deserved it.

But she could still sense Carmen lurking somewhere in the darkness. She heard corn stalks bristling somewhere in the distance, and even farther away, like the echo of a dream, she also heard a voice she was pretty sure belonged to Tess.

The darkness hovered and swarmed over her, but she felt almost safe. Cassie tried to get to her feet, but her body was too weak. Instead, she lay back down on the ground, her body bent in agony, and closed her eyes. She had to simply trust that the darkness was done with her. And she had to believe that her glory belonged to God.

12:57 A.M.

Tess hated that she was crying. She did her best to keep it quiet, moaning or sniffling with every few breaths. The tears cascaded down her face as she ran, her heart slamming and her legs pumping, fueled by fear and adrenaline. She was pretty sure she was running in the wrong direction; she wanted to head to her car, but the darkness behind her was directing her in such a way that she assumed she was running toward the other end of the cornfield—toward the old sewage run off and the manhole Carmen had died in.

She supposed she had known for a few days now that Carmen had been behind all this. But it had all just been so *unbelievable.* Maybe Willa and her crazy Aunt True had planned it all along. Some black witch shit, she wasn't sure. When Miri and Virgie had died, those had been clues. Then there was the occurrence in the shower, that eye in the drain staring at her. She'd managed to deny it, to tell herself she was just going crazy.

But this was real. There was no pinch big enough to wake her from this nightmare. Carmen was here. Nowhere was safe. Everywhere she looked, it felt like something in the darkness just beyond the rows was lurking, hunting. But when she dared a glance behind her, nothing was there. Everything was still, flat. The moon reappeared, and the cornfield looked almost peaceful, faithfully reflecting the pure white light of its core. Whatever had been chasing her was gone, leaving the quiet, still night.

But several feet to her left, running vertically along a row, the tops of the cornstalks rattled. Hurried feet pounded the soft ground, like rough whispers. *Willa …*

Tess ran in that direction, not so much because she wanted to kill Willa anymore. Now, she just didn't want to be alone. Whether she wanted to admit it or not, she *was* scared. Tess maneuvered into the same row as Willa and took off running, her legs moving as fast as they had when she thought she was running for her life. She then released a guttural scream, a mix of terror and rage.

Willa looked back just as Tess closed the space between them and dove at her.

She slammed into Willa's stomach like a running back, and both girls fell in a heap. When Willa was beneath her, Tess responded in a way she had honestly not been expecting. Something inside her went black, and she drew up her right hand and made a fist.

The first blow landed squarely across Willa's left cheek. The impact and feel of it shocked her for a moment but not long enough to prevent her from throwing another punch, and then another. "You bitch! You did this! You and your sick aunt! What did you do?"

Somehow, after the first few punches, Willa raised a hand and blocked her.

Tess stared into Willa's eyes. Blood dripped from Willa's nose, and the sight of the blood—placid in the dark veil of night—was somehow intoxicating. Almost beautiful.

Willa grabbed a handful of dirt and threw it at Tess's face, momentarily blinding her. As Tess screamed, Willa grabbed Tess's shoulders and pushed her off her, sending her sprawling backward into the corn.

Tess cried out and instantly scrambled to her feet.

Willa did the same, bleeding from her nose and a busted lip, but fully prepared to fight.

Screaming at one another like two battle-tested warriors would not fix anything. But Tess had to finish this, for Virgie. For Miri.

Willa rushed at Tess again, her head down, like a ram. Before she could strike, she froze and peered into the darkness.

At first, Tess heard nothing, but then she noticed the corn waving toward her. And laughter.

1:01 A.M.

The wind blustered violently. Willa watched Tess, whose rage was now giving way to something else—fear.

The laughter from the corn, a whispering faint, grew louder and now seemed to surround them.

Willa's eyes probed the field as a shapeless black cloud of gloom rushed through the corn, ripping up the stalks all around them. Willa's eyes met Tess's; the fear had nearly engulfed her. Willa screamed, but before Tess could take one step, something from behind them pushed Willa backward about twenty feet into the stalks and grabbed Tess and lifted her off the ground. Willa watched in shock as Tess hung in the air, clenched by the amorphous darkness, trying to scream.

But when Tess opened her mouth, parts of the darkness sank in, choking her. The dark fist around Tess grew tighter, and her eyes widened in terror and pain.

As tears dripped from Willa's eyes, she turned away, not wanting to see the unthinkable shape that had Tess in its grip. It looked *almost* human in shape, but something was fluid to it as well, like oil.

Tess made a garbled noise, then the cornstalks surrounding her seemed to whisper again as they were brushed aside.

Willa tried to scramble to her feet, but her knees buckled slightly, and a burst of wind brushed the side of her face, blowing back her hair. Slowly lifting her head, she saw Tess hovering about three feet off the ground.

Dried whips from the stalks, almost like tentacles, tightly bound Tess's legs together. Tess was trying to scream, but when she opened her mouth, more of the blackness seeped inside. Something black and oily spilled from her ears, nose, her eyes. The screams she tried to get out became wet gagging whimpers. Her arms were outstretched like a sparrow's wings as it soared into the night. The husks coiled tighter around her, covering her like a mummy ripping her flesh.

Something else caught Willa's attention on the outer edge of the cornfield. Willa watched in terror as a dark figure crawled through the rows toward her.

It was Carmen. She looked almost as she had outside of Willa's window last night, just darker, eviler, like the shadows had devoured her. She slithered toward Tess, grabbed her foot, and yanked Tess into the corn with her. The darkness responded by loosening its grip. As Tess's body was pulled closer toward Carmen, Willa heard the snapping of bones.

Willa, motionless, stared in horror at the ghoul that had once been her friend and now was some evil she could not fathom. The sound that escaped Tess broke Willa—some sort of howling, an old, brittle death cry. Willa turned away and choked on a sob. As she did, the slightest, most pleasant breeze brushed against her face and whispered, "Run."

It was True. Willa had heard her as clear as day.

Run Willa. Run!

Gathering her resolve, Willa obeyed; she ran. She heard another series of sharp cracks and popping. It sounded as if Tess was being crushed, her bones turning to dust. She looked back only once. When she did, Tess was gone.

The amorphous, hovering dark form was gone as well, and the field looked almost … normal. But nothing was normal about this. The dark form had moved on and was now farther off.

She watched the progress of their movement, the bending tops of cornstalks all the way down the row. Willa ran ahead, nearly tripping a few times, realizing where she was going.

Carmen was dragging Tess through the cornfield to the manhole.

Willa lowered her head. She wiped the blood and tears from her face and started for the edge of the cornfield. All around her, the rows had gone eerily quiet.

They seemed somewhat calm.

1:07 A.M.

When they cleared the dirt road, the cornfield came into view, Sam and Mac made a straight line for the field. As they neared the rows, Sam gave a hand signal, indicating she would take the rows on the right and for him to run down farther to take the rows on the left.

Mac nodded and kept running to the far end of the field, about a quarter of a mile farther down.

Meanwhile, she ducked into the cornfield and walked along the nearest row. She knew the rustling of stalks and leaves would give away any hope of sneaking up on the girls, but that was fine. Still, she walked as quietly as she could so she could hear any commotion ahead of her. She chose not to use her flashlight, not wanting to give away her location. But the deeper she went into the field, the darker it got and the harder it became to fight the urge to pull it out.

At a place she assumed to be somewhere near the center, she stopped, looked around, and cut over several rows but stopped when she heard movement nearby. She took off again, leaping across rows and trying to make as little noise as possible.

There it was again. Unmistakable. Footsteps. Someone was moving beyond the rows. The stalks were swaying gently, dead husks crunching underfoot.

Sam moved through the corn, jumping another row, where she saw a figure limping toward the front of the field. It was hunched over, as if in tremendous pain, staggering aimlessly through the rows. Sam drew closer, her eyes wide, hands shaking slightly as she pulled out her flashlight and unholstered her firearm from her belt. "Stop!"

The figure turned slowly. It was Cassie Hollins. And from what Sam could tell, she was alone.

"Cassie," she whispered.

But Cassie simply turned and continued her slow, lumbering pace toward the opening of the field, like a zombie.

"Cassie, I said stop."

Cassie froze, and when she turned around again, Sam turned on the flashlight. Cassie barely blinked in the light. Her eyes were frozen wide, terrified. Slowly, Cassie took two steps toward Sam, and she started to shudder. Tears flowed down her cheeks as she staggered toward her.

"Cassie, oh my god, what happened to you?"

But Cassie didn't answer. She just stood in front of Sam, staring at her like she was looking right through her. Shaking.

"Where are Tess and Willa?"

Cassie's eyes widened, and she pointed into the cornfield.

"Cassie, listen to me. Where are they?" Sam grabbed Cassie's wrist. "Where?"

Cassie seemed to wake from her trance, sucking in a deep breath of air. "Out … Out there. Some … Somewhere out there!"

What the hell happened out there? Sam shone her flashlight at Cassie. Her clothes were torn, and blood dripped down her thighs. She had a bleeding wound on her upper arm, almost as if someone had taken a bite of her. Her hair matted with dark fluid clung to slashes on her cheeks like silks.

"There's … There's something else out there too."

"Something else?"

Cassie's face scrunched in a look of sorrow and horror. "It's her … It's Carmen. Carmen Winstead."

The night and the weeks leading up to this had been so dark and deranged that Sam did not even question it. If anything, it made perfect sense. "Cassie, can you make it back to the dirt road, right outside of the corn?"

Cassie nodded, already looking in that direction.

"Go there, Cassie, and stay there, okay? Listen, I'm here with my partner, Mac. You remember him, right?"

Cassie nodded.

"Listen, one of us will get you as soon as we find Tess and Willa. Okay?"

"Yeah." Cassie started forward again but stopped. She turned back to Sam, her eyes pleading. "I think you might be too late."

"What do you mean?"

"The thing ... The thing out there. I think it already got them. I think they might already be dead. Especially Tess."

The comment may as well have been a starting gun to a foot-race. Sam took off in the direction of the other end of the corn-field, acting on gut instinct. She should have known just as soon as they had started following Tess's car where this night would lead them—where it would end. Slapping away low-hanging corn leaves and husks, Sam barreled toward the end of the cornfield and the forest beyond, recalling that day in the Winstead house, in Carmen's bathroom—the noises, the laughter. Someone had been watching her. It was a feeling she never could shake, and that same feeling was digging into her bones right now.

As she ran toward the back end of the cornfield, she was vaguely aware of a commotion to her right somewhere closer to-ward where she'd last seen Mac. She hit another gear, wondering if Mac had come out the other end yet and, if so, if he had found anything.

It took another three minutes of flat-out running, but Sam finally reached the end of the cornfield. She found herself star-ing at the thin strip of tall grass that separated the Holt family's property from the forests behind it. She looked to the right but only saw the cornfield stretching on, well out of her sight. If Mac *was* already out, she'd have to walk a pretty good distance to find him. She could—

Something moved through the forest ahead—not footsteps necessarily but almost like something sliding across the leaf-covered ground. She did not hesitate though. *It could be anything.* She sprinted toward the trees, keeping her gun at the high-ready. Her legs were already screaming at her from the steady jog through the corn, but she pushed past it. She listened for a scream, for any human sound, as she bolted past the tree line, but she heard nothing. In fact, aside from her footfalls, the woods were eerily quiet. It reminded her of the still sort of heaviness to the atmosphere in the moments before a loud, summer thunderstorm.

She carried on into the woods and reached the gradual downward grade that led to the sewage outpost. As she carefully descended, she noticed a figure just beyond the pines. At first, she thought it was one of the girls. But as she got closer, shining her flashlight ahead, she realized its shape was slightly deformed and somehow fluid.

A long white dress maimed its skin, dragging something behind it as it trudged toward the manhole.

Sam hesitated before looking through the gun's sights, trying to figure out what the hell she was looking at. She ran forward and stopped, then lifted her gun, her brain telling her finger to pull the trigger. But some other part of her was frozen in place, trying to make sense of the scene before her eyes.

Sam paused, knowing the manhole was less than three feet ahead when she heard something rattling on her left. She slowly turned, Glock in one hand, flashlight in the other, and she searched the area. She heard it again, a faint whimpering. She walked closer until her light illuminated a girl lying on her side, gasping for air. Her flesh was ripped from her cheeks, and it was almost as if she'd been tied up by some sort of razor wire that ripped through her skin.

As Sam walked closer, her gun still stretched forward, she recognized the blond hair. It was Tess Todd. Sam rushed to her side, but, as she knelt, something she couldn't see collided with her from ahead, knocking the wind out of her and throwing her backward. She lost hold of her gun as she struck the ground. She quickly got to her knees, fumbling for her Glock.

But whatever it was, it wasn't interested in her. It sped toward the sewer and grabbed Tess's hair. It turned and stared at Sam, its eyes glued to her, its mouth hissing and ravaging like a diseased dog. It drug Tess across the field, and Sam heard the girl's deathly screams as she was wrenched closer to the manhole.

It was Carmen.

Horrified, Sam fell into the fetal position, covering her ears, trying to shut it all out.

And then it was gone. The forest fell absolutely silent.

Minutes later, Sam sat upright and fumbled with her flashlight. She fanned the light in the direction of the manhole, lighting a trembling circle beyond. She was just in time to see a decaying arm reach up and pull the cover over the hole. Before it was closed, Sam saw a pair of piercing black eyes staring at her.

And then the cover slammed shut with a resounding metallic bang, sealing the darkness forever.

1:16 am

As far as she knew, it was over. When the darkness had claimed Tess and pulled her toward the back of the cornfield, Willa sensed her job had been done. She had done exactly what the forces had told her to do; she'd gotten Tess and Cassie to the field, and now she felt … well, *free*.

Yet, as she edged through the forest to the west and farther from the cornfield, the manhole cover, and the detectives, Willa felt a pang of guilt. No, she had not hurt Tess or Cassie. But she was responsible for whatever had happened to them. She had delivered them to the darkness that had been waiting out there, lurking between the rows.

But, in the back of her head, there was a reassuring suggestion—not a voice but an intuition of sorts. And it seemed to be reminding her that she should not feel guilty. All things were even now, balanced. It was the way it had to be.

Maybe that was Carmen talking, the same presence who had guided her out here. She also sensed that if she chose to do so, it could become a part of her for good—if that is what she wanted.

She wept as she ran through the woods. She stumbled and fell on occasion, no longer guided by the urgency she'd felt before. No, now the presence was simply a protective one, a grateful one. Her legs were tired and sore, her lungs straining. More than that, she felt her grip on reality slipping away, trying to process everything that had happened the past several days.

She had no idea where she was or where she was going. Running blindly through the darkness, she just remembered True whispering for her to run, and that was exactly what she had done. Now, scrambling in the dark, she noticed the trees stood strong and tall. At one point, she felt the dead leaves reach down, waving toward her, egging her on, inviting her to push forward, to go deeper into the night. But as the dark pulled her in, all she could think about was True. She had to make it to True. If she did, she would be safe, protected—protected from anything the darkness had to offer, like the shadows she had seen earlier devouring Tess. True would know what to do. She would round them up and put them into her collection box. And Willa would be safe forever.

But she needed to stop for a moment. She ran toward a large oak and rested against its silvery bark, allowing her lungs to rest. Her legs felt like jelly, and at any moment, she thought they would give out.

Willa looked around, her eyes broad; they felt like they would pop out of their sockets at any moment. She searched the woods and slowly pushed herself from the tree and stumbled onward, tripping over decaying logs and dead foliage. She walked as if she was half asleep, her body begging her to stop. But she couldn't; she knew she had to move forward and get herself to safety.

Finally, she heard rumbling ahead—not a big rumbled like thunder rolling across the sky but like marbles being kicked across the floor. She stopped and listened carefully, wondering where it was coming from. *The creek*, she thought as a long-awaited smile creased the edge of her lips. *The damn creek. The road.*

She cocked her head and held her breath. Blood rushed her temples as a slight heave of air burned her lungs. The forest fell silent; it seemed different now, like a shift in the universe. Then a rustle of the wind danced by her as she turned around. The forest was being engulfed in the mist of the darkness all around her. It was following her now. Maybe it had been all along, but she didn't notice.

Willa flailed at her ears as she heard the buzzing of insect flapping all around her. Then she heard something else—the moan of tires beating against the pavement.

Willa cried as the fog engulfed the forest. She ran as hard as she could toward the sounds as a louder rustling crept up behind her. It wasn't the wind this time or snapping of the trees nearby. It was the darkness, the one that had pushed her toward the cornfield. It was here to take her.

Willa filled her lungs as much as she could and ran. Jumping over drenches and logs, she finally reached the stream and fell. The road was just beyond in her sight. She reached for the road, trying to scream as a set of blue and red flashing lights ricocheted through the night sky somewhere in the distance. Her body sprawled forward. Cold water from the stream enveloped her as she crawled up the embankment and pulled violently. She barely got her arms up in time to keep her face from hitting the edge of a road.

The pavement was cool. Rather than trying to get to her feet right away, Willa thought she would just stay there for a mo-

260 | Trace Murillo

ment—her body limp, half in and half out of the ditch. Just for a minute or two …

She opened her eyes to the wailing of sirens and the screech-ing of brakes. When she heard car doors opening and a series of footsteps approaching, she lifted her head. Everything was dark and blurry, punctuated by the red and swirling lights coming from the police car that had come to a stop less than ten feet from her head.

"Hello?" a male voice said. "Miss, are you okay? Can we—"

"Wait, that's Willa Dalton," another male voice said. "Jesus. Kerr and Talbot are looking for her."

"Get them on the radio. Now."

Willa heard the first man's voice closer to her, leaning down, brushing her matted hair from her face, and asking if she was okay again. She closed her eyes and nodded, feeling it was a lie. She was alive, and that's all that mattered.

But more than that, she felt something awakening inside her, something pure. Something from True. A gift maybe.

She exhaled, her lungs still burning, but she rested easy knowing that now she would never be alone again.

NOVEMBER 22, 2008

11:02 A.M.

S am set down the sheet of paper she had been reading for the past three minutes and suppressed a chill. She'd read it six times and tried to find some way to accept what it meant. She looked to Mac sitting on the other side of her desk and sighed. "You see this?"

Mac took it, eyed it, and nodded. He set it down with the same disdain as she'd shown. "Yeah."

"How's it possible?"

Mac shrugged and looked to the ceiling, as if trying to find *anything* that would change the subject.

The sheet of paper in question was the State Maintenance report from Somerdale. The report had been written three days ago, following the death of Virgie Vaughan. It was a detailed description of how the town maintenance crew had installed a steel manhole cover into the concrete block just off the Holt family property. The manhole cover was the sort used in industrial warehouses; it weighed one hundred and twenty pounds and could

262 | TRACE MURILLO

only be removed by using a specialized hex key that only employees of Somerdale City Maintenance had access to.

This, of course, was in complete disagreement with the details in the reports that both Sam and Mac had typed up. Those reports both described the scene as they had found it two nights ago when Tess Todd had gone missing. The manhole had already been opened when Sam had arrived on the scene, and Sam had been able to hear the scraping of the concrete as she had watched Carmen Winstead drag down Tess. The thing that had haunted Sam the most was those eyes staring out at her as the cover slammed shut. It was something Sam would never forget, etched into her mind like the memory of shooting Fredericks. It would just never go away.

"I'm just waiting for the questions to start, you know?"

"I doubt they'll be asked at all," Mac said. "I covered for you on the report. I wouldn't want people to think you have lost your damn mind."

"I know what I saw, Mac. And where is she? Where's Tess Todd?"

"I don't know, but see, that's the thing about these small southern towns. What happened in that manhole is common knowledge at this point. Add in the fact that the entire ordeal included True and Willa Dalton, and people's minds will concoct some pretty tall tales. There will be all kinds of ghost stories to come out of it, cautionary tales that parents will tell their kids to get them to think twice about breaking curfew. Nothing more."

"Yeah, but what about us?" She still couldn't quite believe everything she had experienced. Part of her thought that maybe she would never be the same.

Mac shrugged. "Us? As long as we handle it better than Cassie's father, I think we'll be okay."

He was referring to the fact that Trevor Hollins had already called the police department to complain about the so-called Satanic practices of the Dalton family and how they no doubt had contributed to the string of deaths and his own daughter's trauma. It was total nonsense, of course, but what he did not know was they had interrogated Willa following the events two nights ago. And it had been Cassie who had provided eyewitness testimony that had cleared Willa in the end.

But Sam was not quite as happy that when the manhole cover was removed, Tess Todd was not down there. The only thing they found was a mangled silver tiara lying at the bottom of the manhole, covered in muck. They searched the cornfield and surrounding area for two days and found no evidence that she'd been there at all.

She was pretty sure they never would. The only suspect she could think of was something she wasn't allowing herself to comprehend. She and Cassie had agreed on that point, but unfortunately, Cassie was now doing an extended stay at Moonstruck Country Club.

She knew a very lengthy investigation was inevitable; forensics and the state police would scour the area by the sewage outpost with a fine-tooth comb. And they would find nothing. Maybe it would be chalked up to some strange suicide pact. Or maybe it would silently be blamed on the Dalton family's beliefs and practices.

She honestly didn't care. At the end of the day, it meant a case she'd headed would go unsolved. Usually, that would irritate her to no end. But this one was different. This one, she wanted to forget. With any luck, the entire ordeal would eventually erase itself from the collective mind of Somerdale. And Tess Todd would just go down as a missing person.

"Yo, Kerr, you okay?" Mac asked.

"Zoned out, didn't I?"

"That's putting it mildly. Come on. Let's get out of here. Let's go grab a beer."

"That's the best idea I've ever heard."

They got up together and left her office much closer than they had been two months ago. She'd heard stories about partners who encountered gruesome or violent cases and how a bond formed between them. Given what they had encountered in the cornfield, she thought she and Mac would be extremely close until they retired.

She shut her office door behind her, her desk still cluttered with the notes and images from the scene near the Holt Family Farm. The picture on top, slightly covered by the State Maintenance report, showed the back of Carmen Winstead's head covered in blood-stained dark hair. The attached coroner's report detailed how both of her legs had been pulverized, her right arm broken in two places, both shoulders dislocated, her ribs not only broken but splintered, her spine a tangled mess.

The report also described the manhole where her body had been pushed into as dark and slightly cavernous. To the untrained eye, it might look like some helpless teenage girl had been gulped into the throat of a monster.

Which, Sam Kerr might tell that untrained eye, wasn't too far from the truth.

11:52 A.M.

The snow that had fallen the night before was now iced over. It encased every tree limb reaching over Carmen Winstead's grave. Sometimes Willa thought it sparkled like the stars in the night sky, only she knew better. With True by her side, Willa walked slowly. The snow crunched beneath her feet as she leaned closer to lay a single yellow primrose on Carmen's violated headstone. Winstead had been crossed out with black spray paint, replaced with *Pigstead*. True had told her the primrose was used for protection and love, and Willa thought Carmen could use both.

The sun gloomed above, trying its best to peek through the dark clouds around it, as Willa glanced across the field and felt a reckoning, a rebirth of sorts, as the snow-packed field sparkled. It reminded her of a glittering blanket covering the earth and all its problems. But as she stared into True's eyes, she knew her problems had just begun.

"Joe Winstead is having her grave moved to Bristol. Maybe there, she can finally find peace."

"Willa."

Willa turned to True, and a tear rolled down, moistening her cheek. "Yeah?"

"Are you okay?"

Willa only nodded. She wasn't okay, but there was no proper way to explain why this was the case. She wasn't surprised True kept asking her this. Every time she closed her eyes, she saw the darkness from the cornfield; she saw Carmen. And she was starting to think the darkness that engulfed her was just a part of this town—or maybe some manifestation of the natural spirits and forces True sometimes communed with, the same forces she was beginning to understand and draw into herself. She knew they weren't always dark—in fact, they could be quite joyous and pleasant. And, unlike the people of Somerdale, they could also be accepting.

"Willa, I need you to know something. I don't want to scare you, but I need you to understand."

Willa didn't mind the interruption of her thoughts. Her mind bounced back and forth, and she did her best to keep her mind off things, especially at night when she closed her eyes. She never looked forward to that—closing her eyes and seeing what the darkness had in store for her, the lurking sights and noises that now haunted her dreams. "What?"

"It's not finished."

She would've loved to tell Aunt True that she had no idea what she was talking about, to keep her crazy thoughts to herself, but the fact of the matter was she knew *exactly* what True meant. Worse than that, she could answer without any doubt at all. "No. I don't think it is."

True bowed her head almost reverently and, before walking away, brushed Willa's cheek with her hand. She regarded her niece with something resembling pride. Even in the brief answer Willa had just given, she had admitted a tenuous link to the forces True had spent years trying to get her to understand.

As soon as Willa could hear True's footsteps crunching the snow, she heard her muttering prayers. Now, it made her feel calm. Oddly enough, Willa understood that she was slowly coming to a place where she could identify with Aunt True. She now knew without a doubt that something was out there and that she had been a part of it.

And it had sought her out. Scary or not, something seemed sacred about it.

She knew this because she felt it calling to her. She'd felt it ever since seeing Carmen standing outside her window a few days ago. Maybe even before that. Maybe that was what had led them to be friends in the first place. And Carmen, or whatever had engulfed her that night, still reached out to her. And though Willa had initially tried to avoid it, a small part of her now embraced it.

She felt safer embracing it, letting it become a part of her. Because she felt one thing quite strongly, an inescapable feeling she feared might just stick with her for the rest of her days. While Carmen might be done exacting her own revenge, her essence had become something else. And whatever that was, it enjoyed dishing out fear and death.

And Willa was terrified she might just be getting started.

JULY 7, 2014

12:01 A.M.

Devin's parents had found out he'd been watching internet porn, so they had blocked the sites. The idiots had taken forever learning how to do it, so he had turned his attention elsewhere. At the age of fourteen though, there wasn't much else of interest other than naked women and superheroes. And he and Kyle, his best friend since pre-school, had seen all the Marvel movies and straight up didn't like the DC cinematic universe.

So, bored and refusing to sleep at nearly one in the morning, they used their sleepover time to poke around Reddit for messed-up stories of true crime. There was plenty of it out there, and while Devin found it interesting, it also sort of made him feel a little sick, thinking of the sheer evil humans were capable of.

While Devin scrolled through the site, Kyle was on his phone, checking Facebook. He chuckled, looking up from the sleeping bag on Devin's floor. He would show Devin every funny meme he came across, which was, in Devin's opinion, annoying as hell.

268 | TRACE MURILLO

Devin was about to call it a night. There just wasn't much to do without the dirty sites his folks had blocked, and Call of Duty had gotten boring. He was about to turn off his bedside lamp but saw his town's name buried deep in a Reddit sub thread. "Dude, look at this. Somerdale is mentioned on this thread."

"What's the thread?"

"Unsolved murders." He scanned the story a bit, then made a *pfff* sound. "Never mind. It's more crap about those girls being killed a years ago."

"Never mind, my ass. See if there are pictures of that one chick, that Tess girl. She's fine as hell."

"Fine? She's dead, dude. You're nasty."

"You don't know that. They never found her body. I bet she's sipping a margarita on a beach somewhere."

"More like she's being sipped up by maggots, you nimrod." Devin scrolled through, reading the threads and clicking the links attached to each one. There were, regrettably, no pictures of Tess Todd, but something else *did* catch his attention. "Yo, Kyle. You ever hear of this Carmen Curse bullshit?"

"I don't think so. What is it?"

"This is stupid. Some dumb legend, a campfire story sort of thing."

"It's not like we're doing anything else. What is it?"

Devin snickered as he read the logistics. "Alright, so I won't tell you what it says. I'll tell you what to do. It'll make it spookier, right?"

"Sure."

"Okay, so start a new text message on your phone."

"Who do I send it to?"

"No one. This says it has to be a text message without a recipient."

"Whatever. Okay, it's up. Now what?"

Devin read the rest of it to himself. Yeah, it was stupid and cheesy, but he did love a good spooky story. "Now type in, *Carmen Winstead was pushed*, three times."

"That sounds stupid."

"It does. But that's what it says."

"Okay. There's one … two … and there's three."

"Now send it."

"But I don't have it going to anyone. It won't send."

"Just send the fucking thing!"

"Fine. Sent!" Kyle showed Devin his phone to prove he had done it. "Ooh, it'll bounce back in a second, saying there was no sender! Spooky shi—"

Devin's bedside lamp flickered and went out. Devin heard the inside of the bulb frying and snapping.

"Dude what the hell …?" Kyle said.

"I don't know, it's—"

Something shifted and moved somewhere else in the dark room.

Devin sat upright and looked in the corner. Was something there? Something moving, some figure he—

"Man, fuck this," Kyle said. He was up off his sleeping bag in a flash, leaving his phone. He bolted through the bedroom door and into the hallway.

Devin started to laugh. Under any other circumstances, it *would* have been funny. But now, there was the thing in the corner.

Only, it wasn't in the corner anymore. He could see it moving through the darkness of his room. It looked almost human in shape as it came to his bed.

He opened his mouth, not sure if he wanted to scream for Kyle or his parents.

In the end, he did neither, as the shifting, breathing darkness came rushing at him.

Thank you for reading A Girl Named Carmen Winstead. To stay up to date on new releases, please follow the writer at trace-murillo.com or on Facebook @tracemurillo.

OTHER BOOKS BY TRACE MURILLO

The Patient in Room 432

From the Urban Legend Collection
Hannah Crannah

THE WENDIGO
THE WEREWOLF OF DEFIANCE

COMING SOON!

Please enjoy this insert from The Wendigo available 2021.

THE WENDIGO

He looked down, and all he could see were the tops of the pines and firs. There were other types of trees, but he couldn't think of their names. Besides, they were all whipping by in a blur, the forest a canopy of musty greens. He was flying over it all, and he felt if he reached down, he could feel the very tops of those pines, the needles poking at him, grazing his skin.

But he couldn't reach down. Not consciously, anyway. Because, even as he saw the blur of greens passing below him, Chris knew this was a dream. He was aware of it in some subconscious way that his mind didn't bother to analyze. He knew this was a dream because he had dreamt it nearly twenty times before.

He didn't know what the dream meant, but he knew it felt like a premonition of danger. Peering down into that forest, he sensed something dark, something waiting. Something evil was down there, lurking in the shadows of the trees cast down by the setting sun. But was the sun actually setting, or was it melting? Dissolving? Was the darkness he sensed somewhere on that forest floor so cunning and vile that it had somehow destroyed the sun?

In the dream, it was easy to imagine such an event. Enveloped in fear, Chris felt himself descend. He was no longer floating but falling slowly. His face was nicked and scratched as he fell. And during it all, he was not worried about breaking his back or fracturing his skull on the forest floor. He was more worried about what else waited down there in the darkness among the trees and vastness of the forest.

If he did fall to the forest floor, he could only hope the impact alone would kill him before that living darkness found him and consumed him.

Chris fell and fell, trees sailing by like rockets, and just before he hit the waiting forest, everything went black, and the dream was gone.

And, in the early morning hours, this felt like both a blessing and a curse.

Chris awoke slowly, his head pressed against something hard. He opened his eyes and was slightly alarmed that it had taken him a moment to remember he was on an airplane headed to Anchorage, Alaska. There was a little jolt of excitement at this realization, but a stinging sadness too. He thought of his wife and daughter back home, but mainly his daughter. Brianna was used to him going on trips; he attended at least three pediatric conferences each year, one of which lasted a week. But she'd been particularly unhappy about this trip. She was eight years old and had not quite grasped why four grown men would isolate themselves in the cold, barren wilderness of Alaska. She also did not see the sense in ice fishing—at least in the way Chris had explained it. In that hazy place between emerging from a nap and full wakefulness, Chris rather agreed.

He looked out the window and saw soft, white clouds. Much farther below, he could make out an etching of a road, a gradually rising and falling landscape, and wide swaths of green. It reminded him of his dream, sailing over a gorgeous yet somehow darkly tinged forest.

"You okay, man?" a voiced asked from beside him.

He turned toward Noah Miller, his best friend since college, and gave a sleepy nod. "Yeah. Just thinking about Brianna. She was not happy about this trip."

"Oh, I get it," Noah said. And Chris was sure he did. Noah lived just eight blocks from Chris and had a ten-year-old son. And though his son was more closely tied to his mother, Noah thought the world of him. "What about Vicki? She give you a hard time over this?"

"No. If anything, I think she might have been glad to get me out of the house for a while." He left it at that, not wanting to delve into the hurdles he was jumping over in his marriage. And honestly, there were so many he wouldn't know where to start. So, he just allowed that thought to dwindle from his mind and felt a sigh of relief when it faded.

"Sort of makes me jealous of those two, you know?" Noah said, hitching his thumb to the left.

Across the aisle and about two rows up, the other members of their party sat side by side. Bobby Valencia, the youngest of their group by three years, sipped on a vodka tonic next to Barret Thompson. Barret was a big man, the sort of guy who could appear to be either overweight or just sturdy depending on the angle he was viewed from. He was currently reading the latest Lee Child novel—likely a welcomed break from the classic literature he assigned his high school students back home, Chris supposed.

"Jealous of them?" Chris asked. "Why?"

"No wives. No kids. They can come out here and just enjoy it all, you know? Hell, they can go anywhere, do anything with no guilt or hurt feelings back home."

"Yeah and no responsibilities. Kind of lonely, don't cha think? I mean, who wants to go through life alone?" Chris whispered. "But, hey, what do I know. Did you leave some hurt feelings or something?"

"I'm missing Kevin's soccer tryouts. But, hey, if that's the worst of it, I think I'm okay."

Life alone, Chris thought. Maybe life alone would be better for him. Maybe Noah was right. Maybe Barrett and Bobby were on to something.

They both fell quiet after this. They knew each other well enough to know when to stop discussing something. Chris and Noah, being the tightest of the group, could read this in one another with eerie clarity. Friends since their sophomore year of college at UCLA, they secretly saw themselves as the glue that held their little tribe together.

They had flown out of Sacramento, California, and, thanks to his nap, Chris wasn't quite sure how much longer their flight would be. He watched as Noah took his cellphone and earbuds and started listening to something—probably one of those true crime podcasts he seemed to be favoring these days. As for Chris, he stared out the window at the clouds coasting by and was unable to escape that he felt like he was running away from his problems at home.

Two hours and fifteen minutes later, the cooler air of the North Pacific created some rough turbulence. Bobby was on his third vodka tonic, and, by Chris's estimation, he should have a pretty good buzz going by now. He would either be incredibly hilarious or irritating as hell on their journey from the Anchorage airport to their cabin in the remote wilderness, about twenty-five miles from the stain-on-the-map town of Cox.

Shortly after the turbulence, the pilot announced they would be descending into Anchorage.

After the announcement, Noah removed his headphones and gave Chris another nudge. "Bobby's going to be a handful, huh?"

"Probably. But that's Bobby for ya. Always the attention whore. But I'm glad I'm not the only one who sees that coming."

"Look at Barret." Noah giggled. "He already looks irritated."

Chris had not noticed this. Though, when he looked across the aisle at Barret and Bobby, he noticed Barret donned a somewhat exasperated expression that had been nowhere in sight when he'd joined them at the airport. At the airport, Barrett had seemed eager, but leave it to Bobby to have such a talent to melt away any form of happiness for anyone and leave them feeling—pissed.

"I plan on ignoring him when he gets drunk," Noah said. "Notice I said when, not if. Because you know he will."

"So, it'll be the same as back home, then—just colder and without our wives to use as a rouse to escape. Nowhere to go and no excuse to leave, we are pretty much screwed."

"Pretty much," Noah said as they both eyed each other brazenly and laughed.

It had been the first smile that cracked Chris's lips since he had awoken from his dream descending into anchorage.

They remained quiet until the plane landed on the runway fifteen minutes later. No one seemed to be in a particular hurry to exit the plane, so the four friends milled slowly through the aisle until they stepped onto the airbridge, where Chris watched as Barret showed his true personality.

There was an agenda and a schedule. There were places they needed to be and a timeframe to be adhered to. While he would never claim he was the most responsible of the group—Chris usually got that distinction—Barret was definitely the most organized and forward-thinking. Something about Barret shifted the dynamic of the group a bit. He levelled them out in a way Chris had always felt but couldn't clearly understand. In the past, over beers and games of poker or watching the 49ers play, they'd concluded their little group could be neatly divided, as if they were the cast in a cheesy movie.

The four of them together made something of an odd group, but it somehow worked. Chris considered himself somewhere in the middle, sort of the group's under-the-radar member. He was the responsible one, nearly to the point of being boring—but in the movie, it would be considered a cute quirk. Noah was the passionate one, the guy who got deeply obsessed with whatever project he was working on and also managed to have a very strong marriage. He was the upstanding husband and father, the sort of husband who did not mind kissing his wife in front of his friends or playing action figures with his kid in front of people. And then there was Bobby, the fuckup, by his own admission; he was the guy who could not hold a job, had a penchant for drinking, and still tried to party like a twenty-year-old even at the age of thirty-six, very immature for his age, and still patrolled bars for women ten years younger than him—and often being successful at it. Having held no steady job in the last seven or eight years, Chris often saw Bobby as the group's charity project. Then there was Barret, the intellectual of the group, always trying to get them excited about reading or movies that did not include naked women or things exploding. One look at him and a stranger might assume he was a grizzled outdoorsman, though he was absolutely not. He was a massive man, standing at six-and-a-half-feet tall and weighing two-fifty, most of it muscle. On occasion, Chris had heard Vicki refer to Barret as the Brawny Man, after the character in the plaid shirt carrying an axe on the wrapper of Bounty paper towels. In other words, if there was a plan and an agenda, you did what Barret told you out of fear of being trampled.

"We're supposed to meet our van in ten minutes on the curb out front," Barret said. "So, if you need a bathroom break or something to eat, get to it now."

"How about a drink?" Bobby suggested, already looking up and down the airport's central walkway.

"No time."

"Lay off, Dad," Bobby said, snickering. Still, he quickly fell into line.

They rushed to the restroom before walking outside, and even the hurry of getting in and out of the restroom was a bit exciting. Chris hated to think of himself as free while he was missing his daughter so badly already, but that's exactly how he felt. They were in a hurry, they had an adventure ahead of them, and even if they missed their flights or drivers, they were still four guys away from home; there was an adventure in damn near everything in that situation.

When they got outside to the curb, Chris was surprised to find it was not quite as cold as he'd been expecting. The air held a chill, yes, but it did not have the bite he'd been preparing himself for.

The four of them stood just outside of the airport for a moment before Barret pointed to their left. "Blue van, right there." He started walking without even checking to see if they were following.

Noah, who had paused to tie his shoe, had to scramble to catch up to them.

The driver stood outside the van—a modest blue shuttle type of van that looked to be several years old. He opened the sliding side door for them and greeted them with a smile. He looked to be in his early thirties or so, with dark hair and moustache that perfectly framed his face. "Heading to Delaney Park Airfield, correct?"

"That's right," Barret said, stepping into the van.

Chris got in next, followed by Bobby and then Noah.

When the driver closed the sliding door and dashed to the front, Barret playfully slapped Bobby's knee. "Hot damn, boys, we're actually doing it! You assholes ready for this?"

Bobby gave his usual emphatic cheer of joy, a roar usually reserved for intense sporting events or the opening of another six-pack of beer.

Noah was a little more reserved, giving a little smattering of applause, and a soft "whew-hoo."

Chris, being arrogant as always, just cut a forced smile toward Barrett and turned to stare out the window.

The driver opened the front door and slid in behind the wheel. "You gentlemen ready?"

He got the same response from the four friends: an enthusiastic round of cheers. With that, the driver started the van and pulled into airport traffic, officially starting their adventure.

Printed in the USA
CPSIA information can be obtained
at www.ICGtesting.com
LVHW042323161023
761015LV00032BA/238/J